GIVING IN

THE SHORE SERIES
BOOK 1

M.R. JOSEPH

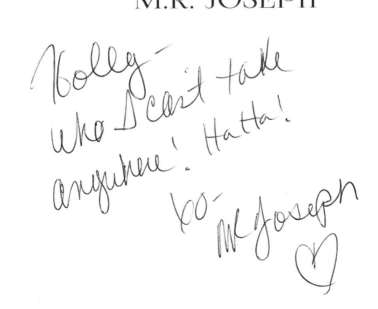

Holly—
who I can't take
anywhere! Hatta!
xo—
MR Joseph

Giving In
Copyright © 2014 M.R. Joseph

Edited by Kathy Krick

Copyright © Jennifer Kearney Photography 2014
http://www.jenniferkearneyphotography.com/#2822

Interior Design by Angela McLaurin, Fictional Formats
https://www.facebook.com/FictionalFormats

ISBN-10: 1496118383
ISBN-13: 978-1496118387

DEDICATION

*To all the Indie Authors who have inspired me
with your words and your stories. Thank you for sharing your
gifts with me and the world. You are the reason I am doing what I'm
doing today, so thank you for changing my life.*

ACKNOWLEDGEMENTS

There are so many words to say, so many people to thank I don't know where to begin. I'll start with the ones who own my heart. Thank you to my husband for putting up with my crazy rants and your lack of clean underwear. You amaze me everyday and I could not have done this without you. Love you with my whole heart. For my kiddos who tell people in school that I'm an author, but they aren't allowed to read my books. Love them so much. To my mom and my sister for sticking by me and encouraging me always. Mommy thanks for reminding me that no matter how many books I sell, I still put myself out there and went for it. Not many people can say that. To my extended family and in-laws, my best girlfriends in the world, you are wonderful supporters and I thank you for all your love.

My readers whom I have grown to know and love. I have developed such a friendship with you guys and I thank you for your dedication and kind words. If it wasn't for you, I would not be writing this.

I'd like to thank my author friends for pimping me out,

encouraging me along the way. Thank you to the following authors who inspire me with their books; Julie Prestsater, Rebecca Shea, Raine Miller, Monica Murphy, Katie Ashley, and Kristen Proby, Emma Chase, and so many more.

To my editor, Kathy Krick for doing such a beautiful job on this book. Thank you for your encouragement, suggestions, and fun talks. You are a wonderful editor and I am so glad I found you!

Thank you again to one of my saviors, Angela McLaurin at Fictional Formats for your beautiful work!

To my cover models Reuben Ondarza and Rosemarie Mount. I love you both so much! Thanks for taking one hell of a horrific day and turning it into something spectacular. I look forward to the next shoot. Ha, ha.

To my beautiful and talented photographer, Jennifer Kearney for your patience, your professionalism, your eye for a good shot even during a monsoon in October at the Jersey Shore. What a day, but what you created goes beyond a thank you.

To John and Lynn Ciminera, my aunt and uncle, for allowing me to use your beautiful home at the shore for the photo shoot. My appreciation goes beyond words.

To my betas. Tina Bell, Sandy Connor, Chrissy Massa, Laura Hash, Lisa McKeown, Tina Moss, and Stephanie Leone. Where would I be without you? No seriously. You all have made this journey so fun. Your encouragement, your ideas, your hard work, your patience when dealing with my crazy moods, your laughter, and the constant stream of 'X-Files' kept me motivated and strong and I love and thank you from the bottom of my heart.

Lastly, to the bloggers and reviewers. Where would any indie author be without you? Thank you, thank you, thank you for all you do!

PROLOGUE

Introducing Harlow and Cruz...
May 2012

"Did you lock the door?"

"Yeah, yeah, it's locked. I checked it twice."

"Oh, God, right there, do that again, ah, that feels so good."

"Put your hand there."

"Where?"

"Here."

"So what's your name? Oh, God rub there, sweet Christ, you're a good kisser."

"Harlow."

"Harlow, what kind of name is that?"

"My mom was a big fan of Jeanne Harlow. I have a sister named Greta as in Garbo and a brother named Crawford."

"Crawford? That's a strange name for a dude."

"He was supposed to be a girl, Mom's a Joan Crawford

1

fan, Oh, God lick my neck there. That's it, suck on my earlobe. Oh yeah, I like that."

"Want to know my name?"

"If you find it necessary."

"Raphael."

"Nice to meet you, Raphael. Oh shit that feels good. Do you have a condom?"

"Of course. I always come prepared."

"Well, thank God for small miracles."

"Shit, what's up with this button?"

"Wait, let me get it… there we go."

"Sweet Jesus, you are huge."

"Exactly what every guy wants to hear, thank you very much."

"Oh God right there. Yes. Yes. Yes. Oh, that's the spot."

"Damn, you are so tight, if my fingers can hardly get in there, what makes us think my dick can."

"Don't think, just do."

"Yes, ma'am. So where are you from?"

"New Jersey. Princeton actually. You?"

"Cherry Hill. Born and… Oh. Yea grip it just like that. Now jerk it harder. Oh fuck!"

"How's that? Never mind I just got my answer."

"These are some hot ass panties you're sporting, girl."

"Thanks, Victoria's Secret does a woman good."

"I'll say. I wish I could rip them with my teeth."

"Oh, I caught myself a kinky one, now did I."

"Oh, sweetheart, you haven't a clue."

"Don't come yet, are you ready? I'll slide it on for you."

"I was born ready, baby."

"Don't call me baby. I'm not your baby."

"That's right. You're just some dirty little girl I just met at a bar, right? Oh, yea, you like that, don't you? That's it, just like that, ride my hand."

"Oh, God, I love it when you talk dirty. Yes, tonight, I'm a dirty, dirty girl about to fuck a guy whose name I don't even know against a bathroom wa… OH, fucking A! I'm ready. Come on and let me put it in already."

"Fine, be my guest, and I told you, the name is Raphael, not God, but if you start screaming his name out as I make you come, then so be it. I've been called a lot worse."

"Wow, seriously dude, this hardly fits you."

"Yea, well, I ran out of the extra-large and this is all they had at the convenience sto… ooo… rrrreee, fuck you are tight as a frickin' vice. Stupendous."

"So what do you do for a liv… liv… Oh yea, harder. Oh Christ."

"A living? Police Academy, as of now. Oh yea, like that, you feel so fucking good."

"You are going to split me in two. Good Lord."

"I bet you say that to all the strangers you fuck in bar bathrooms."

"Nope. Never. I'm a bathroom virgin. I've never done this before. Who in the name of all that's sacred and holy taught you how to kiss? Phenomenal."

"A girl from my neighborhood. She's like five years older than me. I asked her, and she showed me. We kissed a lot. Now she's married to my brother."

"Awkward."

"Not anymore. My God you are the hottest girl I've ever been with, and believe me, there's been plenty, but you, Harlow, are fan-fucking-tastic."

"You are quite drunk, but thank you very much."

"You are most welcome. Oh God ba… aaa… baby, I'm going to come, are you with me?"

"Yes, yes, yes, but I told you don't call me… Oh God,

here I go. Ahhh. YES.YES.YES!"

"Wow."

"Wow is right."

'I've never..."

"Me neither."

"Um, so what do we do now?"

"Nothing. Go back out there with our friends. You go to one end of the bar, I'll go to other."

"That's cold, baby. So can I have your last name?"

"What did I tell you?"

"Yea, yea, don't call you baby. I gotcha. Sorry."

"No need to apologize. And no last names, it complicates things. This was... fun. Let's just leave it at what it is. Well, Raphael, it was a pleasure."

"Pleasure is putting it lightly, don't you think, Harlow? That's what you said your name was right?"

"Yes, or you could name me the random dirty girl you just fucked against the wall of a bar bathroom."

"I'd rather call you the best fuck I've ever had, will that suffice?"

"Well then I take that as a huge compliment, I'm flattered."

"You should be."

"Shake my hand, Raphael, and let's get on with our lives."

"Nice meeting you."

"Same to you."

"Bye."

"Bye."

CHAPTER 1

Don't I Know You From Somewhere?

Cruz

Looks like it's a slow night. You wouldn't think it since it's the beginning of the summer and all. How many God damn crossword puzzles can one person do in one night? How many times can I check my Facebook, or tweet shit? There has to be some dumbass teenager riding his Mongoose somewhere, half cocked off his rear. Maybe two horned up teenagers fucking in a car. I can give them one hell of a scare by banging my flashlight on their fogged-up window and make them shit their pants. That would be hysterical. At the most maybe I'll be able to get a glance at some naked titties. But noooo... I have to stay here at this stupid side street and watch for drunk drivers. Now doesn't that sound like a party? This boredom is almost too much to bear. Maybe I should text the little honey I did doggie style last night. I'd tap that again. What was her name again... Kelly, Shelly,

Melly? Doesn't matter as long as she doesn't get too clingy.

I still have six more hours of this shift to go. This patrol car gets uncomfortable after being in it for a few hours. I should be drinking with my friends. It's literally our second night here. When I got this rent-a-cop job, I didn't expect to be working so soon, but this is a busy place. There are lots of clubs and bars, and that equals plenty of derelicts roaming the streets. So, while all my boys are getting acquainted with the ladies who, apparently, moved in next door today, I'm here, in this car, listening to calls come in over the radio to and from the station. My phone is buzzing. I'm guessing it's Max or Porter texting to tell me how I'm missing out on some new hot pussy.

Oh, wait, never mind, it's Kelly, Shelly, Melly. Fuck me, her name is Stacy. How the hell did I screw that up? Probably cause her name ends in a 'Y', or probably 'cause I could give two shits less what her name is. I was drunk. She was there at the bar, waiting for it. I took her back to my house, and I gave it to her. My motto: get in, get off, and get the fuck out. I've always made my decisions about chicks based on this. It's who I am, and I could care less who thinks it's wrong. I don't do relationships. I saw the constant stream of boyfriends come and go from my crack-head mother's life, including my dad, so I want no parts of them. Zero, zilch, nada. Her text says she wants to know what time I get off, so she can get off.

Classy.

I send a quick text back:

Working till 6 AM. TTYL

I'm putting my phone on silent. I don't even want to see a response from her. Why did I even give her my number? They are usually the ones giving theirs to me. I must have been pretty wasted to do it.

Oh, God, I seriously want to bang my head against this window. If it's going to be this boring all summer long, next year I'll stay home. I'll get a permanent job somewhere in the city. It'll be a lot more exciting with all the drug dealers and gang members, that's for sure. I'll miss this though. The shore house, the summers with no worries. Fuck worrying. Oh, whoa, oh... Oh... Looks like my night just got better. Look at this car driving 10 mph and swerving back and forth. Holy shit, I may just have hit the jackpot. God damn drunks. I have to pull out and start flashing those pretty lights.

Thank God they're pulling over, and I don't have to chase them, although, a car chase would be super cool. Never did one of those before. That will have to wait for another day. The person shut their car off, but left their lights on. The sand and gravel beneath my feet is noisy as I approach the car. I tap on the window. The headlights from my car shine straight through the drunk's car, which I know will piss this asshole off to no end. Drunks have no patience. Ask my crack-head mom. Did I mention she's a drunk too? The drunk rolls down the window. It's a chick, but I only see her profile. The bright lights are blinding her, so she stares straight ahead, squinting at the reflection of my headlights in her rear-view mirror.

"License and registration, please. Have you been drinking this evening?"

She speaks quietly as she rummages through her glove compartment for her car registration.

"No, no sir. I'm lost. I'm on my way to my rental house and I have no idea where I'm going. It's only the second time I've been to this shore point."

Oh, man, I don't need her whole God damn life story.

"Just give me your license and registration first please,

then we can discuss this." She hands it over, her head down. I snatch it from her hands and take a look. I shine my flashlight down onto the license.

Then I feel it. The dropping of my stomach. The undeniable shock as I look at the name on the license.

Holy fucking shit. Her name is Harlow. The name swirls around in my head, makes me dizzy, still. A year later.

Harlow, as in the girl I fucked in the bathroom of one of the bars down here last summer. Harlow... Harlow. Still to this day, I find that name so odd. Guess that's why it stuck in my head, my smaller head actually. Who the fuck names their kid Harlow? Then again, who names their kid Raphael. Oh, yea, that's right. My crack-head mother.

Still, it's her. I will never forget her or that tight as fuck pussy of hers. She never gave me her last name, so I had no idea where to find her. If I can remember that night after the dozen and a half beers I had, I'd go back for seconds. It doesn't happen often, well actually, not really at all, but you don't forget a hot-pocket like hers. What I also remember is that she was cold, bitchy, but she was dominant and had complete control over the situation. I recall the major headache I had later that night, and it wasn't from the alcohol. Instead, it was from the constant pulling of my hair as she hung on to it as I lifted her ass and legs and slid my cock in. It was single-handedly the hottest thing I have ever done in my life; fuck a stranger in a bathroom, not giving last names. I've practically done it all. You name it, I've done it, and then some. Sometimes two at a time, but this was new for me. If I remember correctly, it was the same way for her, just for a fuck, to get in, and you heard it before my friends, to get off, and to get out.

That little light bulb goes off above my head.

Revenge is sweet, just like that snatch of hers. I silently

laugh inside, and I feel like a mad scientist ready to have his experiment come to life. Cue my maniacal laugh.

Harlow Hannum.

Hannum.

"Miss Hannum, will you please step out of the car and make your way to the back of your vehicle."

She starts to protest and with an attitude. Imagine that. I stand with my arms securely crossed over my chest, legs slightly apart, in an intimidating stance mind you.

"Sir, I haven't done anything wrong. I was going slow because I was looking for the street my rental house is on. I may have swerved a few times, but that's because I dropped my phone on the floor of my car and I was trying to pick it up. I'm not drunk."

I clear my throat to scare her. Miss Pissy Pants put her head down and lets out a sigh.

"I'll be the judge of that Miss Hannum. Please step out of the vehicle."

She reluctantly steps out with her head still down and makes her way to the back of her car. I pull my hat down a little further. No way am I having this chick recognize me. Maybe she wouldn't anyway, but I'm not taking that chance.

She tries to turn to look at me as I make my way back towards where she is standing. I can tell she's wearing glasses, and her hair is pulled up in a ponytail.

"Sir, if you would just let me explain."

"No need to right now, Miss Hannum. I'm going to give you a sobriety test. If you fail, you are coming down to the station with me for a blood alcohol test. Do you understand?"

She nods. I notice she's acting shy, not looking up at me, and submitting to my demands. That's a totally different girl than the one I screwed. Do you have any idea how many times over the last year I jerked off to that scenario? Hmm, let me count! ALOT! All I know is this is going to be fun!

"Have you ever had a sobriety test before, Miss Hannum?" Her side is to me, and she's leaning against the car, but is still refusing to look up. I'm praying she hasn't had one before, so she doesn't see straight through my plan.

"No, sir. I have not."

Ohh, her calling me sir makes my cock twitch.

"Then you have no idea what's involved. Is that correct, Miss Hannum?"

"No, sir, I don't."

Thank God.

"I have never been pulled over before. If you just check my driving record, you will see that I have never even had a ticket. I'm a teacher, sir, and I can't afford to have a blemish on my record."

A teacher, she tells me. Now stop and wait a damn minute. Back up the truck. That just made our whole encounter last year so, so much hotter. I fucked a teacher in a bathroom of a bar, didn't know her last name, and now I'm pulling her over. Where the fuck is David Lee Roth when you need him to serenade you?

"Fine, Miss Hannum. You will do everything I tell you to do. First, I need you to face sideways and close your eyes. Then I need you to extend your arms outward, take each of your index fingers and touch the tip of your nose, and return them to the outward position." She sighs. She fucking sighs like she's annoyed. I have to laugh to myself because I'm enjoying watching her be miffed. She does what I say. I bite the inside of my lip as I watch her. That's it, dirty girl, do as I say.

"I need you to walk along the edge of this grass line with one foot in front of the other."

She does what I tell her with a little less annoyance.

"Fine, Miss Hannum. Now please close your eyes and recite the alphabet." She crosses her arms, pushing up those nice, big chesticles as she does so and starts, and I immediately make her stop.

I say in my cockiest voice, "Backwards, Miss Hannum, backwards. You're a teacher. It shouldn't be that difficult."

"Are you serious?" She answers in a high pitched squeal.

"As a heart attack, Miss Hannum. Now proceed."

And she does it. She fucking recites the alphabet backwards. That's fucking hot.

"Very good, Miss Hannum. Now I need you to repeat after me, dum what diddy, diddy dum, diddy do."

"Are you fucking kidding me?" Oh, she's feisty. Me likey.

"Language, Miss Hannum. Now do as I say or I will be forced to handcuff you and take you down to the station."

Side note: handcuffing her sounds pretty cool right about now.

"Ugh, fine." She repeats it, and I so want to laugh right in her face. That's what you get for being a hot, fan-fucking-tastic lay with the blood as cold as a snake.

"We are almost done. Next thing is I need you to stand by your car, turn and face the back of the vehicle, and perform the moves to the Macarena."

She turns suddenly and throws her arms in the air. When she does so, her shirt rides up the slightest bit to reveal her flat stomach and belly button. Her shirt hangs off her one shoulder. Her skin shines from the lights, and it looks soft. My dick so badly wants to escape into her vertical smile, so I do my best not to look at it like it's a piece of taffy I want to lick. I silently plead to Morty; my penis.

Now is not the time boy, behave, and I will get you a treat later.

"Is this some kind of a joke? I've had a rough night. I'm lost. My phone died, and I've been driving for over three hours. My friends expected me to be here hours ago."

She's so flustered, and I'm enjoying every fucking second of it. I lower my voice an octave.

"This is no joke. This is how we do things at the Jersey Shore, ma'am. Now just do it."

And she does. She's so God damn submissive. Guess she's not as smart as she looks. She shakes her ass and does all the moves associated with that stupid-ass dance. I remember those moves, the way her ass shook that night at the bar. My dick was at full attention, and the memory of it is making my pants a little tighter now. Shit, I can't have a boner while I'm giving her a sobriety test. I better bail, even though she keeps doing the dance, jumping from spot to spot, and then repeats it. Oh, God am I going to have some stories for the guys tomorrow.

"Ok. You are finished, Miss Hannum. Please return to your vehicle while I call in your license and registration."

She turns to me, so I turn my head towards my patrol car when she speaks.

"Wait, if I'm not mistaken, aren't you supposed to do that before you give me a sobriety test?"

Oh, crap, she's on to me. Think Cruz, think with that handsome head of yours.

"We do things differently here at the shore, Miss Hannum."

She doesn't argue, doesn't protest. She just goes and sits in her car. I have no intention of calling this in. She's obviously not drunk. Her explanations make sense. I wait a few minutes, check my phone for texts, there are none. Everyone is most likely passed out. I get out and travel back to her car to hand her her things back. I pull my hat down a little more and try not to make eye contact with her.

"Here are your things, Miss Hannum. I strongly suggest

you make sure that when traveling long distances, your phone is completely charged and if it drops on the car floor, either pull over to retrieve it, or leave it there. You should be smarter than that, being a teacher and all."

She looks up at me, and for a nanosecond our eyes meet. My blues with her blues, surrounded by black horn rimmed frames. Hot for teacher, baby, hot for teacher. She still doesn't recognize me.

"Thank you Officer... Cruz. You know, for a split second you looked familiar to me. Do I know you from somewhere?" She looked at my name tag.

R. Cruz. Glad it doesn't say our first names. As soon as she's done looking, I bow my head.

I'm done messing with her.

"No, that's impossible. I live here, and you obviously don't. Have a good night, Miss Hannum. Stay safe." I think I just dodged a bullet. She shrugs and turns the ignition on her car.

"You know I'm still not sure of the way you conduct things here Officer Cruz, but do you know where Barnacle Lane is? That's the street my rental house is on." Now I'm frozen.

Is there a hidden camera here, in the street light, in a tree somewhere? This is impossible, unimaginable, and just plain old mother fucking insane.

"What's the house number?"

"1027."

"I happen to know exactly where that is, Miss Hannum. Just follow me."

CHAPTER 2

Now I Know Why They Call Cops 'Pigs'

Harlow~

Patrol car number… check. Badge number… check. Last name of the bastard who totally embarrassed me with his, 'I'm the law, now bow down to me, 'cause I'm about to make you look like an ass with my fake sobriety test' attitude… check. I know what I'm doing first thing in the morning. I'm reporting the grade-A ass of a cop. He may think I was the deer-in-the-headlights, never getting pulled over before, but when I get his ass canned, he'll know better. That's really all I needed to end this horrific night. I'm tired. I'm cranky, and he messed with the wrong girl. Willow and the rest of the girls are probably so worried, unless they're drunk and don't even realize I'm late. I should have been there three hours ago. Last summer when I came down for the weekend with Willow, she drove, and of course, I didn't pay attention. My nose was most likely stuck in a book. Studying for the Praxis was a bitch. So was student teaching, but I loved it. I had a third grade class. They were amazing, and I'll miss them, but since it all went so well, I pray that they will hire me before the end of the summer. For now, I just want this summer to be relaxing before I enter into the real world. I want to sleep till noon if I want. I want to go to the beach, read, drink, and just have fun. I want a no-worry, stress-free summer. God knows these past few years have been horrific, for reasons I can't allow myself to think about right now.

This cop is going so fast, someone should pull him over. If it's the last thing I do, I'm bringing this jerk down.

Dickcop, yep new name for him, pulls up to the address I gave him. Dickcop is rolling down his window and sticks his hand out to point to the house. It's a three-story twin, with a huge deck on the top floor, spanning the length of the front of the house and the house attached to it. There are parking spots under the deck that are now occupied, so I guess my car will be ok if I park in front of the house. I can still see a few people on the deck. Red solo cups as far as the eye can see cover tables, and the only lights that are on are the ones on the street illuminating the deck. Guess I missed a good party. I get out of the car, and I can smell the salt in the air, and the distant, sweet scent of cotton candy from the boardwalk. I inhale as droplets of memories flood my senses about the last time I was here. They are blurry, but I didn't forget. I can feel my cheeks heat up, and all I can do is shake my head.

I see a guy in a short, black mohawk peek over the railing. He doesn't spot me yet.

"Who's down there?" I look up at him as he notices Dickcop's car. Dickcop is ignoring him. He's now backing up his patrol car, and rip roars it down the street. Nice.

Doesn't even wait to see if I get inside ok. So much for depending on the safety of law enforcement. That just solidifies the fact that cops are pigs. Bacon bits, pork heads, I can't think of another analogy right now. My head hurts.

"Hey, who are you?" Mohawk man yells down to me.

"Harlow."

"Harlow…" He taps his finger to his chin, squints his eyes, and takes a sip from his cup. "Harlow, oh, Willow's friend. You are in big trouble, Missy. She's been having a heart attack waiting for you." Mohawk man smiles. I roll my eyes. I knew it. Willow is so high strung, and I'm surprised she didn't have a search party out looking for me. I pop my trunk and grab my suitcase. When I close the trunk and look back up towards mohawk man, he's gone. Second man tonight who has the manners of a Neanderthal. Twenty three year old guys are assholes. I spin around after retrieving my suitcase, and standing there, hand extended out to me, is mohawk boy.

"Max Vincent. Nice to meet you." I return the gesture.

"Nice to meet you. Harlow Hannum."

"You are in the dog house with that crazy friend of yours. She's nuts, you know that right?"

I chuckle because his statement is right on the nose.

"Yes, this is true. I've known her since the 6th grade." I give him a half-smile.

I know she's nuts. Now a stranger knows it too. Way to make a good first impression, Willow.

"Well, I've known her for less than a day, and I too know this is true. Let me grab that suitcase for you. Anything else I can bring up?"

Max seems like a nice guy. Cute, polite, and I dig the close-cropped mohawk, his 'Keep Calm and Party On' t-shirt, and the black Chuck Taylor's. Heavy, dark stubble aligns his face and an adorable smile that extends from one cheek to another.

"I'm good. Just have to get a box of stuff from the back seat."

"Ok, great. I'll carry this up for you."

Max grabs my suitcase and begins to walk up a flight of wooden steps that are located beside the house I'm staying in. It's dark so I'm not really sure what the house is like. There are a lot of windows, that I can tell. We reach the top, and I follow Max through a sliding glass door which leads to a kitchen. I see Willow sitting there with our other friend, Thea. She turns and just the way she looks at me, makes me think, yep, I'm in big trouble. Max turns to my ear and whispers, "Certifiably crazy. I feel bad for ya." He winks at me and flashes a smile.

"Harlow Hannum, where in the hell have you been? I was ready to call the cops." She hops up and stalks towards me, grabbing my shoulders, and I can faintly smell the scent of hops and barley on her breath.

"No need, I was just with them. I got pulled over."

"Why would you get stopped by the cops? What did you do?" Willow asks in a tone a mother would use to scold a teenager. She flips her long, blonde hair over one shoulder and takes an autocratic stance before me.

"Nothing. He thought I was drinking and driving, but I bent down to get my phone that dropped on the floor of my car. I may have swerved off the road a bit."

"Great, Har. You are in town for five minutes and already have a run in with the fuzz. Am I going to have to put a leash on you this summer?"

"First time in Sandy Cove I take it."

"No, Mr. Mohawk. It's not her first time. We were here last summer, stayed at the Beach Comber Inn," Willow spews at Max, obviously annoyed with his questioning.

"Were you invited into this conversation what's your name… Max is it?"

"Geez, bring it down a notch, Miss Crazy Pants. I helped her with her suitcase."

"Willow, relax. The cop, who pulled me over, led me here. I was lost, and he knew where the house was. Max was on the deck and asked who I was when I pulled up."

It dawns on me that Max called Dickcop by his name outside, which means he knows him. I turn to him and out of Willow's grasp, surprised.

"Max, when I pulled up, you called out to the cop and referred to him by name. How do you know him?"

"Cruz? Cruz lives…" Before he can finish, we are suddenly interrupted by Porter, Willow's cousin, as he pulls open the sliding door and strolls in.

"Harlow, you made it! Wills was going nutso. We were about to send out a search party to look for you." Porter comes up to me, pulls me to his chest, and gives me a bear hug. I love Porter. He's a great guy and has been protecting Willow and me ever since we grew boobs. Porter has the face of a noble dignitary, someone with money, aristocratic even. Tall, well over 6'2" and shoulders that are proportionally fitting for his stature. Chiseled chin, dark hair, thick and wavy, perfect nose, cleft in the chin, and a smile of epic proportions. Porter was it, every girl's wet dream, except for mine. I look at him as a brother. Always have. I think I have serious problems.

"I'm fine. I was lost and my phone died, and I got pulled over by…" Max now interrupts.

"Cruz pulled her over. He brought her here."

"Oh, so you met Cruz?" Max squints his eyes, looking at me intently.

"Wait, you said you came here last summer? To Sandy Cove? Your name is Harlow?" He looks confused, then nervous, then runs his hand over his mohawk and mumbles something along the lines of he had too much to drink tonight.

"Porter, dude, I um, I think we better let the girls get some sleep. It's getting late."

"Wait, Max. You didn't answer my question. How do you know Dickcop?"

"Dickcop?" Everyone asks in unison.

"Yes. Dickcop. He pulled me over because he thought I was drinking and driving, then proceeded to give me the most farcical sobriety test in all of God's creation, when I was clearly sober, and acted like a total ass the whole time." Max looks to Porter. Porter looks to Max, then at me.

Thea looks up at Willow, in her drunken stupor, "She's using the big words again, isn't she?"

Max asks, "What did he make you do?"

My anger returns as the memories of what he made me do resurface.

"The Macarena."

"The Macarena?" Porter asks, and I nod. I take Willow's cup out of her hand and drink some of the contents.

Laughter erupts between Max and Porter, and my irritation grows. Porter turns to me.

"Har, are you serious? Cruz isn't like that, he's pretty cool. You'll meet…"

Max tugs at his arm suddenly with force and shoves him towards the door.

"Um… We better go now. Glad you made it here safe, Harlow. We'll see you girls tomorrow. Beach, badminton, and beers."

"You can count on it after this night. Oh, and Max, this

conversation is not over, but if you see Officer Cruz in the very near future, tell him his ass is mine."

Max looks to me with a smirk. "Oh, I'm pretty sure you already have had it."

He and Porter exit, and I'm left with that absurd statement.

"Is it wrong that a haircut can turn me on?" Willow says dreamily.

"A haircut?" Thea looks at Willow in disbelief.

"Do I stutter?"

I look at Thea and we watch as Willow's head resumes its position in the clouds.

"So you are here for one day, and already in love? Seriously, Wills?"

"Well… Then what about you, Thea? Got your eye on anyone in particular?"

Willow takes a long sip from her cup and points directly at her.

"Doesn't matter," Thea responds quietly.

"And I didn't say I was in love. He's just got that, 'I'm a bad-boy, rock and roll, mohawk wearing, sweet as pie, hot as sin, smart as a whip attitude'. I dig that, and that act of him annoying me, just exactly the way I want it to go," Willow adds.

"You dig everyone."

"That's irrelevant." I give her a look of disgust.

"You're drunk." Thea tells her, jokingly. "Not denying it." Slurs a drunken Willow.

I shake my head and rub my eyes with the heels of my hands. My exhaustion is swiftly taking over my body.

"Oh, God, I need to get to bed. It's been a hell of a long day, and I have to get some sleep, so I have the energy to have a cop fired tomorrow."

"He really made you do the Macarena in the street? And you went along with it?"

"I didn't have a choice, Thea. I needed to do what he said so I could get here before Willow put my face on a milk carton."

Willow gulps down the remaining liquid from her cup and gives me an agreeable eye roll, something she is famous for.

I grab my suitcase and leave the box in the living room that houses my shampoo, makeup and other girly items.

"Point me in the direction of a bed, please."

The girl's stand up from the table, shut off the lights and lead me to my room. I notice the decor of the home. Beach scene portraits line the walls of the hallway leading to the bedrooms. Pale blue paint is the backdrop and light colored plush carpets under my feet. Willow shows me to one of the four bedrooms with the same decor as the hallway. A seashell embossed comforter on the bed, a million decorative throw pillows, and a nice, cozy queen size bed sits there begging for me to lay on top, instead the girls decide to flop on it. Pillows fly off the bed from the force of the 'kerplunk' of their bodies. I unzip my suitcase and begin to place my clothes in the drawers of the nearby chest. My friends lay there, watching and giggling from intoxication, and I'm jealous of their cloudy brains.

"You guys had a party tonight?"

Thea twirls her hair, yawns, and looks towards me. "Not us, Porter and Max. They know a lot of people."

"Porter's been coming down here every summer for as long as our families have owned these homes, so he's made a lot of friends."

Willow's mom and her sister, Porter's mom, bought the twin homes when their father left them a hearty inheritance when he passed away. The sisters decided to buy the homes so their families could enjoy them summer after summer. Willow and Porter are two years apart, and might as well be brother and sister, rather than cousins.

"How do Porter and Max know each other?"

"According to Porter, Max's band played at the same bar Porter worked at when he was in college. They became friends, but Max travels now with his band and goes to school for engineering."

See, I knew he had a big brain. Looks and brains are a big turn on, and totally Willow's type. I have a type as well. Assholes. Write that down. Harlow Hannum has a thing for assholes. I guarantee one of the girls is about to bring up the biggest asshole of them all.

Wait for it, wait for it… It's coming. Which one will say it first? I'm taking bets.

"Well, at least you don't have to see Cha…"

Ding, ding. Leave it to Willow.

Thea doesn't even let her get his full name out before covering her mouth with her hand.

"Willow, he is a name we do not speak. He's like Lord Voldemort from Harry Potter. You know better."

She shoves Thea's hand away from her face.

"Fine. We do not speak his name. So maybe you'll find that guy you got banged by in the bathroom last year."

I reach over and smack her.

"Ow. What was that for?"

"Because, it's something I'd like to forget, and if it wasn't for the constant badgering and questions like did I have diarrhea or something because I was in the bathroom for so long, you would never have known. It's embarrassing enough, and I hold myself 100% accountable for my actions."

Willow takes her hands away from her head and lays her head back on the pillow.

"I wouldn't go as far as to say you were all to blame for it. I'd say Jose Cuervo was also responsible. But all in all, it was super hot!"

The thoughts of that night make me nauseous. I swallow hard thinking of how later that night I expelled the contents of the Jose Cuervo from my belly into the porcelain God. I never get that drunk, and I mean never. But I had just seen the one whose name we do not speak, making out with a girl in the corner of that bar. All the while he was flashing his infamous, sexy glare at me, while his tongue probed the inside of the trollop's mouth. I sat back down at the bar, not returning to where my friends were playing pool with some guys they met and that's when I saw him. He was sitting four stools away from me, ordering a beer, as I was ready to consume my sixth tequila shot of the evening. A totally detrimental decision on the part of a smart girl like myself.

I bounce off the bed and pull each girl up by the hands.

"Time for bed. Summer starts tomorrow and I plan on making it a day of fun and sun, after I get a cop fired. Now, get out." They trail off to their rooms one by one with half-hearted waves. I slip into my tank top and pajama bottoms. I retrieve my toothbrush from my knapsack, find a bathroom, brush my teeth, and I know sleep will claim me in no time.

I wake up to the sun beginning to shine in my eyes. I had forgotten to close the blinds before I fell asleep. I look at my watch on the bedside table. 6:45 a.m. This is only fifteen minutes later than I get up for student teaching. I roll to my back and punch the mattress. Coffee is calling my name, I suppose. I rise and head to the bathroom, run a brush through my hair, splash some water on my face, and brush my teeth. The house is quiet. I seriously doubt anyone is awake. They are normal, unlike myself. I tiptoe into the kitchen. The living room is bright from the sun's rays, and as I go to fill up the coffee pot with water at the sink, I look out the kitchen window to see the calm waters of the bay. There is a large dock that extends outward towards the back. It appears to be in the middle of the two homes. I see a small boat on Porter's side. It's so peaceful.

I need peaceful.

I need relaxing.

I need stress-free.

I need not to be reminded of him. The one whose name we do not speak.

I make the coffee and stalk the consistent drip, drip of the savory grounds, working their way through the filter and pouring into the pot. I tap my fingers on my cheek, as I hold my head in my hands. The anticipation is a killer. I shut my eyes momentarily in the hopes that the coffee will miraculously brew faster if I will it to, and I hear something. A high-pitched squeal of some sort. Sometimes muffled, and I know it's not the sound of a seagull. I walk around to investigate. I hear it again. Where is that coming from? I look out a window on the side of the house, nothing there. I look out the window to the dock, nothing. I walk to the sliding door which leads out onto the front deck. I hear it again, and jump back. Oh, God, someone is being murdered right outside this very door. I run to the kitchen, grab the house phone and a large, sharp knife from the butcher block on the counter. I once again approach the door. 911 is about to be dialed, and now I'm waiting to see the murderer. I rip open the drapes, and swing open the sliding door with the force of a Trojan solider. And I jump, knife in hand, ready to stab, and I scream.

"Oh, my God. Oh, my God. I... I'm so sorry. I had no idea what that noise was. Oh, my God." I turn around after I see in front of me, not a murder, not some kind of sick crime, or a robbery, but a leggy, dark-haired, tanned girl riding a guy on a lounge chair... reverse cowgirl style. Nude. I mean, butt-ass naked. I couldn't see his face, because it was covered by Miss Big Tit's head. All I can see is his big hands grasping her hips, and the unrelenting moans coming from both of them. And do they stop when they see a twenty three year old woman in her Minnie Mouse pajama pants, wielding a butcher knife? No. They continue. Bouncing before me, like my existence has no bearing on their activity. With my back still turned to the couple, Willow and Thea run out the door apparently after my blood-curdling screams were heard. They come to a complete halt and scream themselves. Enter Max and Porter running onto the deck from their house, Porter running over to cover Thea's eyes, (no idea why), and Max yielding an uncontrollable laugh.

Mass confusion surrounds the deck. I still have my eyes covered. The knife I held and dropped sticks up out of the wood on the deck, and I'm annoyed. Thea tries to knock Porter's hands off her eyes, and Willow, well Willow is just plain staring.

"Well, I'll be damned, take a look at those tattoos."

I slap Willow, again, but I don't turn around until I hear Porter yell the one name that has been imbedded in my brain since last night... Cruz.

Son of a bitch.

"Cruz, man, what the hell? Get her off of you. We have girls standing here."

I will myself not to turn. Don't do it, Harlow, most of all, do not pick up that knife and stab that man to death. And I don't. My mind is strong. I try to have complete control. I will have complete control over this situation. I hear some rustling of clothing, and I look to Willow, who has a smirk on her face. I ask Willow, "Are they done, Wills?" She nods.

That's when my body swings around, and I charge forward, bracing myself to tell this bastard what I really think of him.

Dickcop.

And there it is. The bile I suddenly feel rising up in my throat, the jaw dropping moment, the head-spinning, mind-blowing enlightenment when I realize I have seen those inked arms before. I have seen that face. I have seen that wavy brown hair. My hands have been through it, felt it, pulled it, and those striking blue eyes. They have crossed my path, and bore into me like some kind of a hypnotizing coercion. I've looked into them. I know I did.

Those hands, they were on me.

Those fingers in me.

Those lips upon me.

That tongue inside my mouth.

And his... His...

A flood gate of memories sweeps through my head.

Bar.

Tequila shots.

Eye contact.

Head motion.

Bathroom.

Against the wall.

No last names.

Pure, raw, uninhibited, unlawful hot sex.

He knows it. He knows it's me by the cocky smirk on his

face. I'm frozen. My legs are locked, my muscles not allowing me to go any further.

"Hello, Miss Hannum, enjoying your time at the shore?"

From the moment he speaks, it suddenly all makes sense. He's the cop who pulled me over last night, and the guy I had my little tryst with at the bar last year. Things like this happen to only me. That's when I see it.

I see red. Yes, it's true, when anger gets the best of you, you do see red. Flaming red. I am an educated, smart, well brought up woman. I ooze class, but the way he bites his lip, grins at me, and winks, makes all the years of charm school want to fly out the window. The need to claw his face, have my knuckles collide with his chin, overtakes me, but I must keep my composure.

Everyone just stands there, and tall, tanned, and leggy Dickcop-rider whines after she dresses.

"Cruz, you said you would take me home. This scene is creeping me out." She stands there, arms folded, tapping her stiletto-clad foot, while six pairs of eyes stare at her.

"Sure, baby. Give me a few minutes. Why don't you go grab yourself a cup of coffee in the house. I'll be right there."

She exits, and the staring contest begins, until Willow breaks the silence.

"How do you know her last name is Hannum?"

My fists clutching my sides, I move a bit closer. There's a panic in Max's eyes as he moves when I do.

"You... You... You?" My last 'you' is a question.

He rises up from his chair, shirtless, boxer briefs staring me in the face. He towers over me, smirk still present on his face. He licks his bottom lip and invades my personal space. He's so close. I can smell the sex on him. How repugnant. He leans in towards my ear. "Me, me, and yes, me."

He pulls away. I feel my blood pressure rise, and my pulse quickens at the same time. I lunge forward, but Max, who is next to me grabs my arms to hold me back.

I struggle to get myself out of Max's grasp. The girls are rushing towards me, and try to pry his hands off my arms.

"You son of a bitch. You made me look like a fool last night. I knew what you were up to and I am going to get your ass canned for it!"

The look on this brute's face energizes my madness. He crosses his arms and is watching as I struggle to try to claw at his perfect face. He smirks. He's smirking like he knows he got me, that he's proud of what he did to me.

"What the hell are you smiling at, you bastard?"

He comes closer to me, knowing Max won't let me go at him. I stop my struggling, and now we are practically nose to nose.

"I was getting my revenge on you, for not giving me your last name. You know who I am, baby. How could you forget?"

He licks those God damn lips of his.

Oh, now he's done it.

So what do I do since my legs are not seized, no longer bound to the ground?

I knee him in the testicles.

Take that, Dickcop. Those self-defense classes I took in college just paid off.

"And don't call me baby," I scream.

He falls to the ground. Max releases me, and bends down to see how the asshole is.

Dickcop holds himself in between his legs, gasping for air, rolling around on the deck like some kind of wounded animal.

Good.

Max looks up at me, obviously horrified.

"What the hell did you do that for?"

Dickcop still can't catch his breath, and I'm suddenly hit with a case of guilt. Did he really deserve that?

Let me think…

Yep!

"He's pissed because I never gave him my last name."

And the confusion between my friends and Porter continues.

"Har, he called you Miss Hannum. How did he know that if you just said you didn't give him your last name?"

I don't want to tell Porter. What would he think of me, I'm like a sister?

Dickcop raises his head enough to speak, gruffly, "She's the girl from the bathroom last summer."

Porter, God bless him. He shakes his head and studies the air in front of him to try to get around what Dickcop just said.

And just like that, the recognition in his eyes says he knows.

"Holy shit! Cruz? Harlow? Last year? Bar? Missing for a long time? No clue where you went until you came back looking like you returned from a war? I'm going to be sick."

Willow smacks his chest.

"Oh, please. She's still a woman with needs Porter. She's not a baby."

"I know she's not a baby, but I know what went on that night and Cruz said she… and then he said they…" Porter stammers for words, runs his hand through his hair and down towards the stubble on his face. "And then he was like, and we were like… oh, God, never mind. It's Harlow."

He looks exhausted.

Dickcop rises, barely, off the ground, and he's angry. I mean really angry.

"You bitch. I need my balls. Why would you do that to me?"

Now I feel tough as nails, stronger than strong. I'm not afraid of him or his flaring nostrils.

"You made me look like a fool. You made me dance that stupid dance on a street, in the middle of the night. Then you have the audacity, the... the impudence, the insolence to smirk?"

He contorts his face in a confused way and crosses his arms across his chest. He looks to my friends as to say 'help me out here'.

"Does she always use big words like that?"

They nod in unison.

I'm so out of here. I turn on my heels and head for the door.

Thea turns to stop me.

"Where are you going, Har?" Flustered, I turn back to look at her.

"I can't look at him anymore. Porter, I suggest you get your friend to leave and let him go back to whatever rock he crawled out from."

"Yes, Porter. Tell me to go back where I came from. Please. I beg you, dude." Dickcop clasps his hands together as to plead with him. I have one foot almost in the door. I never want to see him again, and I cannot believe that Porter actually hangs with someone this obtrusive.

"Cruz, maybe it's better if you did. It's only the beginning of the summer and it will be a long one if you don't."

The big jerk nods, agreeing and starts for the slider. As I

wait for him to exit, I begin to feel a bit of relief. He turns, still in those tight boxer briefs and as much as the sight of him repulses me, I ponder the reason for the sudden dampness in my underwear. Willow has drool seeping from her mouth, and before I have a chance to, Thea wipes the corner of it, near her lip, and whispers, "Close your mouth, Willow. You're salivating."

"No shit. I'm surprised you're not."

He suddenly turns to me.

"I apologize, Miss Hannum. My balls and I do, actually. I hope you have a very enjoyable and unforgettable summer. Nice knowing ya."

With that, he's gone, and thank the sweet Lord.

Now I just wait for the questioning, but it never comes. It's just a constant state of confusion on the faces of the people surrounding me.

Max glares at me, then makes his way back into the house.

My frustration seizes me. I grumble and go in the house. The remaining people on the deck follow behind.

I go into the kitchen to finally have my caffeine fix. I stand in front of the coffee pot, pour myself some of the dark, smooth liquid goodness, spoon a half pound of sugar in it, and take a long, well-deserved sip. I shut my eyes, savoring the moment it reaches my taste buds. I lean on the counter and feel a presence behind me. Actually, several.

Without turning around I address them.

"What? I feel you all staring at me. You want the run down?"

Three well-orchestrated yes's make their reply.

I shake my head and make my way to the dining table. They crowd me, like hungry dogs waiting for a meal. The events of last year and this morning are things I don't care to repeat, or revisit, but I know if I don't address it, it's going to be a long summer.

"Fine. But first things first. Do not ask questions, do not ask for details, do not pass go, and do not collect $200."

They nod like Stepford wives.

"Last year we went to that bar. We were all having a good time. I had just seen the name we do not speak of making out in a corner with someone. He looked at me and continued the deed. I felt devastated and decided to go to the bar, order something to try to numb what I was feeling and that's when I saw him."

They are looking at me, waiting for the next chapter of the story. They know the rest. I just wish he wasn't part of it. He, I mean the one whose name we do not speak.

"I really don't feel like discussing this. You know what happens next." I bow my head and pass through them towards the sofa. When I think about the events leading up to my bathroom rendezvous, my heart hurts.

It's only been fifteen months, only fifteen. The pain, the mistrust, the lies. I'll never forgive myself for what I did. I'll never forgive him for allowing it to happen. I'll never be the same. The walls are built up. No one can tear them down now. No one. They can try, but I'm just bricks and mortar at this point. When it comes to matters of the heart, that best describes me.

Porter comes and plops on the sofa next to me.

"I'd like to kill that bastard, you know that right?" He grabs my hand in a brotherly sort of way, like he always has and winks.

"Killing him would do no good. I think he'd be more of a God to his disciples if you did, but thanks for the offer, Porter." I give him a half-hearted smile and rise from the sofa. If I stay in this house any longer, tears may come, and there is no way on God's green earth, I'll let anyone see me do that. I need the sun. I need to feel the warmth of it on my face. I need to feel the salt on my skin and not by tears on my face.

"I'm going to the beach. Who's in?"

A show of hands is displayed before me. Porter comes over, kisses my forehead, and whispers, "You are a strong girl, Harlow, and you can handle anything bad that is thrown at you, and I'm proud of you for that, but there's something I need to tell you. Cruz, well, he…"

I hold up my hand in front of his face to stop him.

"Porter, no. He's gone, I don't have to see him if I don't want to. I know he's friends with Max and if he comes to hang out with him, then I will just avoid his presence. Simple. Now off you go. I'll see you at the beach." I shove him down the hall and I hear him calling my name as I enter my bedroom and shut the door.

I sit on my bed, still reeling from what happened not twenty minutes ago. My anger has subsided. I feel calmer. It was just sex I tell myself. Just one night of sex between two consenting adults. Get in and get out. That's what I wanted. I wanted not to feel the pain, replace it with temporary bliss, euphoria.

I didn't care to think. I didn't want to be inside my own brain at that time. I wanted to step outside myself, to not be Harlow Hannum, to not be the doting daughter, sister, and friend. I wanted an escape. The whole ordeal was so unlike me, unlike my personality, but that is what he does to me. I'm a different person around him. He creates a different person within me. Makes me do things beyond all reason. Makes me doubt myself, my self-worth, yet I can't stay away. He pushed me to have sex with a stranger, just so the image of him kissing another girl would diminish from my memory. I did that. Now I see the stranger again. Yes, I was drunk, but not drunk enough not to know what I was doing. I knew exactly what I was doing. I just wanted it all to go away.

Take my pain.

Bury my pain.

Make me forget.

Make it so it was all just a dream.

Too late. I made my bed, now I'll spend my life lying in it.

CHAPTER 3

Let's call a truce, or something along those lines

Cruz

My fucking balls. My mother fucking balls. I'm probably sterile. Fine with me, don't want any rugrats running around my life anyway. Fuck that shit. This ice is just not cutting it. I need booze. I need booze now.

"Max, get me a whiskey, please." I still see stars when I open my eyes. The pain is unbearable. Sometimes I wish it was ok to hit girls. Yea, I said it, so. Sue me. I would never, but what gives that royal bitch the right to do that to me?

Here comes Porter. Oh, great, a lecture. I ain't got time for this shit.

"Harlow, Cruz? Really? Fucking Harlow?"

'Yea, really Porter, Harlow.'

"So what?" And really, so what? I fuck girls all the time. This one, in particular, stuck with me, but still so fucking what?

"She's like a sister to me. I've known the girl since she was ten. Our parents belong to the same country club together. They travel to Europe. I took Harlow to her first Cotillion. This is so fucked up."

Max and I stare at him, wondering what the fuck a Cotillion is. He rolls his eyes, knowing just from the looks on our faces what we are thinking.

"Jesus, it's a ball for rich people, ok. You dance and do fancy shit, but that's beside the point."

I don't really want to hear his point. I just want my balls not to be shoved up my throat anymore, and I want to go crash on the beach until I have to be back at work by six.

Porter is pacing, annoying me. Max is biting his nails like a chick and not getting me my whiskey like I asked. Some friend.

"Ok, so here goes. You fucked my cousin's best friend in a bathroom down here last year. You bragged about it, profusely, I might add, then you pulled her over, made her look like an idiot, and then you brought a girl up here and…"

I stop him because I totally forgot that my Saturday night special is still here. Probably in my bed, naked, legs spread, waiting for me to give it to her. Outdoor sex was hot, but she needs to go.

"Porter, no need to remind me what happened, but Max, dude, I need you to go into my room and go kick what's her name out of there."

The expression on his face is priceless, comical even.

"Why should I do it? You're the one who brought her home. Come to think of it, you worked till six a.m. How'd you score that?"

"I bailed her out when I got off. Saw her in a holding cell." I recall seeing her, a hot mess of a woman, sweaty, lipstick smeared, mascara running down her face. That's hot.

"She beat the shit out of some girl in a bar. They called the cops. I took my opportunity to help the poor damsel in distress. She sucks dick like a vacuum." I lean back on the sofa, my Morty suddenly sporting to life from the memory. Hands linked behind my head, I shut my eyes and wince a bit at the pain still radiating throughout my balls.

"So you brought her here and fucked her on my deck?"

Pretty much.

"Yea. So? I thought this is the kind of shit we talked about. Getting blasted, having fun, hooking up with as much random snatch as we can. We're twenty four years old. We have the rest of our lives to be serious and work, and for some of you, get a… what do you call it, um, the thing where all you do is bone one girl for the rest of your life. Ew."

Man, that's a scary thought. One pussy for the rest of someone's life. I always say 'variety is the spice of life.'

Porter stops pacing and looks at me with all the seriousness of a priest.

"Maybe, just maybe, some of us do want that, one person to be there for you. When you're having a shit day, someone to come home to every night, to wake up to, to laugh with, to live with."

He is making me nauseous. If he says the 'L' word, I'm so outta here.

"Someone to love, someone who's going to love you back."

And… I'm gone.

"Where are you going?" He asks.

I turn to him after I throw the damn bag of ice that was on my balls on the counter.

"I'm going to go get my suit on, grab a towel, and go

take a nap on the beach. I haven't slept yet."

As I make my way to my room, Max yells, "That chick is still in there. What do you want me to do?"

Shit! I forgot. I'll let Max have a go at her if he wants, but first he's got to go get my stuff out of the room.

"Go get some from her, dude, but before you do, grab my swim trunks on the table in there and a towel."

He lets out a frustrated sigh, but heads to the door anyway. His hand on the knob, he says without looking at me, "What do you want me to tell her?"

Interesting question, so I just go with the first thing that pops into my head. "Tell her I had to go on a secret mission for the C.I.A."

"C.I.A.?"

"Yea, she thinks I work for them and that I was just undercover as a cop, trying to solve a case of corruption among the police force."

Max scrunches up his lips, thinking of how that worked, and Porter shakes his head at me, as usual.

"That worked?"

I give him a sly smile.

"She rode my cock outside at the break of dawn, what do you think?"

He gives an agreeable look, making his own sense of the whole thing, and makes his way into the room. I wait around the corner until Max comes out with my stuff. I hear a loud crash when Max opens the door, and I only see his face.

"Dude, she's pissed, you better get lost. Here's your shit."

He throws it at me. I'll just go get changed in my car. I rush down the hall, with Porter on my tail.

"Cruz, there's just one more matter we need to discuss before you take your, um, nap. Harlow still doesn't know you are living here, and when she finds out, she's going to want to leave. I know her, she won't stick around."

I forgot she doesn't know. Oh, man, she is gonna be pissed. She's a feisty one, seems like the littlest of things sets her off. I don't really care. I like a challenge. Not that I plan on revisiting her hotdog highway again, but I'd like to think it would be fun to get under her skin, try to make her want me again, then blow her off.

"Listen, P, I paid you a thousand bucks to stay here this summer. I'm not going anywhere if that's what you're thinking. I have a job here this summer, and possibly permanently, 'cause God knows I'm not going back home."

He nods, agreeing with me, but I know he's not done with his little tirade.

"You're right, but I have to tell her. She paid my aunt too, you know, so if she wants to leave, I have to try to convince her to stay, it's only fair, and the two of you will have to learn to live with it."

I can live with it, but the question is, can she?

"Fine, man. I'm ok with it. I won't give her a hard time. I won't even be here a few nights a week, so she won't have to deal with me. Sound good?"

I'm not sure he's convinced. Porter and I are friends, but he knows what I'm like, and I'm not like Max. Max is smart. He has brains. He has a bad temper, but he's not a man-whore like myself. Yes, I call myself a man-whore. Hello… Proof is in the pudding. Max doesn't do the shit I do. He has more self-worth than me, more to lose. If he says he's going to do something, he does it. I can't keep a promise to save my life, but I'm a loyal friend. I'll give myself that. I learned that in the Marines. Stand behind your fellow brothers, there's a code of ethics that I'll carry on for the rest of my life.

"Cruz, just take it easy on her. The girl has been through a lot this past year and a half, and she needs a break."

That's interesting. Wonder what that's all about. Wait, I don't care. She kneed me in the gonads.

I salute Porter, and then we hear the subtle moans of Max and the chick in my room. Good for Max. He needed a little pink cookie to start off the summer.

I run out, go to my car and make a quick change. I lock my car and make my way down the four blocks to the beach. Between work and working my dick out, I'm exhausted. As soon as I find a nice, sandy place to crash, I'll be out of it in no time.

OW! What the fuck! What is that pain shooting in my leg? I throw the towel off that's been covering my head and feel a little confused. How long have I been sleeping? When I open my eyes and squint into the sun, I see an image standing in front of me. I can't make it out, between the brightness of the sun and the pain traveling through my lower limb, so I quickly scurry backwards on the sand. That's when I hear it. The voice of the ball-kicker.

"What in the hell are you doing here! Of all places on this beach, you have to camp on my beach block?"

Damn her.

When I adjust my vision and the pain in my calf begins to subside, I get a look at Harlow Hannum.

In a bikini.

Mercy.

Doesn't matter, 'cause this chick has now injured my nuts and my leg. No freaking way it's going to happen again.

"Listen lady, who do you think you are? I'm not some punching bag you can take out all your sexual frustrations out on."

She clenches her fists at her side. I'm well aware that her long, strawberry blonde hair is blowing around her like a wind tunnel. I can make out her freckles that are splayed across her nose. I didn't notice them last year or this morning. I like freckles, but this one's a pain in the ass, so I try to pay no mind to how cute they are.

"I am not sexually frustrated, you puerile neanderthal. But why is it that everywhere I am, you are? I thought I told you to get lost?"

What's with her and the big words? She sounds like Max and his big brain.

"I did get lost, Little Miss Mike Tyson. I left the damn house to get away from you."

"Me? Get away from me? Of all the asinine things. I don't even think you fathom the extent of the things you have done to me."

I am who I am. I'm not a revenge kind of guy by nature, but pushed far enough, I can easily be persuaded.

I inch a little closer to her. Her friends are by her side, but I lean into her ear so that only she can hear me.

"Listen, baby, let's not forget about the things that you have done to me." I wiggle my eyebrows up and down and slowly trace my lower lip with the very tip of my tongue.

I can see it, the steam coming out of her ears. The color in her cheeks is heating up to a nice dark pink, and it's not because of the sun. I can really get under her skin, rouse her up. Drive her absolutely, bat-shit crazy. This is going to be a fun summer.

Porter and Max make their way down to where we are and they stand beside me. Boys on one side, girls on the other, and it looks like a standoff. Shit, the tension is fierce. I like a little heat. I like a little drama. I'm the king of it.

"Well guys, Miss Hannum here thinks she owns the beach. I am here just being innocent, trying to take a nap, and my cojones were trying to rest as well. They've been through a war today thanks to you, baby."

She seethes me, despises me, and has a true distaste for me and my words. She shuts her eyes as tight as she can, rolling her lips between her teeth. She speaks through them, not opening her mouth much, but the words are clear.

"I told you, do not call me baby. I am not your baby. I loathe the word. It makes me ill. I will, however, apologize for my impetuous assault on your... well, those." She motions towards Morty and the boys.

"Fine. I accept, now I will also apologize for making you look like a total ass the other night. It wasn't professional of me. Truce?" I extend my hand to her, and she is reluctant to take it, so I repeat my mantra.

"Come on, Harlow. Truce?"

She does take it. I squeeze and allow my fingers to graze, gently, the top of her hand, which makes her pull away from my grip, fast. She acts like my hand was on fire. Jeez.

Porter lays his hand on my shoulder and squeezes it.

"Cruz, I'm proud of you man. It's going to be a long summer, and I really don't want any trouble in my parent's house, and Willow's mom will go ballistic if anything happens to hers. If we all have to live next to each other this summer, we all have to get along."

Everyone nods, except for Harlow.

Ha!

She figured it out.

She knows.

Awesome.

Oh, shit. Nevermind.

Her calmness is now replaced with a look of terror.

"What do you mean, Porter, if we have to live next to each other? Who? Us, you and Max? Please explain before I go mad?"

"Oh, I forgot to tell you. Cruz is our roommate. He's going to be living in my house with Max, me, and…"

Harlow is grabbing her towel and beach bag, stuffing the contents that were on her towel into her bag. When she's done, she swings the bag over her shoulder and starts to walk away, fast.

Her friends begin to yell at her to come back.

Harlow turns and walks back, well, almost running towards us.

"I'm not living here, Willow, with that, that, that man-whore." She motions to me, and I have to agree once again.

My name is Raphael Patrick Cruz, and I am a man-whore.

Yes. My middle name is Patrick, my crack-head mother is a mick. So!

She gets in my face (ohh, how I have a newfound love for freckles) and gives me a look of pure disgust. Her tone is quiet, but her delivery is spectacular.

"If you think I'm going to live next door to you for the next ten weeks, watch you parade around with skanks, listen to you have sexual encounters with them inside or outside of that house, and watch you and your caveman mannerisms, I will be put in a mental institution for the criminally insane, because I will kill you by the end of summer!"

Yikes, she can scream when she's angry, and if memory serves me, when she's coming too.

Mind… meet gutter.

She takes off and her friends look pissed. Porter's cousin,

Willow, the crazy one, gets near and starts to poke my chest.

"Listen here dickwad, you are not going to be the reason that girl leaves here. She is so deserving of this summer break. I can't even give you enough reasons. Just let me warn you." She takes my nipple, ouch, and starts to twist it. "If she leaves, and you don't try to rectify it, I will cut off your precious dick and serve it to the fish restaurant up the street, have them cook it up real nice, then shove it down your throat. You got me, copper?"

Ow, that hurts, and I'm pretty sure this is not a threat. Think Cruz, think.

Do the right thing?

Let her rip off my nipple?

Let her cut Morty off my body?

I love Morty, we have been friends since birth.

Ugh. Doing the right thing sucks. Totally.

"Fine. Ok. I will, but please stop twisting my nipple."

She releases me. Points to her eyes with her index and middle fingers, then at me, like a sign as to I'll be watching you. The girls walk away, and I'm left with a bruised nipple, calf, and balls.

Life's not fair.

"Guess I better go apologize." The guys nod to me.

I hate being a grown up. It sucks.

CHAPTER 4

Introducing Turnip

Cruz

By the time I reach the house and make it to the girls' sliding glass door, I'm really re-thinking this whole apology thing. Why should I? Because I tried to have a little fun with her? It really wasn't a big deal. I thought it was funny to see her dance around that street.

My conscience is battling with me, the angel on one shoulder, the devil on the other. The devil usually wins, but I'm seriously afraid of Willow. I'm pretty sure she means business, so I guess in this case, the angel is defeating my horn-clad friend. I just need to figure out how to give Harlow a reason not to leave, and I really have no idea how I'm going to pull this off. I've never had to apologize, admit I'm wrong, or at least be wrong. I'm close to perfection in my eyes. I need to stay here, do good at this rent-a-cop job so maybe I can get a full-time position with the force.

After chickening out about two or three times, I gently knock on the door. Willow comes to the door, opens it gently, and motions for me to come in. I follow her as she gives me the death glare.

"Where is she?" I say quietly.

"Packing, what do you think she's doing?"

Shit. I better make this good.

"Can I go talk to her?" She nods.

"Last room on the right, and remember what I said asshole, she needs to stay, so do your best to keep her here. I know being a nice guy may be new to you, but you better try, if your genitals know what's good for them."

This chick is scary, and if I don't make Harlow stay, I'll be afraid to go to sleep at night.

I take a deep breath in, as I pass two very pissed off broads, and make my way to Harlow's door. I reach it and quietly knock a few times. This is really not my thing, but here goes nothing.

I hear her faintly tell me or whomever she thinks it is to come in.

I slowly turn the knob and make my way in. She's turned so her back is to me and the rest of her is in her closet, taking out items of clothing. A large suitcase is on her bed, open, with a few things already in it.

I close the door behind me and lean against it. When she turns and sees me, she looks shocked, but surprisingly calm. Her eyes only meet mine for a split second, and she goes back to doing whatever she was doing. She addresses me without another glance.

"What are you doing here? You got what you wanted, I'm leaving. Hope you're satisfied."

Why do I suddenly feel bad? That's not like me. I don't

feel bad for anything. Not even homeless kittens, but when she looks at me, I can tell she's been crying.

I push off the door, arms still crossed and go to sit on the edge of her bed.

"I'm not satisfied, actually. I'm... I'm sorry, ok. I've been hard on you, and we've only been in each other's company for a few hours. I haven't been, well, I haven't been fair to you."

She snorts and gives a small 'ha'.

This isn't going as planned. I better step up my game.

"No, I'm serious. I'm just not used to girls being so..." She stops me.

"Cold?"

And I have to agree with her. That night, as hot as she was, she was cold as ice. I've bagged dozens and dozens of girls and very few stick in my mind, she was one of the few.

I smirk, "Yea, I guess you could say that."

She continues to throw shit in her suitcase, this time with a little more gusto.

Yikes.

"Listen, your friends want you to stay, so does Porter, and I'm trying to be honest with you."

She stops the assault on her clothing and places her hands on her hips, giving me an amused look.

"Well, I'm guessing that's a first for you, Officer Cruz."

I give my best one-sided smile and fiddle with her scarf that was meant to be thrown in her suitcase, but missed.

When I don't answer, she turns back to her closet, picking up shoes and emptying hangers. I bring the scarf up to my nose. I don't know why. It smells like a chick. It's soft, silky even.

Like a chick.

Actually, it smells really good. I don't remember how she

smelled that night, but I imagine that's what this scarf smells like. Is this what Harlow Hannum would smell like?

Does that sound sick? Maybe.

I throw it in her suitcase, and now I need to plead my case.

"Look, you're right. I'm usually the one who's right in a situation, and I'm not a nice guy sometimes, but I don't deliberately go around hurting people." I pause because what I want to say next may not go over very well, but I have to try before Morty is served on a bed of lettuce.

"Um, your friends and Porter tell me you've had a rough year and that you need a break, so I have to convince you to stay."

She turns around quickly and her eyes look weird, and she looks incredibly nervous.

"What did they tell you about me? What did they say? Tell me, you asshole. I need to know." She's close to my face, taking a fist and punching the bed next to where I'm sitting."

What the hell?

"Nothing. All they said was that you had a rough year. They didn't get into specifics. Chill."

This is getting weird to me. She smooths out her shirt and looks calmer now that she knows what her friends said. She shuts her eyes and swallows so hard, I can hear it.

"Fine." She slowly reopens them, but our eyes don't make contact. She looks at her suitcase, stares at it, and bites her lip.

"I do need this break. I don't want to go home."

There's a sadness when she says it, and for some unexplained reason, I kinda feel something I'm not sure of.

Sympathy? Is that what it's called? I dismiss it quickly. I stand up when I see her trying to zip up her suitcase and lug it off the bed. When it hits the floor, I still her hand with mine.

"Stop for a minute and listen. You should stay. I think maybe we can come up with some kind of solution, so we can both live here and enjoy the summer without being at each other's throats. I'm really trying here."

I grab the suitcase from her and throw it back on the bed.

"What the hell do you think you're doing?"

She's so difficult. In less than twenty four hours, I can tell.

"I'm trying to tell you let's figure this out. I work a few nights a week. You won't have to see me. You don't even have to talk to me when you do see me. If we are on the beach, ignore me. I can do it, if you can. It will be like we're strangers."

She closes the closet door and turns back to me. She's quiet for a moment, almost like she's thinking what she should say next. "We are strangers."

I laugh, and I'm thinking that yea, we are. Strangers, who had sex. How funny is that? I never even thought about something like that. People say it's such an intimate thing, and I've never thought of it that way. It's always about how it makes me feel. The pleasure of it, not the... what's the word Porter uses... intimacy? What a weird word.

It's all about the pussy.

"Yea, I guess we are, in a way. Guess I didn't think of it that way even though we, you know... did the nasty."

She rolls her eyes at me. "Do you always have to be so crude?"

What does she mean? That was crude for me to say? Wow, we really are strangers then, because I can be a whole hell of a lot cruder than that.

"No, baby, I'm not always that crude, but when it comes to the ladies, I can be a bit… free with my words and actions." I wink at her.

She grabs the handle of the suitcase and tries again to pull it off the bed.

Did I say something wrong?

"Wait, what are you doing? I thought I was getting through to you?"

She's quiet, now pulling the suitcase towards the door, I get out of her way, and I'm about to just let her go.

Then I think about Morty, and the thoughts of him no longer being with me, and now I'm scared. Shit.

"What did I say this time?"

She stops before she gets to the door. She looks so small with that big suitcase in her hands, so petite, so fragile.

"I think I've told you at least a half dozen times in the last few hours, not to call me baby. It's insulting, and it sounds like something only a male chauvinist pig with a small mind would say."

Not this again. What the fuck does she have against guys calling her baby? This is so not worth it. I'll ask Porter for my money back and sleep in my car for the next ten weeks. It's all bullshit.

"You know what? Forget it. Letting you leave is worth getting my dick chopped off for… well almost. Maybe I'll run away to Siberia. Eskimo chicks are hot," I mumble.

She turns to me, confused, but amused.

"What in God's name are you rattling off about? You are the most vexatious person I have ever met."

Is that English? The vocabulary on this girl is unbelievable.

"Ok, so I have no idea what that means, but it sounds like you are insulting me."

She lets out a frustrated groan as her hand goes to the knob of the door.

"Wait." I make a sudden move for her hand to stop her. I can't for the life of me figure out why I'm doing it, but I do. She stops, and I hear her let out an exaggerated sigh.

"Willow said she would cut off my dick. I… I mean penis and sell it to a seafood restaurant if I didn't convince you to stay. I really like my penis, and I'd like to keep it, so please, let's come to some kind of agreement, learn to get along with one another, and make it a nice summer." The room is silent. Eerily silent, and I wait to hear her reply. Then I hear her giggle. She giggles. She fucking giggles.

"She really said that?"

"I wouldn't lie about something like that, trust me." And I wouldn't. Morty is like a brother to me. "I'm not a bad guy, really. I'm not once you get to know me. I'll behave."

"Ok. Fine. I have a few conditions."

She turns around and motions for me to sit on the bed. I do, but she remains standing, and I feel like I'm about to be scolded. She paces in front of me, looking at the floor and not at me.

"First things first. No more deck sex, please. I'd like to enjoy the view from it without seeing you and your flavor of the week engaging in sexual acts."

"Ok, I can deal with that."

"Second, when you are entertaining someone of the female persuasion, please keep the noise down to a minimal roar. I fully understand that this may be a difficult feat for you, being the man-whore you are, but have some respect for the people living next to you."

Oh, God. Is she serious? How the hell am I supposed to keep a chick I'm banging quiet? I mean, I get the deck sex thing, but damn.

"Now wait just a minute, baby, how am I…"

Shit. If I could eat that last word, I would, because now I know what's next. Just the look on her face says it all. She crosses her arms and inches her way a bit closer to me, actually a lot closer.

"And then there's number three." Her tone is soft, but what she's about to spew at me, I'm betting is not.

"At no time over the next ten weeks will you use the term 'baby' when you address me."

Air quotes are gestured around the word baby.

"I cannot begin to depict how much I despise it. I have a name. It's Harlow, in case you have suddenly forgotten. It means meadow of the hares. People with the name have a deep inner need for quiet, and a desire to understand and analyze the world they live in, and to learn the deeper truths. That's me. It's not sweetheart, or darling, or cutie, and it's certainly not baby. Learn to address me correctly, or we are going to have a problem."

She leans in, hands flat on the bed beside my body, arms stiff, her hair flows in the front of her shoulders, towards her chest. I can feel her breath on my face, and I smell her. It's the same scent as on the scarf. Sugar cookie, maybe?

"Do I make myself clear, Officer?"

I bite the inside of my cheek, tasting the blood from my teeth, and I nod. It's all I can do at this point. She doesn't linger in front of me. She straightens up and crosses her arms in front of me.

"Ok, fine, but why don't you like anyone calling you baby? What's the deal?"

She stares at me, then moves to her suitcase and begins to drag it across the room, back towards the bed. I grab it from her and fling it back on the bed, but she still hasn't answered my question.

"So are you going to tell me why you don't like it, or do I have to guess?"

She unzips her suitcase and starts to pull things out, still not making eye contact with me.

"I… I j-just don't like it. It's not cute. It's n-not sexy. It just makes me feel…" After stuttering her words, her voice trails off, and I don't hear the last thing she says. I'm not sure what her deal is. I stand up, fishing out some of her shoes out of the suitcase, and I begin handing them to her. It's a simple gesture, and she looks confused by it. I shove a shoe in her hand, rolling my eyes at her. She looks at it, then at me and places it in the closet.

"Ya know. I'm not a monster. We can be friends, if you want. Just because what happened between us last year, happened, doesn't mean we can't get past it. We both know it's never going to happen again."

I hand her another shoe, and a small smile shows up on her face.

"True, and I guess we could be, as long as you follow my list of demands. Especially the name calling one."

I smile back at her, wondering what is going on in that all-too-big brain of hers.

"So last year, why did you tell me your name was Raphael?"

"'Cause it is."

"Why does everyone call you Cruz then?"

"'Cause it's my last name. I'm not really sure why I told you my real name. I never use it. Even my brother calls me Cruz."

"That's weird. I think it's pretentious, and I'm not calling you Cruz.

"Not as weird as the name Harlow."

She laughs. "Harlow isn't weird. It's not common either, but it's not weird."

"Well, I'm not a fan, and I'm not calling you it, and don't you dare call me Raphael."

She yanks a pair of shoes out of my hands and groans at me.

"Oh, really? Then what are you going to call me? Not the 'B' word that's for sure."

I laugh at her. This is all too comical.

"Something not at all cute, or sexy, or funny. I'm going to nickname you the most un-sexy name in God's creation."

She places her hands on her hips, cocks her head to the side, and waits for the name I'm going to give her.

"Now once I give you this name, there's no going backsies. It sticks."

"Backsies?" She asks.

"Yea, backsies."

"Ugh, fair enough."

I hold out my pinkie for her to take. Harlow doesn't seem to get what I'm trying to do. Did she live a sheltered life or something?

"Pinkie swear. You link your pinkie finger with mine, and we shake on it. Have you been living under a rock or something?"

She shakes her head 'no'.

"Well, whatever, just do it. It's cool."

She links her tiny finger with mine, and I pull at it, startling her.

I start to think of a name, a really good name, one that I know she'll hate. I rub my temples, shut my eyes and mumble, "A name, and un-sexy name, hmm."

I peer open one of my eyes to see her becoming more aggravated the longer I take.

"Would you just get on with it, please. I've already wasted enough precious vitamin D sunlight because of you."

Ok, she's had enough, and I think I've got it.

I stand up. My body towers over hers. She's not short. She's not tall. She's right in the middle. I extend my hand out to hers to shake.

"It's nice to meet you, Turnip."

A puzzled look shows up on her face, and I grin. She hates it.

I, on the other hand, love it.

"Turnip?"

I grab her hand, place it in mine and forcefully shake it up and down.

"Yep, damn glad to meet you, Turnip. I'm Cruz."

She pulls out of my hand, clearly aggravated by the name, and it is the most un-sexy name to come out of one's mouth. That's why I chose it. Before she gets a chance to protest, I make my way to the door, planning my escape.

"You pinkie swore, Turnip, it sticks, no backsies."

"Fine." She growls through gritted teeth. "You are so immature."

I stand there, very satisfied with my decision. I could pat myself on the back right now if I could. I affected her, again, in a different way. A non-sexual way. I'm not really used to that, but I think it's something new to try. Maybe I could be friends with Harlow Hannum. I'm not really friends with many chicks, but if I have to live next door to her for the summer, maybe I should try. I don't have to be a dick all the time.

I give her a glance over my shoulder and give a quick wink.

"I'll see you later, Turnip."

"Later, Dickcop."

Wait, what?

CHAPTER 5

The Grown Up & Ms. Loosely Goosely
get to know each other
Harlow~

It's been almost two weeks since Cruz and I made our little deal. It's ok so far. I just continue to do what I'm doing, what he told me to do. I ignore him, pretend he doesn't live here, and go about my business. He works a few nights a week, so I only see him at the beach during the day. He mostly sleeps when he's there. Not a problem for me, although the tattoos are a distraction on occasion. I mean... What I mean is, they are there, so you kind of can't help notice them when he's laying on his towel... shirtless. I'm not blind. I know he's good looking. I'd be a fool not to notice. But in no way, shape or form would I entertain the thought of being in an intimate situation with him again.

I know him now... well, sort of.

He keeps to himself and hangs with Max a lot. When Cruz isn't on duty, they go out and only one time, so far, have I heard the moans and groans of one of the barflies they have brought home. I can deal with it. I just stick my earplugs in my ears and turn my iPod on, problem solved.

When we do see each other, it's a polite nod. Some nights when I'm alone and sitting out on the patio, which faces the dock and the bay, I sometimes see him bring a bar floozie home and watch as he tries to impress her by telling the trollop that he owns the house. Then I may hear him tell one of them that they need to be ever so quiet, because there may be spies listening in on their conversations. I listen to him go on and on about how he's a spy for the C.I.A, or part of some undercover operation for Homeland Security. It's comical, really, bordering on ridiculous, no wait… let me re-phrase that, it is ridiculous. Girls are so gullible.

I don't think I've been this relaxed in a long time. My meds are helping, which is a good sign. I love sitting out on this dock watching the soft ripple of the water on the bay. Early mornings here are my favorite. I'm not a sleeper, so I'm always out here with my coffee by six. Insomnia has its pros and cons, you see. You don't sleep much, but at least you don't waste your day in bed, and you get a few extra hours to be productive.

The applications I'm filling out for positions in the school district I student taught at ask for a lot of information, and the teachers and mentors at the school gave me glowing recommendations. I'd be thrilled with just a substitute position right now.

I'm beginning to type away entering all the info the schools are asking for, when I hear footsteps behind me on the dock. I turn around and find Cruz standing there. He has a fisherman's hat on with things hanging off of it, a fishing pole and a tackle box.

A smile as large as life is displayed on his tanned face. There goes my peace and quiet, right out the door.

Stretching his arms over his head, he addresses me, "Good morning, Turnip. Ahh, what a day." He makes himself comfortable on the dock, placing his items on a towel he has spread out. He hooks his line, pulling out a worm for bait, and I cringe.

"That's really disgusting to look at this early in the morning. Speaking of such, why are you up?"

He casts his line and dangles his feet off the dock into the water.

"I just got home from my shift and I thought I'd do a little fishing before my nap. What brings you out here?"

I take a long sip of my heavenly Starbucks and go back to typing, ignoring his question. It's really none of his business what I'm doing.

"Well, ok then, be rude why don't you."

What happened to us ignoring each other? We did come to some kind of agreement or did he forget.

I speak to him while reading all the fine print of the applications, "I'm not being rude, I'm just... well I'm busy. That's all." My tone drips of annoyance.

This mumbo jumbo I'm looking at can be quite confusing, so I really need to take my time and concentrate on the task at hand.

"Fine, I don't want to know anyway. It's probably something smart, like an I.Q. test."

"None of the above."

"Fine," he snaps.

"Fine," I snap back.

Silence sets in as I go back to the tedious job I was just performing. I sit. He sits. The sound of seagulls and my fingers tapping the keys are the only sounds heard.

"Would you mind? You are scaring the fish."

I roll my eyes. He can't see me, but I do, and continue, this time I pound them just a little harder.

"I don't mind at all." I smile to myself, pleased with my comeback.

One down, two more to go. I somewhat have the hang of it, all the information I type in is the same, so I copy, paste and repeat.

Then I hear whistling. Annoying whistling. His whistling. It continues, high notes then low ones. The tone is obnoxious and infuriating, and as it continues, I no longer have a grasp on my concentration. I slam the lid to my laptop shut with fierceness.

I turn towards him against my better judgment, and his back is to mine.

"Would you mind? What I am doing requires extreme meticulousness, so I would rather you go whistle your tune somewhere else."

Cruz rotates his head over one shoulder slowly to me.

"Was that English? What the hell are you talking about?"

This man infuriates me. So I stand, laptop tucked under my arm and clutching my coffee cup in the other.

"Oh, I'm so sorry, big words scare you? Poor guy. It's ok, Officer, your lack of knowledge of the English language is hard to comprehend. I mean you being a caveman and all." I pat the top of his head and he shoos my hand away.

"You always have to talk like that? Why don't you loosen up a little? This isn't college anymore."

He mumbles something else about being a tight ass as he goes back to focusing on the water.

"I am loose. I like to have fun like the next person. I just choose to use a large vocabulary while doing it. It suits me. It proves my intelligence, unlike some people."

He pulls the rod out of the water, stands and throws it on the dock, and now I know I stirred something up inside him. His body stalks over to me. His hat is now flung off his head and lands on the dock. His hair a wild mess of brown waves, and if I'm not mistaken, steam is coming from his ears.

"You wouldn't know a good time if it sat on your face and did the Macarena."

Oh, no he did not just say that. I can feel the anger pulse through my veins like a high-speed train, and I'm not going to allow him to affect me with his useless words.

"Really? Well, maybe if you didn't always have a party sitting on your face, then maybe you wouldn't have to settle for being a rent-a-cop at the age of twenty four. You uneducated, unintelligent simpleton."

He curves his lips into an angry hard line, shutting his eyes tightly.

Oh, Lord, I pissed him off.

"Listen here, you snot nose, rich brat. You don't have to use big words to make people think you're smarter than the average person. I was an Officer in the Marine Corp as a Staff Sergeant, organizing a platoon of men in Afghanistan and Iraq. I've seen and experienced things you have only read about in books or have seen on the news. So do not stand there and insinuate that I am not intelligent because I don't always use an extensive vocabulary to explain myself."

I'm rendered speechless. I swallow hard, feeling like a fool. He didn't deserve that. Maybe these meds aren't working. I feel bad. I'm really not sure what to say next. I stand there, bewildered. I place my mug and laptop down on the dock, then stand and place my hands on my hips.

He crosses his arms, looking quite satisfied that I have no words. He inches towards me, his nose to my forehead.

His breath streaming across my face. He's biting his lower lip, waiting for me to look up. He takes my chin, raises it up with his finger to meet his gaze. I feel my breathing pick up its pace. I swat his finger away, and I'm not sure why I'm still standing here.

"Cat got your tongue, Turnip?" He licks the lip he was just holding between his teeth. His blue eyes brazen as he asks the question. My jaw agape, I want to say something, anything, to disturb his thoughts. He holds a stare like he's summoning me to talk without actually telling me to.

"My, my Miss Hannum, for once that pretty little mouth of yours has nothing coming out of it. What a welcomed surprise."

I hear it in my head, my sub-conscience is telling me to speak Harlow, say something, do something damn it!

"Since there's nothing coming out of that smartass, sassy little mouth of yours," he growls sexily, hungrily, "maybe I should put something in it?"

What?

My natural reaction to what's about to transpire, does not stun me; it frightens me and with all of my might, all the strength I have in this body, I shove the pig off the dock into the bay.

He crashes into the water, flailing his arms and legs, gasping for air.

"You bastard! How dare you? You are nothing but a self-righteous pig!" He sinks into the water, bobs up and down. What is this game he's playing?

"Help, Harlow, please, I…" Back down he goes, then up again, coughing, splashing, then back down.

What is he trying to do?

Then he goes under again. And not resurfacing. I wait, and I wait. I peek over the dock to see where he is. Nothing but a few bubbles pop up.

Shit!

Did he drown? I look to the opposite side of the dock, nothing. I feel panic in my chest, so I yell for help.

"Someone, help. Come quick!"

My anxiousness overtakes me, and I pull at my hair, pacing until I see Max fly out onto the upper patio.

I get on my hands and knees and peer over the old wooden boards.

Oh, no! I can't see him. The water is too dark.

I'm suddenly grabbed by my arm, thrown in the water, and I'm confused, not breathing correctly, gasping as I feel the water enter my lungs. I can't stand, nor can I yell. I'm going to die. This is how I'm going to die. I can hear muffled sounds of people talking, yelling, splashing all around me, as I begin to sink deeper and deeper into the salty water. I close my eyes, wishing for a quick end and not a long, drawn-out, dramatic death. Flashes of my past come to play. Weaving a movie about my life, the good, the bad, the tragic. I don't want that to be the last thing I think before I die. I plead with God, not that, oh, please, not that.

I feel my body jerk. There are arms around my waist, hauling me up from the water, and I feel my body hit a hard surface. I blink a few times after my cheek has been slapped and hands turning my head towards the side of my body. I expel water from my lungs. I shut my eyes again because of the sting from the remnants of the salt due to the saltwater.

"She can't swim. God damn it! How did this happen!"

I can hear Willow yelling and hands making contact with bare flesh, the slapping sounds, the cries, and then two hands grasping my shoulders.

"Harlow, Harlow, can you hear me?"

I take a deep breath in. It hurts my lungs, but I do so,

and momentarily I cough and spit more water from my mouth. Willow is looking at me, my face in her hands. She is focusing on my face.

"Oh, thank God, Har. Are you ok? Do you want to go to the hospital? What happened?"

There's much confusion surrounding me. Lots of faces, in my face. Willow trying to pull me off the wooden boards. Her screaming at Cruz.

"You asshole. How could you do that to her? She can't swim. Never learned how and you go and do this. If I thought you weren't much of an asshole a week and a half ago, God, let me tell you what I really think of you now."

She leaves me, gets in his face, they are shouting, pointing at me, to the dock, to the water, and to my... oh my God! My laptop! It's soaked, ruined. Simply drenched. And then I feel the tears prick my eyes, sting them, and I regurgitate the salt from the bay. A heavy mixture of emotions is going through me. Sadness, anxiousness, and I'm just tired. So tired, I want to go back to bed, and it's only seven a.m.

I hug my knees and rock like I always do when I'm anxious. Max comes to my side and bends down so he's level with me. His hand rests on my knee.

"Harlow, are you ok? He didn't mean it. He had no idea you couldn't swim."

I don't reply. I'm still in shock, still shaking from seeing my life flash before my eyes.

I rise, and Max helps me up. I grab my laptop, water drips from it, and I feel defeated. Willow and Thea look at me. They come to my side and link their arms with mine as we make our descent back to the house.

Cruz stills my arm as he speaks, "Turnip, wait, I'm... I'm, well, you know."

He can't find the words. The only words that will make this ok, but he doesn't have the power to say them.

Willow smacks his chest and follows the rest of us into the house. He remains stoic, and I faintly hear Porter yelling at him as we walk.

I need a shower. I smell like the bay. I need the warmth of the water on me, speedily. As I make my way to the bathroom, Willow asks what I want to put on after my shower. I just want my sweats, because when I get out of the shower, I'll be packing to go home. I can't stay here with that asshole.

I turn on the water, and I feel the temperature of the spray. I peel off my wet clothes and step in, automatically feeling the constant steady stream of water from the shower head on my body. I just keep telling myself over and over: 'You're ok. You're ok. You are alive.'

All these emotions stirred up by one person. Now, I'm a sensible person. I know he had no idea I couldn't swim, but it's his insatiable need to play, to kid around, to trick, and to use sexual innuendoes every chance he gets.

I stand there, hands against the cool tiles of the shower, thinking of what I need to do when I get home. Buy a new laptop, re-do all the applications I began. Damn it, I should have pressed send sooner.

I'll get a simple job until I have a teaching position. Maybe Daddy will let me fetch coffee for him at the office. All I know is I have to leave.

I'm finished my shower. I wrap a towel around myself, make my way to my room, dress quickly and throw my suitcase on my bed, again, for the second time in less than two weeks. I hear a knock at my door.

"Come in." Willow enters and sees what I'm up to.

She stands there, hands on hips, and a look of disapproval on her face.

"Gonna run again? Go home and sulk, let him win? You're stronger than that, Harlow. Since when do you wimp out?"

That stings, but I don't care. I can't enjoy myself here knowing that immature ass lives ten feet away.

"Leave me be, Willow. It's just not working out. I'm going home."

She kicks the door closed with her heel and grabs the clothes I'm trying to pack out of my hands and throws them on the floor.

"What the hell!"

She grabs my wrist and turns me towards her, her eyes pleading with me.

"And what's going to happen once you get there? Stay in your room for the rest of the summer, avoiding the outside world, risk running into him? You know what will happen if you do? I can't go through that again with you, Harlow. I'm your friend, but I won't allow another slip up with him."

I think about it, about her words. What would happen if I did? What would happen if I fell back in? Under the spell, under the pull, under his forcefulness. It's so easy for me to cave. She thinks I'm strong, but I'm as weak as they come, especially when the one we do not speak of is involved.

"I know, but I can't stay here. I hate Cruz. He ruined my laptop. I was in the process of filling out all the online applications for the districts in our area, and it took a long time. I never sent them, now I have to start all over again."

She tugs me down to sit on the bed next to her. Her

demeanor softens, and she wraps an arm around my shoulder.

"You have been through so much, Har, and you have overcome a lot of it for the most part, but you can't let him win. I want him out. Not sure why Porter hangs with someone like him. All I know is, you can't let him win, and if you go home, that's exactly what's going to happen."

She's not talking about Cruz either.

We sit in silence for a few moments. I'm thinking about what she said. If I go home, he wins. He'll know I'm defeated, that I came crawling back. I can talk to my brother Craw about things but Greta, my sister, no way. She's way too caught up in her wedding plans to hear my sob stories. Mom and Dad aren't aware of anything, so I can't go to them.

Someone knocks at the door, and Willow gets up to answer it. She automatically slams it again, not giving me a chance to see who it is, but I have a pretty good idea.

She leans against the door and rolls her eyes. "Son of a bitch."

I smile. "It's fine. Let him in. It can't get any worse."

She eyes me for a second, not believing I just said that.

I nod my head as she pulls at the doorknob.

Cruz walks in, looking as pale as a ghost and holding a cardboard box in his hands. He looks awful, and that's unusual for him.

Willow eases up to him, gets inches from his face, not saying anything. She just stares at him, because in the case of Willow, sometimes her scowl is worse than her words.

Oh, God this is uncomfortable. She's so good at it.

She turns to me and winks before exiting.

The room is still, so is the air between us. I look to the floor, playing with my fingers in my lap, as he continues to stand.

"You're leaving?"

I nod.

"I don't blame you. I haven't made this easy for you."

I look up at him, pursing my lips together, my eyes agreeing with him.

"Look, I'm not a jerk. Really I'm not. I'm just not good with sorry's or hello's or goodbye's. I've been really hard on you, but you don't make it any easier."

I start to speak to stop him, because I'm pretty sure I'm not the cause of this.

He holds his hand up to stop me.

"Let me finish talking, please."

I let out a sigh. "Fine, continue."

"You think I'm a stupid person, well I'm not. Just because I didn't have an extensive education like you, doesn't mean I haven't been educated. The Marines paid for me to go to community college. I got my Associates Degree in Criminal Justice, and I haven't pursued a full time position with a force because I just got back from my third tour in Iraq. The world has educated me."

Oh, no. God forgive me. I had no idea.

"I'm sorry. I didn't know."

"Damn right, you didn't." His voice raises and appears a little sterner.

"I'm sorry. I didn't mean to raise my voice. I'm just sensitive about it. I'm not usually, but for some reason, you bring it out of me."

He told me he was in Afghanistan and Iraq when we were fighting on the dock, but I had no idea how many tours he accomplished. I owe him an apology.

"Cruz, I don't what to say. You're right. I haven't been fair to you, and I guess I jumped to conclusions. I apologize."

He comes to sit on the bed next to me. I flinch when he does, like I think he's going to hurt me, and when I do it, he is a taken back.

I sweep my hair behind my ears, feeling uncomfortable, and I'm not sure why. I mean I had sex with him. You'd think I wouldn't feel like that, but in reality, I think that is the reason I'm feeling like this.

"I'm not going to touch you, don't worry. I'm not going down that road again. No offense."

I laugh. "None taken."

He smiles at me, as I try to dodge my eyes from looking at him.

"Is that a smile I see? You actually have teeth? My God, I thought you just forget to put your dentures in all the time."

I shove him and let out a small chuckle.

"Jerk."

"You should do it more often."

"What's that?"

"Smile, it looks good on you." He smiles broadly at me. I wish I could allow myself to smile the way he does.

I'm up. Time for me to try to make amends.

"I think maybe sometimes with you. I remember what happened between us, and I realize I didn't know you, and I did what I did..."

He interrupts, "What we did. I was a part of it too."

"Ok, us both, but I think I was angry with myself because I had never done anything like that. I disappointed myself, and I was well, embarrassed. It was totally out of character for me."

He laughs and runs his hands through his already tousled locks.

"Yea, you're right about that. Getting to know the

Harlow this summer is totally different than the one I didn't know last year."

What he says is a little confusing, but I get it. I was a different person last year. Someone who sort of had an out-of-body experience.

I can't tell him what encouraged me to do what I did with him. I have to try to put it behind me. Put behind me the circumstances which in turn brought Cruz and I together that night, but with this brain of mine, I hear the voices in my head, taunting me, fucking with my subconscious: 'You can run, Harlow, but you can't hide.' 'Fall into his spell.' 'Feel his spell.' 'Follow his spell.'

I shake my head, making the voices go away. Cruz is still talking.

He looks at me, and I must have just looked like a nut-job.

"Where'd you go? Looks like I lost you for a minute."

I'm not sure where I just was. Lost in my thoughts, listening to the words in my head I do not want to hear.

"I'm sorry, just deep in thought. What were you saying?"

He shrugs and dismisses my daydream.

"I was saying that the past is the past, and maybe we can actually get to know one another and be friends. I can be a grown up and not torture you, actually be a stand up guy."

I hear the sincerity in his voice. I believe him, and I have to allow myself to give him the credibility.

"And I can relax a little. I'm not as wound up as you think I am. I can be loosey goosey."

He lets out a small 'ha' sound, and now I'm the one he doesn't believe. I swat at his arm.

"I'm serious. I am a lot of fun, even though I'm very serious about life. I can party with the best of them."

He has a glimmer of hope in his eyes when I tell him

that, a combination of cautiousness and challenge.

"I'll believe it when I see it."

I stand up in front of him, and I feel relaxed, the most relaxed I've felt in a while. It's odd that I feel like this talking to him, but I'll take it for what it's worth. This can work. We can try to put our differences aside, make this a great summer, and maybe, just maybe develop a friendship out of this.

"Oh, I should say the same about you, Mr. Grown Up. I'll enumerate that when I see it."

He gives me the proverbial eye roll.

"And let's start with that, Ms. Loosey Goosey. Women who are fun and carefree don't use words like enumerate. Believe me, don't believe me. Just try to sound a little less stuck up, ok?"

He knows what enumerate means. Interesting.

I sigh. "I suppose I can try. Loosey Goosey is the name of the game. Soon enough I'll be in a job where I have to be serious all the time. No better way to give myself a break from it than try to loosen up."

He rises from the bed and begins to walk away, leaving me with my thoughts.

Cruz turns back to me. "Oh, I almost forgot. I went and got you this." He hands me the cardboard box. "This is my first attempt at being a grown up."

I slide my nail over the strong tape holding the box shut, and I stick my hand in and pull out a brand new laptop.

He replaced it.

I'm transfixed on it, relishing in his thoughtfulness.

"Porter told me what you were working on when it got wet. I'm, uh, really sorry all your work was ruined, but hopefully it won't take you too long to get your information together again, and you can submit your applications again in no time."

I run my hand across the sleek black cover of the laptop, and I realize that there's hope for Raphael Cruz.

"Listen, I'll let you get to it. I just wanted to do the right thing."

I look up at him and give him a toothless smile.

"I'm glad you did, thanks Cruz. It was a real grown up thing for you to do."

He winks at me and turns the knob for the door. He says over his shoulder, "I'm glad you're staying, Turnip. See ya later."

Yea, there's hope for Raphael Cruz yet.

CHAPTER 6

So you're the King of the Douchebags?

Cruz

I need to get laid. It's been over a week. This job is a killer when it wants to be. All this overtime is worth the cash, but I feel so bad for poor Morty. He hasn't gotten enough exercise. I need to change this and fast. Tonight I'm off, and we are all going out, so I'll hold out hope.

It's hard to believe that it's almost 4th of July. The last few weeks have been great since my neighbor and I have been getting along.

Harlow's not so bad. She's thawed a bit, snickers at my inappropriate jokes, acknowledges my existence, and actually has conversations with me. She's still using the 'big words' now and again, but I give her a look, and she gives me one of her infamous eye rolls, and a knowing look to turn it down a notch. We hang out at the house, having drinks on the dock with the rest of the crew. As everyone swims, she sits with her toes touching the water, just a little. Maybe I should give her a few swim lessons. She doesn't know what she's missing.

I found out she's not really a snot either. Her parents, Joe and Annabeth have money, and she explained to us one night when we were all sitting around how her mother was some sort of a hippie. Harlow's mom worked for social services, grew her own vegetables and shit like that. Her dad, on the other hand, came from money, old money, and lots of it. He's a lawyer. Had to do the whole 'follow in daddy's footsteps' type thing. They met when her mom was a social worker tending to a case her father was part of. She said he was a free spirit like her mom. Telling us about them being soulmates and shit like that. One pussy for the rest of your life. Yea, that's a no-no.

Harlow's grandparents hated the fact that their son was going to marry a commoner or whatever, and they had a set of conditions, which her mom made her father abide by because she didn't want any trouble, or lose him.

The conditions? Send them to private schools, make them go to charm school, and be raised with class. That's so different than the way I was brought up. My crack-head mother's idea of class was sitting at the dinner table, (when we actually ate dinner) with a shirt on.

My mom, not us.

So Harlow grew up having an after school job at a diner and paying for things on her own. It sounds like just being raised to work for things you need, not things you want.

Good Motto.

I want to save as much as I want to spend, but I need to live on my own. I can't live with my brother Antonio and his wife, Bella, anymore. There's a spawn on the way for them, and there isn't enough room for me. If I don't save, I'll be forced back to the old neighborhood with the crack-head, and that's not an option.

Max and I talked about getting a place, but he'll be traveling a lot with the band this coming year as well as finishing up Engineering school. Porter is going up to Boston this winter to get his Masters.

So it's just me. But that's ok. I'm sort of used to it.

I like mornings on the dock when I don't have to take a nap as soon as I get home from my shift. This morning, I take my coffee outside, go sit in one of the Adirondack chairs, watch the boats go by and wave to the people on them. I walk down and see Harlow on the phone. I don't want to listen in, but she knows this is what I like to do in the mornings, and I'm not budging, so I can't help it if I do hear her conversation.

"Yes, Greta. I know, Greta. Relax. It will… Greta, it's not a big deal. No, no I'm not saying that it's not a big deal, of course it is."

She rolls her eyes, points to the phone and brings her hand up to her throat like she's choking herself. I laugh because I know she's on the phone with her crazy sister about her wedding.

She motions for me to give her a sip of my coffee. She must be out. I hand it over to her. We take it the same way. So much sugar that the spoon stands straight up in the mug.

She takes a sip and closes her eyes, like it's the first time she's ever tasted it. I laugh.

"Ok, well Craw is coming for the 4th, so I'll give him what you need. No, Greta. I didn't… ok, ok, fine. I'll speak with you next week. No worries. Ok, I love you, too. Bye for now."

Bye for now? She's so formal sometimes. But Greta is not like her. From what Harlow tells me, she's like her grandparents where Harlow is like her mom.

She throws the phone on her chair and lets out a growl.

"More wedding planning fiascos with your sister?"

She drinks the rest of my coffee like she's doing a shot of Jack Daniels. She hands me the empty cup. I turn it upside down to see the slightest little drop fall on the wooden planks.

"How'd you guess?" She smiles.

"Well, over the past few weeks you get this look about you when you're speaking to your sister. You chew on your already chewed down nails so they bleed."

She's doing it now. She pulls them out of her mouth as soon as I say it.

"Oh, well thanks for noticing."

She plops on her chair, exhausted, and her body acts like it has run a marathon.

"So what's the deal?"

"You really want to hear this?"

Not really, but I'll let her talk.

"Sure, shoot." God, I wish she didn't drink all my coffee.

"Well Greta doesn't like the fonts I sent her for her invitations. I found them on a website, and I picked several out for her to try. She hated them and wants me to search for new ones."

"Can't she look on her own? Why's that your responsibility?"

"Because she's too busy with other things."

I straighten up in my chair, lean over the arm rest and look at her confused.

"Wait, didn't you tell me she doesn't work, that her fiancé said it wasn't necessary? So why doesn't she have time?"

"Because she's extremely busy with her wedding planner.

What's the word you say when I appear to be clueless about something... duh, is it?"

Smartass.

"Fine. I get it, she's nothing like you. She's the one who never got out of that bratty rich kid routine no matter how hard your parents tried to sway her away from it."

Harlow winks and points at me. "Ding, ding. Correct answer, sir."

"So you're stuck with the dirty work. Too bad. You need to stand up for yourself, Turnip."

She stands up and sits on the dock, toes inching towards the water.

"I'm working on it. I told her I'd give the samples to my brother when he comes next week. I'm not jumping on it immediately."

I get up and go to sit next to her. I land my feet in the water with a small splash that reaches her.

"Oops, sorry."

"Caveman," she mutters.

"So beach volleyball game today? Guys versus girls?"

She doesn't answer. She's focused on the water.

She sticks her big toe in, pulling it out immediately. Her fear is crazy to me. I take her foot and try to ease it into the water, very carefully. She flinches, not fully understanding what I'm trying to do. She tenses under my hand, pulls back, and gives me a look of warning.

"It's just water. Put the rest of your toes in, not the whole foot, it's not going to bite you, neither will I unless you ask." I wink at her knowing that when I talk like that it gets her in a tizzy.

She creases her brow, smacks my arm and her expression's not anger, just worry.

I grab the instep of her foot and slowly ease it in, a bit at a time until all her toes are submerged. She looks at me, trusting me, but with caution, great caution. She doesn't fully trust me yet, and that's ok. We're working on it. It's not going to be cotton candy and clowns right from the start, but we'll get there.

"That's it, it feels good, right? Now just a little more."

I lower her foot a bit until the top and all of her toes are under. I can feel her relax, the tension starting to dissipate.

"Good, Turnip. Now just lower it a bit more, like you're getting into a bath. She does what I suggest, and struggles, but does it.

"See, not so bad, now try the other one."

Harlow pulls her foot from under her and painstakingly dips the toes of her foot in, like the other. I have to encourage her, bit by bit. She tenses up again, and I don't feel bad. She has to try to conquer this fear a little at a time. Her foot eases into the water. Her eyes, tightly shut, but she does it. Her body is stiff as a board, but she does it.

She leans back a bit, still with her eyes shut. Once her foot is all the way in, she peeks one eye open, looks to me, and I give her an encouraging smile.

"You did it," I whisper.

She grins back at me, and she's pleased with herself.

"Now move your feet around. Just a little to get a feel of the water."

Slowly, she does it, just an inch or two, and I can tell it's still hard for her.

Her eyes aren't focused on the water, there's still fear there. However, she looks to me when she sways her feet back and forth, letting the water surround them.

"Thanks," she says quietly and without glancing my way.

Ok, tender moment over. Back to being me.

I stand up, and she does the same, carefully.

"Well, I'm outta here. Gotta go surf the internet for porn."

She groans, and it's glorious.

"Ugh, just when I think you're actually attempting to be a human being, you go and screw it up with your mouth. You. Are. Gross."

I have to laugh, 'cause she still doesn't get me. I wonder if she can hear me banging my random muff, when I bring one home?

I should ask her.

Nevermind. I'm trying to be a grown up.

"So why do you say I'm gross? You didn't think I was gross about a year ago. I just so happen to have a large sexual appetite, and if I just so happen to bring home a little company to help satisfy it, then so be it. I'm twenty four, not forty four."

"Do you have to remind me that I fed into that sexual appetite? I would rather you not."

Aw, that makes me sad. I gave it to her good if I remember correctly. It was certainly memorable to me. May I remind you how many times Morty stood at attention and found his happy place with that memory.

I place my hand over my heart and act like it's breaking. I turn my mouth into a frown.

"You hurt my feelings, Turnip. I thought it was something you'd never forget."

Cue, eye roll…

There it is!

"Don't flatter yourself, you incorrigible ass."

I shake my finger at her.

"Tsk, tsk, Miss Hannum. Using big words again. What's a guy going to think when he tries to pick you up and you go all smart on him. He may not understand what you're saying."

She starts to walk away from me. I see the hard line her mouth was in before she turned. I yell out to her as I watch her stomp up the dock to the house. I laugh. She hates me.

"Where ya going?"

She doesn't turn around fully, but she yells to me over her shoulder.

"You are impossible."

Oh, my how I love to get this chick all riled up. It gives me great satisfaction. But I only try to kid with her. She needs a sense of humor.

Poor girl.

Her stomping away is like an open invitation to apologize.

This grown up things sucks the life right out of my balls.

So, after I apologize for the umpteenth time, she forgave me, and now we are all at the beach, soaking up the rays, and playing a mean game of volleyball. I hate to admit this, because I am in no way, shape or form a fucking pussy, but the girls are actually good. We finish the last game (we won, by the way), and I'm in need of some sort of refreshment in the style of one with hops and barley. I motion for Porter to hand me a beer from the cooler he's sitting on, but he is involved in some sort of deep conversation with Thea. Maybe he's trying to dazzle her with his vast knowledge of draft beers. Who knows? Don't care.

"Porter, man, get your ass off the cooler and grab me a beer, pronto. I worked up a sweat kicking the girl's ass's right out of their bikini bottoms."

He grabs me a beer, I flip off the cap and take a long sip.

"Do you have to be such a douche all the time, or is it just when you haven't gotten any in a few days?" Willow blatantly calls out from under her oversized sunglasses.

"Why is my sex life any concern of yours? Maybe you should try to get one."

Several noises I'm not sure of come from her mouth. Pauses, sighs, and then a few others.

"I am perfectly content with my sex life."

"Or lack thereof," Thea mutters to her not as quietly as I think Willow would have liked.

"Thea Thornton! Whose side are you on anyway?"

Thea looks like she just realized she put her foot in her mouth, not sure what to say next.

"Your side, silly. I was kidding."

Willow gets up and goes to the cooler Max is sitting on now.

"And how do you know I haven't been getting any?"

Her hand moves from her side and extends one of them towards me.

"Well, for starters, the pictures in our house have been securely fastened to the walls this week. No against the wall banging has made them crumble to the floor, unlike last week's boink fest you had in your room. Tell me again, Cruz, are two vagina's really better than one?"

Oh, she's fierce.

"Actually, Willow. It's kind of hard sticking it into two vagina's at the same time. I mean it's big, but I let my fingers do the walking in one, as the big guy here is in the other one."

I motion to Morty. I make him proud with my comebacks.

Of course, I get the ew's, and the ah's and the 'Oh, that's so gross'.

"Move it, or lose it, mohawk man." She thumbs for Max to get up so she can fish out some kind of girly foo-foo drink for herself. Most of the girls drink them, except for Harlow. She's the beer girl of the group, with the exception of the occasional shot of tequila.

Max pouts, but does what she says.

"You are so mean to me. Want me to get my flashlight and find that bug that crawled up your ass?"

Bad move Max, bad move. She's already in a mood. I can tell.

Willow comes eye to eye with Max. She is a few inches taller than him, which is funny. I always enjoy it when a girl pokes a guy in the chest as she gives him an ear full of shit, oh, and when he's shorter than her.

"Listen here, short stack, I have no bug up my ass. I am not mean, and you want to know the truth, yea, I need to get laid, just like the rest of you. I need a good, old-fashion fuck fest. Happy now?" The scowl on her face is one I'd rather not mess with. She's terrifying.

She downs the pink-colored contents of her bottle in what seems like one big gulp, swiping at her mouth after.

Everyone stares. It's not the words a debutante like her uses, but I don't think she's like the others.

It's quiet, I mean really quiet.

Porter, obviously embarrassed by his cousin's choice of words, shakes his head, and looks at the sand beneath his feet. Max is looking at her like a hungry tiger, and she's the helpless gazelle, ready to be eaten. Well... maybe it's the other way around. I see him lick his lips.

Oh, no buddy, red flag, call the guards, we are at def-con one here.

I have to stop this, stop the madness, I see that is about to unfold.

"Ok, people. Enough. Max, what time does your band go on tonight?"

Max snaps out of his staring contest with Willow long enough to answer me in a tiny, pussy like voice.

"Ten. That reminds me, I, um better go rest up."

Max grabs his towel, his eyes still on Willow, and yea, I think I may vomit. He trips over his own two feet and stumbles. I hit my forehead with my hand, closing my eyes tightly, because Max is an ass, and I'd rather not see him fall on it. His ass I mean.

He jogs up the beach onto the boardwalk and disappears. Willow flops back on her chair, and sighs.

"I'm so going to have him before the summer is over."

Porter jumps up from where he was just firmly planted.

"The hell you will, Willow. He's my friend. He's your friend, and friends don't sleep with each other's friends, or whatever. It's just wrong. It complicates things."

She stands again, meeting Porter's eyes, nose to nose, and I think the shit may hit the proverbial fan, again.

"Oh, yea, well Harlow had sex with Cruz, so what's that then, huh?"

Oh, no she just didn't say that.

Harlow jumps up, spins Willow around by her arm, and if I was a betting man, I'd say some big, huge, monstrous words are about to fly out of Harlow's mouth.

"Willow Taylor! How could you!"

Oh, I was wrong. I'm shocked.

Porter has his fingers in his ears, saying 'la, la, la' in a sing-song tune, and mumbling, "I didn't just hear that."

"That was classified information, Willow. And in front of him. Plus we weren't friends back then." She gestures to me, and then turns her icy stare back at Willow.

This. Is. Classic.

I'm waiting for them to start ripping each other's tops off, and then kiss. That would so make my day.

"Well, my God Harlow, that's the first thing you said to us after we got back to the house that night. Star tattoo this and star tattoo that. Besides, you guys are passed it anyway."

Harlow's anger doesn't seem to dissipate. Willow's words only fuel her, and I feel as though I may have to get out of the line of fire.

"You're a real bitch, you know that? How immature can you actually be? Now he's (she means me) going to get off on what you just said. Look at the smirk on his face. Thanks a lot."

I do have a smirk. I like that I have a smirk, and I have every reason to have one. She talked about my stars. Oh, yes, my stars. All the ladies want to lick the stars, and then go running to their girlfriends to tell them about them. The stars are almost as good as my C.I.A. story. Almost.

Gets 'em every time.

All's quiet for a few seconds until Thea saunters up to Porter. Her voice is quiet, like it usually is. She plays with her hands, not really looking up at Porter when she speaks.

"So friend's hooking up with friends is wrong?" She meets his eyes for a second. Her lip looks like it's quivering, and then she looks back at her hands.

"I'll keep that in mind, Porter. Thanks."

She grabs her stuff and walks off the beach. Porter looks like he's waging a war with his thoughts. I'm not about to ask what the deal is. Not my concern.

"Hey, Turnip, relax. I'm not going to bust your chops about it. What's done is done, right?"

That's really not what I'm thinking. I'm going to use this

information to my advantage. Now listen, I know we are getting along and trying to find some kind of friendship in all this, but I never said I can't tease her and get her angry as hell at me. It's a turn on. I like to see Harlow Hannum a little hot under the collar.

"I'm sorry I have to apologize for Willow. I didn't expect her to betray me like that." Harlow looks genuinely sorry, I almost feel bad for her... almost.

"Ok, girls. Let's go back to our houses, rest up, then go out tonight, have a great time and hear Max's band play."

I grab Harlow's beach chair before she has a chance to stop me, but before I do, I give her a little show.

I reach up, stretching my arms over my head, letting my swim trunks drop slightly, to reveal, yep, you guessed it...

"Oh my, oh my. I wonder if the stars will be out tonight. What do you think, Turnip?"

She's not paying me too much mind, so I cough. She turns around and gives me the eye roll.

"I knew it was too good to be true. Put those things away."

She gives me a half smile that I didn't expect, and her cheeks have a touch of red to them. I'm not sure if it's embarrassment, recognition, or the sun.

Tonight Max's band is playing at Jax. It's the most popular bar here in Sandy Cove. It gets pretty packed, but Max is good friends with the owner, so he reserved a few tables for us, right near the stage, so we can see Max. The girls are late, as usual. They told Porter and me to go ahead without them.

We saunter up to the bar, grab a few brews, and make our way to the reserved tables. Damn, this place is crawling with hotties tonight. I tap Morty a bit through my jeans and say to him, "Tonight's going to be a good night for you, bro." I'm giddy like a school girl. I nod to some of the girls I see. I wink, and graze my upper teeth with my tongue. I flex without doing it like a body builder and adjust my arms a bit to get them to notice, not like they didn't already.

I mean, really, look at me.

The tables at Jax have banquet seats that are aligned enough that everyone sitting at them has a great view of the stage. Porter and I raise our beers, and I make a toast.

"Here's to good friends, good music, and the ton of pussy we're getting tonight, cheers." Porter doesn't return my sediment. "What the fuck is up with you man? I'm kind of getting tired of your Mr. Rogers, quiet as a church mouse attitude."

He scowls at me, not immediately looking at my face, and trying to avoid the question.

Then he raises his head, looking right past me like I didn't exist.

"Holy shit." He drags the phrase out, jaw agape, and eyes widened to the point of bugging out of his head. I crank my neck to one side, nothing, but then when I move to the other, I realize what the blank expression on his face truly means.

I repeat after him, "Holy shit!" I emphasize the holy. And with all good reason, which at the moment has my head spinning like the rinse cycle of a washing machine.

In walks the girls, but they don't look like our girls. They look... well, they look hot! Dressed to kill. Some in short skirts, some in dresses, and some in shorts. Legs. All I see are legs.

"My God, are they the same girls we live next door to?" I say it out loud and I had no intention to.

Willow steps up first. All five feet ten of her, then Thea steps up after her in a short little skirt. Porter looks like he's about to go ape shit. He doesn't look too happy, but what I see after Thea walks in, stirs something down below, and makes me take a long, hard drink of my beer. I blink, several times for there is a sight to behold. Harlow Hannum looks like she just stepped out of a fucking magazine. Like the kind I see in the convenience stores.

Her hair cascading around her shoulders, with soft, wide curls flowing down to lay across her supple breasts. The purple color of her sundress is unusual, but compliments her skin tone. But her legs? It's her fucking legs that make Morty stand at attention.

It's not right, well it is, but it's not. I'm guessing it's my natural male testosterone playing part in my sudden boner, but for Harlow, it's got to calm down. A sudden bulge in my pants is not an option. Also, I'm not dead. I will admit to thinking a girl is pretty, even if it is Harlow.

Sorry Morty, old boy.

"Hi," she says placing her hand on my shoulder.

"Yo. Beer?" I turn to her, not meeting her eyes.

"Sure." She replies, and I spin on my heels to the bar and wait to be served. I reach the bar, and I'm still in shock as to the way she looks tonight and how my body reacted to seeing her dressed up that way. I feel a hand on my shoulder, this time I feel the nails of that hand slowly touch me, from shoulder to wrist.

"Wow, you have some serious ink. I like it a lot."

I glance to see who's speaking. I come face to face with some exotic looking chick, maybe Polynesian. Long, dark hair, bronzed skin, and her lips all pouty and needy. Wonder how they'd feel around my cock? Maybe later, first I have to get Harlow her beer.

"You like them now, do you baby?"

She continues to trail her fire engine red nails up and

down my ink, alternating between licking and biting her lower lip.

"Oh, yea, I like a lot. You have them anywhere else."

The bartender hands me my beers. I throw money on the bar and turn around, but something catches my eyes, and my brain goes from zero to sixty immediately, observing the scene in front of me.

It's almost like when a swarm of flies zeros in on a piece of crap, although instead of flies, they're guys. Around the girls, smiling, talking to them, licking their lips, and getting ready to go in for the kill. Especially Harlow. I study all of them for a few moments, surveying, waiting to see what their next moves will be.

My eyes go to Porter, who is standing next to them. I notice the girls not paying any attention to him, but his eyes are on all three of them. I start to make my way over, but the beaut next to me stills my arm.

"Where are you off to? I want to find out where your other tattoos are."

Damn, I could have her right now, and she's fucking hot, but the big brother vibe in me needs to go over and give the guys flirting with the girls a bit of warning, without words that is.

"Maybe later, baby. I'll find you. What's your name?"

"Leilani."

Polynesian? Sounds hot.

"Sounds good. And you will get your answer about the rest of my ink."

She releases my arm, and I stroll over to the gang. The guys around the girls aren't as big as me, some are built well, but my stature towers over them. I make my approach, methodically, intimidating even.

I hand Harlow her beer after I tap her arm. She doesn't

even take her eyes off this guy she's talking to, she just holds out her hand for me to place the beer in it.

What the fuck is that all about?

"You're welcome, Turnip."

The guy she's talking to snickers.

"Turnip? What is that?"

Harlow laughs forcefully at his question. I mean such an exaggerated attempt at a laugh that even I think it's comical.

"Oh, that's just some silly name my neighbor came up with. Oh, I'm so sorry, but I didn't get your name." She asks the genius standing next to her.

"Elton. Elton Joel."

Now see, that's my cue to laugh the way she just did, but mine won't be forced because you have to be kidding me. Elton Joel? Were his parents smoking crack when they named him? Oh, wait. I'm not going to answer that, but it's not going to stop me from laughing right in his face.

"Elton Joel? Seriously?"

Harlow shoots me daggers from her eyes, clearly ready to kill me. Elton Joel smiles when Harlow looks at him after she shoots me her fiery gaze, but when she looks back to me, his expression is less than welcoming.

"Yes, I know. My mom was a huge Elton John and Billy Joel fan. You gotta take what you get. I'm used to it."

Harlow's grin spreads so wide, her jaw is going to hurt.

"I know exactly how that is. I was named after an old movie star my mother loved."

Elton Joel moves in a little closer to her ear, and I inch a little more towards Harlow to listen in. It's loud in here, so I bend down a little. All I hear from him is, "Harlow's a beautiful name for a beautiful girl." He picks her beer-free hand up and kisses the top of it.

Oh, come on! That's a line I use, and a move I make.

Can't he be original? I'm the king of the pickup lines, and that is by far one of the cheesiest. This guy is a grade-A ass. My dilemma is do I intervene, or let Harlow step into his pile of bullshit. I'm not going to think. I'm just going to speak.

"Hey, Turnip, Max's band will be going on in a few. He got us a few booths reserved so why don't we go sit." Again, not eyeing me, she speaks in an even tone.

"Cruz, I'm perfectly fine right here for now. I'll come over in a bit." All the while she's still grinning at this asshat like he's Santa Claus or something. Then she shoos me away with her hand, like I'm bothering her or something. Like I'm one of the swarm of guy flies, but with me, I annoy her like a typical fly. I guess I'm lucky she didn't swat and smash me like one.

I mutter out a 'fine', and I'm not really sure she even heard me. Guess it doesn't matter.

I reach one of the booths we have reserved, and I'm surprised to see Porter sitting alone.

I throw my body in the booth, kind of pissed off at Harlow, for which I'm not sure why, but even more angry that Elton Joel is feeding her lines that she clearly doesn't know are lines.

I guzzle my beer as I sit, Porter is very quiet.

"What's up with you?"

Porter stares over my shoulder, obviously perturbed about something.

"I'm fine," he says with his mouth in a hard line.

"Don't look like you're fine. What's the deal?"

He snorts, "I guess I could ask you the same thing. Looked like you were burning a hole right through that guy talking to Harlow. You use your x-ray vision to see if he was a jerk? We all know you have Superman like powers."

I glance back to them, watching as Harlow continues to laugh at Elton Joel's come on's.

"Nothing," I say, feeling offended he would even ask me such a question. It doesn't bother me she's talking to him, why should it? I can just smell a load a crap a mile away, and Elton Joel is full of it.

"Girl's seem to be having fun and making new friends. Good for them. You see some of the chicks in here? We should be doing the same stuff, instead of sitting here with our dicks in our hands."

Porter just shakes his head.

"I'm fine. I need another beer." He signals a waitress to come to our table.

The lights dip, and Max's band takes the stage. The kid is so damn talented, and the girls have never seen him play. This was the perfect opportunity for them to watch Max and the band, but as they began to play, the girl's interests appear to be on other things. The guy flies move to the beat along with the girls, and by the looks of it, the girls like the music, but could give a shitless that it's Max up there.

Max plays his heart out, singing backup on some vocals. The crowd pushes towards the stage, some dancing, and some even gyrating to the beat of the music. Hands up, swaying back and forth, beer bottles raised, with some patrons singing along to the covers the band performs. The guys and I stay in our booth because we have a pretty perfect view of the stage from where we are. The waitress keeps the beers coming, and we throw them back like they're bottled water.

The band continues to play, and I've been trying to keep an eye out for Harlow, but I don't see her. Porter looks like he's going out of his mind, for some reason, and my head, my poor big head goes from one shoulder to another, searching for her, wondering if she's ok with Elton Joel. And now I spot her.

Her sundress-clad ass rubbing up against Elton Joel's khaki panted front.

Fuck me.

Harlow's arm is draped around his neck from behind, she reaches up running her fingers through his hair. His lips graze her bare shoulder, his one arm resting across her belly, pulling her in closer. Their rhythm matched, step by step, never seeming out of sync. She eases her head to the side so he can have better access to her neck, as he plants a row of kisses from behind her ear, down the length of her neck. Harlow's eyes are closed, her hair swinging from side to side to the charge of the electric bass. I bite the inside of my cheek, hard. I taste the coppery-flavored blood, feeling the sting of it. I wonder why watching her move makes me angry. Her moving with him, against him.

I'm willing myself to turn around, to look away, but this girl is stepping outside her shell. She seems free, moving her body in ways I have never seen. The fluency of her arms and legs, the way she dips her knees down, gracefully messy with the sway of her hips, grinding into him as she rises up again.

She moves like a swan, not like the stiff, too-large-of-a-vocabulary girl, who tolerates me.

The night we were together, she moved like a hungry tiger, feral and cold, waiting for the kill. Tonight, her body is relaxed, no weight of the world bearing down on it. It's just freeing her to move without worry, without stress, just to be a sexual object, and I don't like it. I don't like it one fucking bit.

My knee won't stop shaking. My head is foggy from the beer. My body, tense and ready to strike at a moment's notice, and that time may be now.

As the beat of the music pulses through the air, and the sound of drums beating within my ears, I see Elton Joel's hand snake from around her waist. It languidly makes its way down to her thigh, and she doesn't seem to notice or care. He inches her dress up when he reaches the hem. Her hand is still resting on the back of his neck. His fingers make their way to her inner thigh, while he licks the side of her neck. Her eyes are still shut, and her lower lip is sucked in, as she is enjoying whatever it is he's doing to her. When I don't see his hand any longer, as it disappears under her dress and out of my sight, my body betrays me and it makes me fly to her.

I push my way through the sweaty crowd, towering over the bodies, not caring who I'm shoving until I stand in front of them. Elton Joel looks up at me with his face buried in her neck, sensing me watching them, and his face grins, as he pushes his hand further up her dress.

I don't have time to react because Harlow does. She pushes his hand from underneath her dress. Not really looking anywhere but at his arm.

"Hey, not here, ok," she says, and it's not a good enough answer for him. He has guts. I'll give him that. With me still standing in front of them, Harlow's eyes shut again, he tries it again, and now I know this cocksucker doesn't have the sense he was born with.

My reaction has to be swift. I'm not hesitating, so basically, I won't. My hand grabs onto his wrist, the only visible part of his hand so to speak, and I yank it down.

"I'm pretty sure she said not here, so I suggest you get your fucking hands off of her."

Harlow looks up, hair sticking to her sweat-soaked forehead, the sheen of it covering her chest, shoulders, and neck. Her eyes sparkling in a beautiful blue haze, but it turns into fury.

"Cruz, I can take care of myself. Get lost."

"Yea, you heard her, leave us alone. She's in good hands."

Oh, I bet she is.

Elton Joel should keep his fucking trap shut.

"See that's where I think you're wrong, Elton. I know guys like you 'cause I am one. I know what you want from her, and you ain't getting it." I grab Harlow's arm and pull her to me. She resists, and she yanks her arm back.

"How do you know what he wants, and maybe, just maybe, I want the same thing tonight. You do it all the time, so go away, Dickcop."

Her speech is slurred, her attitude unlike herself, and I'm pretty sure the alcohol is giving her the liquid courage to defy me. She grabs Elton's face and smacks her lips onto his, forcing her tongue between his lips, parting them, and he doesn't resist; it only brings her closer to him. Watching their tongues mingle forcefully, his hands snaking down to her ass, grabbing a hold of it enrages me even more, but she made her decision. Fuck it.

"Fine, Turnip, it's your life."

I turn away from them and run into Willow and Thea dancing.

"Hey, Cruz. Max's band is great. This is so much fun. Where's Harlow?" Thea asks.

I thumb in Harlow's direction, and she's still making out with Elton Joel.

"She's all yours, girls. I tried to get her away from that guy, but she's being stubborn as usual."

They look at each other, then back to me, and laugh, wiping the sweat from their heads.

"Cruz, maybe she doesn't want you to get him away from her, maybe she wants him to get under her?" Thea laughs at what Willow says, and it's so obvious they're drunk, falling into each other and laughing like maniacs.

"Whatever, I'm out of here. Have fun."

I walk away from them and go back to the booth where Porter is. I finish what's left of my beer.

"I'm leaving," I announce to Porter.

"What do you mean, man? The night is just getting started."

"Well, my friend, mine is over. I'm going back to the house. Let Max know where I went when he's done. Later."

I walk away from him squeezing my body through the crowd. I feel someone grab my arm and tug. It must be Harlow coming to her senses, and she's done with Elton, but when I look in the direction of the pull, it's the exotic looking chick from the bar, and I already forget her name.

"Hey there handsome. Going somewhere?" She smiles at me and licks her lips. I feel her nails graze my skin. I don't really look at her. I'm too preoccupied with finding a parting in the crowd to make my escape.

"Home," I simply say. My tone is flat.

"Aw, well what a shame. I was hoping I could see where the rest of that ink is." She winks at me, and my head is suddenly clouded with thoughts of seeing if those tits of hers are as gorgeous as I imagine they are. "Wanna get out of here?" She whispers into my ear.

Now, as much as I want to say yes, and take her somewhere and fuck her into oblivion, I'm choosing the latter. This decision shocks even me, and as horned up as I am, the more I look at her, the more I sense trouble… and I don't know why.

I take her hand away from my arm, knowing when I get

home I'll probably regret my decision, but something in my fucked up head tells me here and now that I should leave.

"Maybe some other time baby."

She backs up, looking disappointed as she adjusts her shirt, and pushes out her breasts even more.

"Suit yourself, hot stuff. I'll be around." She spins on her high heeled feet and slowly walks away. I get a glimpse of her heart shaped ass in that skirt, and I suddenly feel bad. Not for me, but for Morty.

This house has never been so quiet. Usually it's filled with people. Either my roommates are here, or the girls come over to play a game, or just sit around having a few drinks with us. I welcome the silence as I make my way outside to the deck, and crack open my beer and my laptop, so I can do a bit of work for the online class I'm doing this summer.

There's a shift in the air temperature, it's not as humid as it has been, which means a storm is coming. Laying on this lounge chair with just the illumination from my laptop screen, I begin typing swiftly on the keys, reading, and gathering the information on the screen into notes. It's only midnight, and I, Raphael Cruz, am home doing homework. What's wrong with this picture? I should be banging that chick from Jax right now, and making her all sweaty as she screams my name. I'm still not sure why I did what I did. I walked away and came back here, alone. That jerk dancing with Harlow had some balls grabbing her the way he did. She's a different girl with a few drinks in her. Case in point: last summer. Sometimes when she's around and we are just sitting here, talking with the others, the memory of that night comes to mind. It's like she has split personalities or something. It's not that I don't like her personality... well, sometimes I don't. I mean the more we talk, the more I do like it. It's just that if what happened last year didn't happen between us, would I still want to get to know her?

Ah, fuck, I should have taken that girl home from the bar.

I slam down my beer and pull at my hair with my free hand. Frustration makes its way to my brain, and I feel like I need to relieve this pressure building up in my pants. How could I have let this happen? I do make some pretty shitty decisions, and this one by far, was the shittiest of the night. I need to concentrate on what I'm doing, figuring I'll take care of my business with my hand and a bottle of lotion later.

I see the lights of what looks like a cab pull up in front of our house. I peek up from the lounge chair, not seeing anything, but I hear the door of the cab slam. It pulls away before I have a chance to inspect. I go back to reading the assignment I was given, when I hear footsteps coming from the wooden steps beside the girl's house. There goes my peace and quiet until all the drunks get home in a few hours. I sit up a bit, adjusting my body and my laptop resting on my legs when I see it's Harlow. She doesn't see me as she goes to unlock the sliding glass door to her house.

"Where's Elton Joel? He dump you to go to an after party with Lady GaGa?" She jumps at the sound of my voice, dropping her purse in the process. I hear the contents fall onto the deck, her change spilling and bouncing on the wood, and I see something roll towards me. I stop it with my foot. It's a small can, so I bend down and grab it from underneath my toes.

It's mace.

"Jesus, you scared me. What are you doing out here?" I

look at her then back to the can.

She carries mace. I'm not surprised. She's a smart girl.

I set my laptop down on the lounge chair and get up to give the can back to her.

"I should be asking you the same thing. Why are you back so soon?"

She doesn't answer. But she begins to pick up the things that spilled from her purse from the deck floor and stuffs it all back in.

"Um, hello? Can you answer me?"

"I wanted to come home, that's all. My God, why do you care anyway. You made me look like an ass in front of that guy tonight."

"Well, no actually, Elton Joel made himself look like an ass tonight. Why aren't you with him and before you even answer that, why did you take a cab home by yourself?" She struggles with the key to the glass door and appears frustrated.

"Damn it, just get in there." Harlow's talking to the door, twisting and turning the key in the lock, and she yanks on the handle.

I grab the keys with my free hand and pass her the can of mini mace. She looks at it, then her eyes raise up to mine. I unlock the door, slide it open and usher my hand towards it for her to go in. She does without looking at me, but I hear a faint 'thanks' come from her.

She walks in and throws her purse and the can of mace on the dining table. My question still hasn't been answered as to why she's back without her friends. She goes to the fridge to get out a bottle of water, with her back to me she opens it, tosses the cap in the sink, and takes a long drink.

"You can go now." She tells me in a cold tone. It angers me because I did nothing wrong. I was trying to help her.

That guy was an asshole.

"You know I was only looking out for you. The guy just wanted in your pants, and if I didn't interrupt the two of you, that's where he would have gone. I know guys like him." I want to say 'cause I am one, but I think she knows that already. Then the thought comes to my brain, and I remember what Willow said earlier.

Maybe she did want what he was going to give her. Maybe he did the deed. Do I waste more time trying to defend myself if it already happened?

Yes. Yes, I do.

"I'm trying here, Turnip, but you don't seem to care that I am." I stand there, arms folded across my chest, waiting for a God damn reply. "Well?" I say after about a minute of complete and utter uncomfortable silence.

She turns, looking at me with an expression I haven't seen before. One of maybe, agreement? A slight smirk on her face, then it softens.

"Well, you were right." She finally looks up at me, a touch of sadness in her eyes as she does.

"About what part?" I ask.

She strolls over to the couch and plops down on it sighing.

"You are right. Albeit I hate that you are. He tried on the dance floor, I told him to stop, he did. Then I excused myself to go to the ladies room. When I came back out, he grabbed my elbow, tried to lead me to the back hallway beyond the restrooms, and stuck his hands in places I didn't want them to be." She tells me this very matter-of-fact, not changing the level of her voice, there's no anger in her tone, just telling me like I'd imagine she would if she were talking to the girls. I'm guessing it's the alcohol, but her speech isn't slurred, and her eyes are clear.

I'm mad at this situation, and I'm going to do my best to keep my cool. I clench my teeth, and I shut my eyes tightly.

"You mean to tell me he forced himself on you? He tried, again, to do what he tried to do on the dance floor? Did you use that can of mace on the mother fucker?"

Silence again. She looks every which way but at me.

"Turnip, I asked you a question. I know I'm not your best friend, but still, I got this big brother type vibe going on with you I think, so I kind of want to know so I can either bash his face in, or I can bash his face in."

She smiles when I say that.

"I didn't use the mace."

I bunch up my face in confusion.

"Then what did you use?"

A devilish grin turns up on her face, she pulls at her bottom lip with her teeth, and drinks from her water bottle.

"Turnip?" I say with my voice raised an octave, then a lower one. "What did you use?"

She finishes her sip, flashes me an unbelievable smile, and says, "My knee."

I laugh. I mean I really laugh because for as tiny as she is, I'm not surprised by it. Not the least bit shocked at her confession. When I laugh, she laughs, tears coming out of her eyes. A good, old-fashioned belly laugh, and it's really adorable. The suit of armor she usually wears is off, and she's open with me, joking, laughing, being herself.

Maybe.

I make my way to the sofa and park myself next to her. She twirls her hair, and I've noticed she does this when she's tired.

She turns towards me and sits crisscrossed on the sofa.

"So what were you doing out on the deck, and by the way, what are you doing home?"

She looks tired, but seems to be in the mood to talk, so she's asking, I don't have a problem telling her. We are still doing the baby step thing here.

"I was tired. Didn't want to hang out anymore." I keep my answer simple, not wanting her to know she pissed me off with Elton Joel earlier. She had a bad night, so why tell her because I think it would have only caused us to argue about it, whether I was right or not. But I was.

She doesn't believe me. Her face tells me so.

I snicker at her. "Seriously, I worked a lot this week, plus I had some work to do."

"Work?" She asks.

"Yes. I'm taking an online class to keep up with the latest past and present case laws and any recent changes to them."

"Case laws?"

"Yes. It's all kinds of legal shit for when I have to be present at a hearing. It's for future reference, when I get a full-time position, I'll be somewhat up to date on things."

She gets up and goes to the refrigerator, grabs a new bottle of water for herself, well at least I think it was for her until she makes her way back to the sofa and hands it to me.

"Thanks." The gesture was nice, so I take it from her.

"So with this class, what else does it entail?"

"You really want to know?" She nods. She really wants to know.

"Well, I have to stay updated on probable cause, reasonable suspicion and vehicle investigations." She begins to laugh.

"What?" I ask. "What's so funny?"

She wrinkles up her nose and her freckles spread out onto her cheeks when she does. She continues to twirl a strand of her strawberry blonde hair.

"Nothing, except the tables are turned right here and right now."

I'm not understanding what she means. She rolls her eyes and continues to speak.

"You and I. Tables turned, because I have no idea what you just said. Big words, you used big words that I have no idea their meaning. It's usually the other way around."

She means cop talk. Funny, isn't it? She's right. Sometimes when we are all sitting around, talking, and she uses a big one, I pretend I'm checking a text, but I use my smart phone to Google the word she's referring to.

"Sorry, it's to keep updated on new laws. So what about you? Have you heard anything else yet about any teaching positions that opened up?"

She lets out a frustrated breath and eases back on the sofa.

"Not yet. I just don't want to go back and have to get a job that I don't want to do. I know that sounds bratty, but I just want to teach. It's my dream and all I've ever wanted to do."

When she tells me that, she gets a dreamy look in her eyes. Like if a chick talks about a hot movie star, or a new bag she wants, or some shit like that, not about teaching, but it's cool.

We are talking like old friends. She's telling me about how her brother is a junior in college, is also going to be a teacher and how he's coming to visit next weekend for a few days. How her sister is still driving her crazy with her wedding plans, and how her grandmother, the rich one, is paying for most of it. She tells me she disapproves of her and her brother's career choices that she wished they had gone into law and worked within the family firm. Her dad never wanted to be a lawyer, but was sort of forced into it.

He made a good living from it, but does very adventurous things with his spare time. Sky diving, zip lines. He climbed Everest once, and almost died. He's very into his family. He taught his kids the value of a dollar, never spoiling them, but taking them on extravagant trips to Europe. And a few years ago they went to Australia, so they could explore a new continent, and a new culture. She tells me how he wanted his children to stay grounded, grow up with privileges, but with the values of Harlow's mom, who came from nothing.

Harlow's been everywhere. I've been places, but the places I've been to ended in death and destruction. Never for pleasure, or relaxation.

The five of them, plus her sister's fiancé, always volunteer at a homeless shelter on Thanksgiving, donating and cooking all the food. Her grandmother hates it, but it's something they look forward to every year.

I've never heard of a rich family doing something like that. When she talks about her parents, she lights up. They are the sun and the moon to her. She's extremely close with her brother, has little in common with her sister, but they get along well.

"So tell me about your family? I'm going on and on about mine, and I feel bad I haven't even asked you about yours."

"Well not much to tell. Mom's great. She's a homemaker. She's beautiful, kind, loving. We are close, and dad, well he's a real jokester."

These are lies.

All lies.

I tell them because she'll never find out the truth anyway, so to keep the conversation light, I lie.

"Yea, my dad loves having a catch in the yard with my brother and me. He works really hard. He's a VP at a printing company, has been for thirty years. I'm going to be an uncle in a few months. I'm not into kids, but I'm happy for my brother and his wife, Bella."

Her face lights up when I tell her about being an uncle, then it turns into something else for a moment. Girls get that look in their eyes when you say baby, but the light that was just there, went out.

"That's um… that's great for them. This will be their first?"

"Yes. My brother told me they tried for a few years without success."

She gets up from the couch abruptly and goes to the cabinet which stores DVD's and games. She rifles through it while speaking to me.

"Well some people aren't as lucky as the ones who don't even plan on pregnancies. It's a shame, really. It comes so easy for some. I'm glad they are getting their little miracle."

Her voice is distant. It seems to not even be her speaking. Like another person said those words. Sometimes I don't get this chick.

"Bella is great. When we were younger I had a crush on her, but my brother snagged her from me."

She looks at me, like she's heard this somewhere before.

"I remember."

Did I tell her that? I can't remember.

"You do?" She comes to sit by me again and holds a DVD in her hand.

"I do. That night last summer when we um, when we…"

"Did it?" I say with a grin. She smacks my arm.

"Yea, whatever. I told you, you were, a um, a…"

I know what she wants to say, I'll finish it for her.

"Good kisser."

I'm aggravating her.

Score and I've earned a blush from her.

"Yes, yes, yes. Ok. Fine. A good kisser, and you said you practiced on a girl who is now your sister in law."

She remembered that? But she was drunk. Totally wasted. At least she seemed to be.

"How did you remember that? It was so long ago, but I did tell you, now that you mention it."

She doesn't want to say, which is fine. She looks uncomfortable, so I won't press the issue. She changes the subject quickly.

"Um, I'm not really tired, and I was going to watch a movie. You want to watch it with me?"

She wants me to hang around? I think she may be bipolar. One minute she's kicking me in the balls, the next minute, she wants to know my life story. I'm not really tired anymore either, so what the hell, I'll just keep working on being a grown up.

"Sure. What do you have there to watch?"

She holds the DVD close to her chest, closes her eyes, and lets out a breath, a dramatic one.

"My favorite, A Song In My Heart. I knew Mrs. Taylor, Willow's mom still had to have it here. I turned her on to it."

"Sounds like a chick movie to me. I want blood and guts. Can't you find Rambo or something like that in there?" I point over to the cabinet.

"Ugh, Neanderthal. Why'd I even ask." She shakes her head at me, basically aggravated at my reaction to her choice in movies.

"What I say wrong?" I grab the box from her, look at the cover, read the synopsis on the back, and toss it on the table.

"That is fucked up. It's sad. She's a singer with this awesome career, and she gets hurt in a plane crash and practically gets her legs cut off. She's a cripple. Why would you want to watch something like that?"

She stands up, puts her hands on her tiny, little hips, and taps that foot of hers.

"Well then why would you want to watch something like Rambo? Didn't you get enough of that stuff when you were in the Marines?"

She's got a point.

Damn it.

She continues talking. "I was raised on the classics, my mother was a…"

I interrupt her. "Huge fan of old movies, and movie stars, hence the name Harlow, because you were named after Jeanne Harlow. Your sister Greta, was named after Garbo, and your brother after Joan Crawford, which I still don't get."

She looks startled. She stops tapping her foot, and looks at me like I have a parasitic twin growing out of my neck.

"How do you remember that?"

Oh, shit, how do I remember that?

"You, um, you told me that during one of our conversations out on the dock one morning."

She shakes her head.

"No, no I never said that to you, this summer. I said it to you last summer during our little, you know…"

No need to hesitate.

She's right.

I scratch my head, wishing I didn't say it all out loud, but I did. No turning back.

"So. Your name's weird. Of course I'd remember a story like that."

She waits a second, takes a step forward, and then retreats. She thought of something, contemplated saying something to me, but backs away, still standing near the sofa, but a few inches away.

My sudden urge to cover this up makes me take desperate measures.

"Ok, fine. I'll watch your stupid chick movie, full of sappy love shit and tragedy. But if they break out in a musical number, I'm fucking out of here." She claps her hands in an exciting way and shoves the DVD into the player.

I like playful Harlow Hannum.

When the music for the intro of the movie starts, I already know I'm in deep shit. I hope there's a knife handy, so I can slit my throat. Harlow sits at one end of the sofa, hands me a blanket, and grabs one for herself. She covers herself in it and snuggles down to make herself comfortable in the crook of the sofa. I look at the blanket, then to her.

"What am I supposed to do with this?"

"Cover yourself up with it, get cozy, and enjoy the movie. That's what you do. That's what I always do."

She smiles at me, and for some ungodly reason, it makes me feel… I don't know how to explain it, a little warm and fuzzy maybe. So I do what she said, hoping there are no hidden cameras for anyone to take notice at what a pussy I am.

The heat from the blanket suddenly wakes me from my sleep. I can feel more weight on me, around my chest, and a softness under my one hand. I shake my sleepiness and open my eyes, confused and not remembering where I am at that moment, until I look down. Then I remember. I see the top of her head. The thick strawberry blonde hair of Harlow, and when I shift my body, her arm tightens around me, and she purrs. Soft, little snores come out of her with every breath. I can smell her hair under my nose, a scent that awakens me even more than the feel of her soft hair. Do I wake her up? Do I tell her to go to bed, or do I just fall back asleep, which is what I really want to do because the heaviness in my eyelids tells me so. Leaning my head on the back of the couch, I contemplate what to do next. I try to pull my arm out from under her neck, and when I do, the strands of her hair go through my fingers, and it feels like silk passing through them. I've never felt anything like it. I've felt and pulled a lot of hair in my day, but this feels different. My fingertips spark at the sensation. It flows up my hand to my arm, and I'm awake more than I was five minutes ago. Harlow doesn't move. She's so still and so deep in sleep. I'm not sure what my next move will be.

Do I even want to move?

I'm exhausted, but I don't do this. I don't cuddle with chicks. How'd she even get this close to me anyway? She was on the opposite side of the sofa when the damn movie started. I can't even remember when I fell asleep, or when she did for that matter.

I push any thoughts I have of staying on this couch out of my head. I look at the clock which reads 2:15. I didn't hear anyone come in, so maybe they went to an afterhours place, or decided to stick around Jax for a bit after closing. Her friends will get the wrong idea if they see us this way, hell my friends will get the wrong idea if they see us, so I make my move.

I gently nudge her arm, making sure not to startle her.

"Turnip. Turnip, wake up. Time to go to bed." I stroke the top of her head, thinking this may not be a good idea.

She doesn't make a sound, not even a stir, or a flinch, nothing. The only thing left to do is carry her to her room and leave.

I struggle to get her body off of mine and slip out without disturbing her. I slide an arm under her legs and support her back with the other. Gently lifting her off the sofa, her arms find their way back to my chest. I cradle her as I carry her to her room. When we reach it, I lay her down, trying to pull back the comforter from the bed, and one by one I take off the shoes that are still on her feet. She moves her body involuntarily to her pillow and tucks her hands underneath it, supporting her head even more. I pull the comforter over her body, and my hands do something my mind tells me not to do. They make their way to her hair again, stroking it, feeling the softness I felt out in the living room, waiting for that sensation. As soon as it hits me, she moves, and I pull away.

A little too soon.

"Chad?" I hear her croak out.

Who's Chad?

"Chad, I'm sorry. Please. Stay with me. I'm so sorry."

She's dreaming, but who is the Chad she's dreaming about? I don't remember a Chad from the movie we watched tonight, and the guy from earlier wasn't Chad. I'm too tired to figure it out. She's still asleep, and no longer talking to this Chad person, so I get up from the bed and make my way to the door. But before I leave, I take one last look at this tiny person lying there, looking so young, so innocent as she sleeps.

I walk out of her room, lock her doors to the house, and go back to mine. I lay in my bed, wondering who Chad is, and why just a few strands of hair made me feel... something. Not knowing what it is, or what it was, I know I saw a softer side of Harlow tonight, one that I liked. One that could make us be better friends, closer ones even. I think about the way she looked in that bed, so vulnerable, warm, content. I'm too tired to jerk off tonight. Morty will just have to wait till tomorrow.

The last thing I think about before I fall asleep is the peacefulness I saw in her as she slept. Her hair splayed across her pillow, the soft sounds she made as she breathed in and out. She looked like an angel, and here I am, thinking of her like the devil.

CHAPTER 7

Fireworks

Harlow~

I can't believe the 4th of July is in two days. The summer is flying by. It's somewhat the idea of what I wanted it to be like. Hanging with the girls, relaxing on the beach, going out at night. It's everything I wanted out of this summer and needed. I see that it's almost time for my first scheduled call of the week with Dr. Goldberg, my therapist. So I tell the girls I'm headed for a run. I take my phone with me and run to the spot on the beach I always go to when I have to speak with him. I dial in, and his secretary puts me through to him.

"Hello there, Harlow. How's your week going?"

"Hi there, Dr. Goldberg. It's good. I'm feeling ok."

"How have you been sleeping?"

"Not too bad, as long as I take the meds. I did miss a night or two, but I realized I didn't need them, and slept for a solid six hours."

"Good, good. Glad to hear it. Have you heard back from any of the schools you applied to for a job?"

As much as I want to tell him yes, I can't and it frustrates me.

"No not yet, but I'm not worried, just anxious."

"Are you feeling the anxiousness only with the job situation, or are other things making you anxious?"

I look out at the water, which is far enough from me not to make me anxious, and I tell him about the feet in the water incident with Cruz. I conquered a fear and Dr. Goldberg seems pleased to hear about it.

"I think you are making great strides, Harlow. Now about this friend you talk about so often, Cruz is his name? The cop?"

"Yes, that's him. What about him?"

"Well, you talk about how in the beginning of the summer you were ready to leave because of his antics, and you weren't comfortable with him living next to you because of what transpired between the two of you last summer."

Yes, I told Dr. Goldberg about Cruz. About the night we got together. About the one whose name we do not speak was there making out with that girl. I had a session with Dr. Goldberg a few days later and told him what I did. I needed to get it out and tell him, which in hindsight, was actually progress considering I wasn't locked up in my room somewhere, rocking back and forth like a mental patient.

"Correct, and believe it or not, we have settled on some kind of friendly ground."

"I'm glad to hear that."

The one thing I'm so surprised at out of this whole summer is the relationship Cruz and I have established. I've never really had any guy friends, well, except Craw, but he's my brother and one of my best friends. However, the more time I spend with Cruz, the more he's, I don't know, what word should I use to describe him… let's call it human?

I tell Dr. Goldberg all of this, and I can tell he's writing it all down, making notes, and just listening to me.

"And does he know about what happened and about him?"

Oh, God, I wish I never have to tell him.

"No, he doesn't. Only my brother and Willow know." And Cruz will never know.

"You know, Harlow. It sounds like from what you tell me, this young man is having quite a good influence on you. I hear a change in your voice when you speak about him. I know he gave you a rough time in the beginning, but sometimes the ones who we least expect to open us up to a new way of thinking, a new way of learning. Then there are the ones we feel so comfortable opening up to and having conversations with that make you feel calm and at peace, that's therapeutic."

Maybe Dr. Goldberg is right.

Our conversations are great. We have a better understanding of each other's personalities. I'm not much of a talker at times, especially when I'm in a down stage, but for some odd reason, beyond my comprehension, when I feel that way Cruz seems to be there, making me laugh, or grossing me out.

"I guess, Dr. Goldberg. I do feel myself opening up a lot more around him. I'm not used to doing that with a guy. I mean Craw is different, but still, I'm not so sure how it's therapeutic for me."

"It's therapeutic because it's the unknown. He's the unknown. He doesn't know what happened to you and can't judge you for anything. You say he listens to you. He knows about your dream of becoming a teacher, how hard you worked for it. He knows about your family, the history there, so by just talking to him about random, daily events or things from the past, not directly related to why you speak to me, that's therapeutic."

As I sit on this beach, listening to the waves crash on the shore, the sun beating on my face, I shut my eyes, take a deep cleansing breath, and think about it all. I think about what I've been through. The things that 'he' has done to me. He left me with no self-worth, leaving me to think I'm just not good enough, and sometimes I think he's right. But lately there are those times when I'm around Cruz, he can make me feel like I am good enough.

My session with Dr. Goldberg goes on for a little bit longer. He tells me no need to up my meds, that he thinks I'm making great strides and he will talk to me after the holiday, but encourages me to enjoy the new found friendship I've found in Cruz.

We are still doing our little morning ritual when he's not sleeping from working a long shift. We sit on the dock, drink coffee, watch the sun rise sometimes and talk. I attempt to dangle my feet in the water, if I'm in an up mood. The water is somewhat therapy for me. Even though I don't go in it, just the movement of it, the calmness it distributes, makes me feel a sense of calm inside this unbalanced head of mine. That and the combination of Cruz's and my early morning talks. He's almost like Dr. Goldberg. It's as though I'm in session, but now it's this guy I live next to, who I had sex with a year ago, without knowing him.

Jesus, I did that and didn't know him.

Sometimes that seeps into my brain, and I can't shut it off. I've never been a highly sexual being. Only being with one person besides Cruz, that's what you can call me... quite inexperienced.

But I was a different person that night. I was uninhibited, lustful, greedy even. My dominate side shone through in my actions. Actions I can't take back if I tried, and once in a while Cruz will remind me of that.

Craw is coming in today for a few days. We are going out tonight to this new place on the bay, The Boat Stop, where people can drive their boats up to its docks, park, and walk to the bar. I'm excited for Craw to meet the guys.

The blissful morning sun is warm and inviting on my face. Just the sounds of the seagulls is better music to my ears than any song on the radio.

"Mornin', Turnip."

I turn to see it's Cruz, still in his uniform from his shift.

I peer up at him, swallowing hard. A feeling enters the pit of my stomach, it's unfamiliar and ever present for some unexplained reason.

The uniform. It's just the uniform.

Blue is his color. It brings out the color of his opulent eyes.

I ignore my stomach.

"Good morning to you too, or am I about to say goodnight?"

He laughs and takes a sip of his coffee.

"Goodnight, yes. I just got back. It was a busy night. Two calls for bar fights, and one domestic, and a shitload of paperwork."

Poor guy. He looks tired. He's been working hard trying to prove himself to the precinct he works in so they may hire him on a permanent, full-time basis.

"Then if you're so tired, why are you out here."

He shrugs. "This is our thing, that's why. I didn't want to miss it."

Ok.

"So what time is your brother getting here?"

"Around ten. We are headed over to that new place tonight on the bay. Are you coming?"

He nods and stands up, stretches and starts to unbutton his uniform shirt.

Wait. What. Huh?

Cruz peels it off from his body. A tight, white undershirt reveals the muscular outline of his body. I can see the ripples from his strong stomach muscles, his inked arms, and the crest of his pecs. He strips it off swiftly, but my brain is processing it as methodical, inching it off his body, displaying one inch of skin a centimeter at a time.

I'm awakened suddenly from my slow motion brain activity when he throws the shirt he just took off at my face.

"Hey!" I throw it back at him.

"You looked like you were in some kind of dream state there. I had to wake you up. You had this weird look on your face."

My thoughts go back to him being a jerk. I wasn't making a weird face. My thought process just slowed down momentarily.

"I'm fine. Tired I guess. I didn't sleep well last night."

He looks at me, inquisitively.

"Really? Two nights ago you said you slept like a baby, and the night before that too. That kind of sucks. Did you drink too much coffee or something those nights? I was working twelve's, so I didn't know if you guys were just staying in, or if you headed out."

He's right. The nights he worked, I slept like crap.

Tossed and turned all night.

"We went to dinner one of the nights, and the other stayed in and played board games. No coffee and just a few drinks when we were playing games."

"Oh, well. Too bad. Ok, well, I'm going to hit the sack for a few hours. What time tonight?"

"Ten."

He smiles and makes his way over to the chair I'm sitting in. He bends down and kisses the top of my head and strokes my hair with his hand. I'm rendered speechless, my mind not processing this display of affection correctly.

"Goodnight, Turnip. I'll see you later."

Cruz turns and walks up the dock back to the house, and I'm left thinking of his simple gesture. Then I have it, what it was, what that meant.

Yes, it's the brother/sister thing.

I hear Willow call to me from the deck.

"Harlow, Craw just pulled up."

My little brother is here. I haven't seen him in over a month. Craw and I are so close. I consider him one of my best friends. He was there for me so much over the past year and a half. His support has meant so much to me. He was my mind when I didn't have one. I run out to the deck and peer over the railing. My brother gets out of the car, closes his door and looks up at the house. I wave my hands and jump up and down.

He smiles when he sees me, and I feel warm and happy when I see his face.

He reaches the deck and I run to him and hug him with all my might.

"Oh, Craw. I'm so happy you're here. I missed you so much."

He squeezes me back, lifts my body and spins me around.

"I missed you too, Har." He lets me go and steps back, grabbing my hands and surveys me.

"You look fantastic, sweetheart. The shore has done wonders for you."

He brings a smile to my face. Every time, without fail.

"Thank you very much. The sun has been kind to this pale skin of mine. Come on in and I'll get you something to eat."

We walk into the house. The girls greet him with hugs. We have a brief conversation about what we all have been up to since we've been here. Craw tells us about how he is taking summer courses, so he can graduate a few months earlier than expected. I ask how my mom and dad are, and if Greta is driving him crazy, which he tells me yes. He calls her the 'Princess of Princeton', which I always laugh at. I ask how Grandmother is, and if she knew he was coming here. He tells me she didn't say too much because she is so wrapped up in Greta's wedding. It's the social event of the year, so she's preparing for her mirrored image debutante granddaughter to put on quite the show.

After an hour of conversing, the girls leave to go to the beach, and Craw and I stay behind to catch up some more, even though I talk and text with him all the time.

We sit on the sofa and he kicks off his shoes and lounges.

"So, you look terrific on the outside, how's it going on the inside? Still talking with Dr. Goldberg?"

Craw is constantly on me about therapy, which is a good thing. He worries, especially with me here and him being at home.

"Yes. Two days a week. I've been feeling so good. I am still taking my meds everyday."

He pats my knee and grins.

"Good girl. It's important, Harlow. You're down to two days a week, maybe in time you can go down to one. I'm proud of you."

"Thanks, Craw."

"How's living next to Porter's friends?"

He sort of knows Max but hasn't met Cruz yet. I think I kind of have to tell him the truth, who he is and what happened between us before someone else does.

"Good. You know them, well most of them, they're great."

He crinkles up his forehead and smirks.

"All of them. I thought it was just Porter and Max."

"Well, not exactly."

I go on to tell him everything, from me falling in the water to me kneeing Cruz in the testicles. He already knew what transpired between Cruz and me last year, how I didn't know him, or his last name, or the fact that he doesn't go by Raphael. At one point during our conversation, Craw's eyes bug out of his head.

"Well you little slut."

I smack his leg, and he smacks me back.

"I am not a slut. Every time I think of what I did I cringe, Craw. That wasn't me that night."

"You were so a slut, at least for that brief time. I told you when you told me it happened I was glad you let go. It's sometimes fun not being yourself, Harlow. Embrace it."

That's such a hard line for me to cross. I was with one

person for so long. It was almost like I had an out of body experience.

"So did you guys hookup again? Are you interested in pursuing something with him?"

"Absolutely not. He's a man-whore. We are just friends. Actually getting to be great friends. We are getting along really well. He's a cop down here, well a rent-a-cop, but he's trying to get a full time position. I can't wait for you to meet him."

Craw stares at me. He's focused on my eyes, and I don't know why.

"Why are you looking at me like that?" I ask him.

"Because."

"Because why?"

"Because in eighteen months I haven't seen your face light up like this until this moment."

He's crazy. I smile all the time, at least when I'm having a good day. And we are just having a conversation, and I'm telling him about Cruz. What's the big deal.

"What are you talking about."

He inches closer to me, rests his face on his hand, and his elbow on his knee. He studies my face.

"You talk about this guy like he's a superhero. The smile on your face when you said his name says more to me than I think even you know."

His words are farcical. I don't demonstrate any of the characteristics he's talking about. Cruz and I are friends. We have great conversations, we talk about everything under the sun, and we respect each other, for now anyway.

I brush past his comments and suggest we grab some stuff for the beach. I tell him we are going out tonight to a new place, and the cabs will be here by nine forty five.

Craw and I head down to the beach for a little bit. Porter and the girls are there. Cruz is sleeping after his exhausting shift. He works very hard. Sometimes it surprises me he has such a good work ethic, but from what he tells me, he inherited that trait from his father, who is also a very hard worker.

After an hour or two of soaking up the sun, we head home to get ready for our night out. Our ritual for going out always consists of loud, get you on your feet dance music, a few cocktails and chips, greasy, salty potato chips. After we are all done with our hair, makeup and consumption of fattening chips, I see Craw outside smoking a cigarette on the deck. I step out to tell him the cabs will be here any minute.

"I thought you were going to quit, Craw." I sound like my mom, but I hate that he does it, and I hate more the reason why he started in the first place.

Me.

"I am, I promise. When you go down to therapy one day a week, then I will."

"Therapy? Who's in therapy?"

I hear a big, monotone voice behind me, and it jolts my body.

It's Cruz.

"Oh, hey. I want you to meet my brother Crawford."

Craw sticks out his hand to Cruz.

"Please, call me Craw."

Cruz takes his hand.

"Oh, hey. The brother, right? I'm Cruz. I've heard a lot about you from Turnip here."

Craw turns to me with a scowl.

"Turnip?"

Oh, great. More fuel to add to the fire of Craw's

accusations that there's more than friendship here. I need to defuse this, now.

"It's a silly nickname he gave me. Don't mind him."

Craw looks to me, then back to Cruz, not really believing it's just a pet name. That's exactly what it is. A friendly joke.

"Well anyway, it's nice to meet you, Cruz. I've heard a lot about you from my sister. A lot."

I'll kill him for emphasizing the 'a lot' in that statement. I feel my cheeks redden, as I feel the need to turn this conversation to something else.

Cruz knows what Craw meant, but he doesn't say anything. He winks at me and continues to ask him questions.

"So Harlow tells me you are in your last year of college. Teacher, right?"

Craw nods. "Yep, just like my big sis. Hopefully she'll get a position soon, and then she can put a good word in for me when she does."

"Well, good luck to you. I have no doubt your sister is going to make an excellent teacher, and from what she tells me, you will be one too."

I'll have to admit, although I don't want to, but that was probably the sweetest thing to come out of Raphael Cruz's big mouth.

Porter yells to us that the cabs have arrived, so we make our way down to meet them. Craw grabs my arm in the process and whispers, "Just friends my ass, Turnip." He winks at me, and I roll my eyes. He's dreaming.

We pull up to the new bar/restaurant called The Boat Stop. It's a bit posh, unlike the places down here we usually go to. The place is a bit crowded, and it's a mixture of young and old. Money comes here. This I am sure of because I come from it. I can see by the clientele. We step in and make our way to a few tables we spot over near the docks. It's a beautiful night to be outside. A light breeze flows off the bay, and I love watching the boats pull in. I love boats. I don't like to be on one, actually I hate it, but I can appreciate their architecture.

Craw goes to hang with the guys, and the girls and I sit at a table. We talk about the place and about how Willow's dad is going to love it when he comes down. The area used to be the site of an old boat yard for fishing vessels in the late 1800's. There's a lot of history here, and I remind myself to research it more. I'm a history buff. I like old things. I take an interest in the past.

Cruz makes his way to our table and asks us if we need anything from the bar. We give him our orders, and thank him as he arrives back after a few minutes. He hands us our drinks and slides into the seat next to me. My seat is situated so I have a perfect view of the boats docking. Their lights and hard lines, the sleek, sexiness of the boats captivates my attention. Craw comes over to join us and takes a seat next to the girls. Cruz turns and talks into my ear, "You look nice tonight, Turnip. I like this preppy sweater thingy you have going on here." He picks at my cardigan sweater, and I swat at his hand. He chuckles and turns his head to look at a few girls who just walked in the door. Craw mouths to me, "Friends my ass." I kick him under the table, and he laughs. We keep the conversation light, discussing nothing in particular. How tomorrow is the 4th of July, and the activities we all have planned. A bar-b-que at our houses and fireworks on the beach at night. Sounds like a perfect day. There's something to be said about fireworks. They surprise you, coming at you without warning. They are full of color and vibrancy, displaying their brilliance as they capture your attention. There's an intimacy about them as well, I interpret them like that. Even though thousands of people see the same thing, I feel like they can be my own private show. Bursting out in the sky just for me.

My thoughts of fireworks and bar-b-ques suddenly turn to panic. My gut clenches. The acid in it turns, and my eyes well with unshed tears. Willow looks at my face, knowing damn well that I see something I don't care to see. My solitude is suddenly lost in an image, and as it approaches, it seeks me out like a hunter who finally spots his next meal. My mind whirls around at the sight of his eyes, the way they hold me captive, his lips, and the way he sticks his tongue out to graze his own top lip, and the way he saunters over towards my table. The hunter appears to be ready to strike, and my breathing becomes heavy and labored. Willow leans over and whispers, "What is it, Harlow? What's wrong?" The sheer panic in her voice makes her whip her head around to every angle until she spots the hunter.

"Oh, Christ. Harlow look at me."

I can't.

I can't tear my eyes away. She grabs my hands and tells me sternly, "Harlow, I said look at me." I do. I focus on her face, seeing my reflection in her eyes due to the fact I'm focusing so hard. She speaks to Craw without breaking her eye contact with me.

"Craw, I think we need to leave, slowly, without making a scene. Do you understand me?" I don't see Craw's face, I only hear his words. "Mother fucker."

Then I hear Cruz's voice. "What the hell is going on?

Turnip? What's wrong with her?"

I do something again so out of character for me. It's difficult to comprehend why I do it, but I do it anyway. I break my eye contact with Willow, pull my hands away from hers, and turn my head to Cruz. He looks just as panicked as I am. He searches my eyes for an answer, but I don't give him one. I only say what I feel I must at that moment.

"Cruz, kiss me, now."

He pulls back, trying to understand the question, or rather the demand.

"Kiss me now, quickly."

He smirks. His facial expression bordering on annoyance, and he sits upwards in his chair with defiance.

"I am not kissing you, Harlow. You've got to be crazy."

Wrong choice of words at this present time, my friend.

I search his blue eyes, suddenly taking my hand to his broad, hard chest. I snake it upwards towards his thick neck, scraping my nails on his taut skin. As I do so, I say strongly and without fear, "Maybe I am, but if you don't kiss me now, I'll be forced to make you. I'll be the one." He hesitates, his mouth slightly parted, and he manages a sigh. I look to my right and see that the hunter is almost at his target, and in a desperate move to convey to him the importance of this act, I whisper, "I warned you." And I pull his face to mine. My lips touch his, and my tongue darts out to part his lips. The stubbornness of his lips infuriates me, so as my hand reaches up to lock in his unruly brown locks. I feel Cruz's body relax, and he parts his lips for my welcomed tongue. I slip it inside tasting him, whipping it around inside his mouth, his tongue bathing mine. The twists and turns of them together, almost in a battle it seems. The subtle moans I hear coming out of his mouth, and I taste him. My eyes are tightly shut, and his hand grasps my hip, pulling me towards him even more. One more inch and I know I'll be in his lap. I can feel his teeth hit mine, biting at my lower lip, teasing it. As I feel a familiar ache begin to build between my thighs, I see stars. My eyes are shut so steadfastly, temporarily making me forget the purpose of my actions. I see. I see…

Fireworks.

That's until I hear the hunter speak.

"Baby, I've missed you." My eyes spring open like a jack-in-the-box, but I still keep my focus on the man whose eyes are before me. He licks his lower lip, bringing his free hand up to touch it, and I break my gaze from his when he does so. I look at Willow and Craw, whose expressions I'm not sure I'm reading correctly. Theirs is a mixture of anger and disbelief.

"Baby, did you hear me?" The hunter's words then bring me back to the reality that he is here, the hunter has found his prey. I turn my eyes to him, not being able to escape his voice as it reverberates through my soul. I need to maintain cool composure and act like his presence is like that of anyone else who says hi to me.

"Oh, hey. What are you doing all the way down here?"

The hunter leans both his hands on the table, gripping it, so he can steady his long, lean body.

"Daddy let me take his boat down here this weekend. He heard about the opening of this place, and told me it was good for her to stretch her legs down this way. What's, um going on here?"

Craw stands up, his chair falling behind him from the force of his abrupt move.

"None of your fucking business. Get out of here, asshole, before I throw you out myself." Willow grabs hold of Craw's arm, pulling him down, as she sets the flipped over chair up, willing Craw to sit.

The hunter straightens his body up and waves his hands at Craw.

"Whoa, just relax little brother, I only came to say hi to Harlow. I'm meeting a few friends here so I'm not staying, unless she wants me to. Do you want me to stay, baby?"

He sounds like he's asking me, but he's not, he's actually telling me. To the outside world, it appears he's asking, but I know him and his games and how he lures in his prey.

I don't answer him, but the hunter's curiosity about the man I was just kissing comes full circle.

He extends his hand to Cruz. "Hi there. I don't think we've been properly introduced. I'm Chad Knox." I sneak a glance at Cruz, who looks confused, but takes Chad's hand anyway, and I hear Cruz say, "Chad... Chad. Nice to meet you."

"Don't say it's nice to meet this son of a bitch. Get the hell out of here, Knox. I'm not fucking kidding." Craw never holds his words back when speaking to Knox. Chad exudes a small laugh and seems to back away from the table the slightest bit.

"Fine, have it your way. Baby, when you're done playing around with Mr. Tattoo, I'll be at my Uncle Dan's house on 4th Street, if you want to talk. I'll be there all week. I hope you do come to see me, baby. I've really missed you."

He acknowledges Willow, then Craw, who remains silent, but provides him with the standard one-finger salute. When he retreats and walks to his party, I relax just the slightest bit in my seat. I touch my lips, feeling the swell of them, and I remember what I just did. I turn to Cruz.

"Oh, God, Cruz, I'm so sorry. I'm so sorry." He runs his large hand over his face, scratching at his stubble. His eyes wander around the room, and every time he opens his mouth to speak, only sounds I'm not sure what they are, come out.

"I'll fucking kill that mother fucker, so help me God. Har, are you ok?"

"I'm... I'm fine, Craw. Cruz?" He doesn't look at me, and I think I may have just ruined our friendship. My hands finds his arm, and I grasp it.

"Cruz?" He finally looks at me, his eyes tense.

"An ex-boyfriend I presume?"

"Mother fucker is more like it," Craw says as he pulls out a cigarette to light, but just holds it between his lips. I wait with baited breath for Cruz to say something, anything. Tell me to fuck off, whatever.

"You let him call you baby?" When he says it, it stuns me, and I can't help to feel a pang in my heart when he does so.

With those words, he gets up out of his chair, throws a few dollars on the table and walks away.

So he met the one we do not speak of, and I wish he hadn't. I had to kiss him. I had to show Chad he doesn't have me. His powers are useless against me, and I can move on.

But in actuality, I didn't. I just used Cruz as a decoy, a distraction from reality. The reality that I caused. I wanted to go talk to Chad, but I have to be strong, fight the forces of evil that invade me. I need to talk to Dr. Goldberg tonight. I need my therapeutic sessions with him on the phone, or even more so, my early morning therapeutic session on the dock with a cop.

But will he give me the therapy I deserve, or did I lose that too?

When I touch my lips, I try to hold back the ache that has surfaced. A familiar one. I never thought a kiss could set me on fire, especially one that I initiated. My belly rolled. I lost all sense of reality, thinking and feeling things that I haven't in a very long time. Not since last year. But how could that be? I grabbed him and brought his lips to mine just like that fateful night a year ago. It was that same feeling of excitement, adventure, raw sexual emotion, passion, lust, and any other words I can use to describe in a sexual nature. However, thinking of Cruz in that way has rendered me confused. I can't stop touching my lips. They burn, the blood coursing through them, throbbing. I know what he tasted like, what he smelled like. What it was like to have his tongue dual against mine. Sharing a kiss like that so intimately, but yet surrounded by so many makes my pulse quicken. Again, I did something out of sorts for me. This is what this man does to me, he makes me do things beyond my control, and I have to be in control. I am reckless when I'm with him, I am not the girl who hid under her blankets for over a year. I am not the girl who uses big words to impress people or scare them off. I don't need to be that way around Cruz. I can be me. Harlow Hannum.

My lips still ache and I wonder when the feeling will leave me, or would I want it to.

"Hi, Dr. Goldberg. I know it's not one of our regularly scheduled sessions, and I know it's late but I needed to speak to you."

I had called Dr. Goldberg's answering service, and they told me he would call me back. I know it's well past midnight, but when you're desperate, you'll go to any length.

"It's fine, Harlow. Really, it is. What can I do for you."

I touch my lips again, feeling the strength of Cruz's lips still on them, and every time I close my eyes, that moment plays again in my head like a movie. A good one with some sort of climatic moment and then thoughts of Chad pop in and the panic sets in. Immediately, I lose all forms of serenity. The way he made his way over to my table when I spotted him and those eyes. They know how to hypnotize me and reel me in like bait on a hook. I don't want him because he never wanted me. I used to do whatever I could to please him, but no matter what, I'd always come up short.

"I was out tonight and I saw Chad."

Dr. Goldberg sighs, not that he is annoyed, but in a way that says he wishes I didn't.

"I see. Did you exchange words with him?"

"Yes, it was brief, actually my brother said more to him than I did."

Dr. Goldberg laughs. "Oh, my. Good old Craw. I like the boy. I like how he always has your back, Harlow. So then what?"

"Well, I think I handled it well. He asked me to come and see him, but I didn't answer. I kept the conversation short."

"Good, good. That's exactly what I told you to do, knowing you are both from the same town and your fathers' are friendly, you are bound to run into him."

I know I have to tell him the reason why I handled it so well, and I'm still not sure it was the best approach seeing the way Cruz left. I think confused is a good word to describe it. I, myself, am bewildered by it all.

"I kind of did something else that I'm not sure was the best thing to do."

I shut my eyes tight, feeling guilty for what I have done.

I'm always feeling guilty for something. I wonder if that feeling will ever subside.

"And what was that, Harlow?"

"I kissed Cruz in front of Chad to… I don't know, make him jealous? But I don't think that's it. I think maybe to distract myself from his presence? See, this is why I'm calling, Dr. Goldberg. I don't know what made me do what I did."

I sound whiny, like my sister Greta.

A moment goes by before he speaks again.

"Harlow, what transpired between you and Chad is something I feel you will never fully recover from. What went on will remain in your thoughts no matter what you do, no matter what you say. You told me before he has a powerful grip on you, always has, but I don't think you did what you did to make him jealous. A distraction, quite possibly, but for some unknown rationalization I think from the things you tell me about your friend Cruz, you wanted to kiss him."

Now I think Dr. Goldberg is the one who needs to be on crazy pills.

"Oh, no way! I didn't mean for the kiss to end up like the way it did, and I didn't set out for it to happen, either."

Or did I? Was it premeditated?

Still feeling the after effects of the kiss, I question myself.

"Harlow, I'm not saying you set out to kiss him, but maybe in your subconscious mind it was… the logical thing to do. I hear you speak so highly of the man. Although I am a licensed doctor and therapist, I am also a man who has been happily married to the same woman for thirty five years, and I know how women think."

Here's Dr. Goldberg giving me his take on the female psyche. Typical male.

"I understand that, Dr. Goldberg, and Cruz is becoming a near and dear friend, and we have a past, but I'm not sure in the back of my mind I wanted it to happen."

This time.

I hear him clear his throat.

"You once shared some sort of intimacy with the man and clearly you have not forgotten it. Can you open your mind to the fact that there may be more here between you both? Is it out of the realm of possibilities?"

It has to be, doesn't it?

My lips still burn. Is that normal?

We are friends who were one-time lovers. A case of at the right place at the right time, I suppose. Besides, even entertaining the thought is out of the question, not even sure I would. No. No, I wouldn't. I couldn't. We are developing a friendship, a mutual understanding that it is possible for a woman and a man who have slept together, but no longer have the desire to be with one another in that way again can, in fact be friends.

I'm too damaged anyway.

Nobody wants me.

"No, Dr. Goldberg, I like being on my own. I like the person I am becoming. I like myself again."

I lie a little because I no longer can listen to his psychobabble.

It's too hard to pretend to not care how damaged I actually am, but with Cruz, I forget that. Maybe he's bringing me out of that way of thinking. I need to explain it all to him, and I know he will listen, but only when the time is right.

CHAPTER 8

All the worlds a stage,
and I'm the best actor around.

Cruz

No matter what my dick is doing right now, which is a lot, I still can't get the image of what happened at the bar out of my head. It was like Harlow was a different person. She was like that person last year in the bathroom, taking charge, dominating the situation, stepping outside of that God damn shell of hers.

I never said I liked it, though.

My mind is still reeling from the time her eyes changed their shape, the color blue turning a bleak gray when she saw him walk through that door. I don't think I've seen anything like it. I've never seen eyes do what hers did. There was nothing there when she spotted him. They were lifeless, like when her focus was on him, he sucked the light out of them. It scared me and as fucked up as that sounds coming from me, it did.

And I don't get scared.

I've got this girl, Leilani, who I met at the bar the other night, riding Morty so hard right now, I may need to soak him in a tub of ice tomorrow. For some strange reason, I can't get Harlow's kiss off my mind. The way she grabbed the back of my neck and forced her lips on mine, the sensation I felt going through my body just from that is enough for me not to give two shits that I have this animalistic, exotic looking piece of ass going bunking bronco on me.

And that scares me even more than the look in Harlow's eyes.

I don't get scared. I don't feel things. I was born and raised on the streets by a crack-head. My father left when I was two. I never knew him. I only knew the John's that walked in and out of my mother's life. She used to make me call them uncle. Uncle my ass. The final straw was when I was ten and one of them told me that my mother wouldn't suck his dick, so I had to step into her place. I threatened him with a butcher knife and hung his bag of crack over the toilet, threatening to flush it and slit his throat if he even tried to touch me. Never saw that fucker again.

My crack-head mother blamed me for ruining her life once he left, of course. All she ever cared about was the drugs. She didn't love me or my brother. She didn't show compassion or care about us. We were basically on our own. Bella's, my sister in law, parents would make sure we were fed on holidays and would check on us frequently. They were our neighbors and looked out for us. I wish we could have lived with them. Not like we saw a lot of our mother. During the day, she slept off her high and at night, she was out selling herself or trying her damnedest to score.

We lived in filth, felt like filth, we were just that.

Filth.

Feelings weren't expressed in my house. I feel what I want to feel, physically, not mentally. Like I can feel this girl's pussy going up and down on my cock, and it feels good, don't get me wrong, but that's it. I don't feel like kissing her, touching her skin, feeling her lips on me. I just want to get off and show her the door.

I don't show emotions, but for some reason, I showed some tonight. It was a mixture of them. The look on her face, the way her body tensed, the way she looked at me, the way she… Kissed me. I wasn't prepared for that.

I'm not prepared for anything that has to do with Harlow, but the one thing… the one fucking thing that still has me spinning is she let him call her baby, and she didn't bat an eyelash when he did. There was no, 'don't call me baby', she just let him say that word. The word she hates, no let me rephrase that… she fucking despises. I say it to her almost every day without even thinking first and every day she corrects me in her teacher voice, like scolding a child. Except with that douche bag, it was like it was just another word. When I say it, the woman shoots fire from her eyes. I mean it. It's like the word is poison. I don't get it. I don't get her.

Am I even supposed to?

I can't come. The faster she rides me, the more I think about tonight. I should just fake it, but how am I going to fake it with a condom on? It's dark in here so maybe I should at least try.

"Oh, Cruz, you are so fucking big. That's it baby. Give me what I want." Breathlessly she tells me to fuck her harder.

It does nothing to change my thoughts. All that dirty talk coming from her mouth actually takes away from my hard-on, plus I'm not even doing anything. She's the one fucking me for Christ's sake.

"Are you close, Cruz? I'm gonna come baby. Here I go. Oh God, yes! Yes! Yes!"

Now I've heard that somewhere before. A lot, but I'm going to put on my acting skills.

Ready.

Here goes.

"Oh yea, baby. Here I go, yea. Oh God, yea!"

I buck up and down, once, twice, and that's all she wrote folks.

Faked it.

Never in a million years would I have thought I'd have to fake it with someone who looks like her. Perfect tits and ass. I deserve a round of applause for that performance. An Academy Award even. She needs to get off me, not nuzzle her face in my neck. I need to pull out and run to the bathroom and flush this empty rubber down the toilet.

I somehow manage to wiggle my body from underneath her, practically rolling off the bed onto the floor. I almost feel the need to run to the bathroom.

"Where you going, baby?" She says to me in a sultry voice.

She called me baby. It makes me sick.

Irony.

"Bathroom. I'm not feeling so good, so… Um… this was fun. You know where the door is, right?" I don't even give her a chance to say anything, and I don't take a glance back at her after I basically tell her to get lost. My head is not where it should be. Where it should be is in between that chick's legs, but I'm not feeling it.

I lean against the bathroom door for support, flick on the light, and rip the rubber off my dick so fast, like a Band-

Aid. I can't catch my breath from the smart of it.

Sorry, Morty.

I wait until I hear the door close and exhaling never felt so good. The water I splash on my face both shocks me and suffocates me, and I know I need air. I have no idea what time it is, or if anyone is home. Didn't notice any sounds coming from the living room or any doors slamming. I didn't hear any bodies slamming, for that matter, either. Not that what was going on in my room a little bit ago stopped me from paying attention. That little tryst didn't even hold my interest long enough even to realize what was, if at all, anything was going on in my house. The thoughts of Harlow took the place of it. There could be a hundred people in that living room right now for all I know. Not that I even care. I bust open the bathroom door, and go to my room and put on a pair of gym shorts. I'm too hot right now to stick anything else on.

The house is dark and quiet. I really don't think anyone is here, if they are, they're all passed out. I step out onto the deck, the salt air hitting my nostrils. I close my eyes and take a deep breath, running my hands through this unruly hair of mine. I lean on the railing of the deck, scratch at my chin, feeling the stubble, and wondering why Harlow reacted that way to that guy.

Chad Knox.

The name Harlow whispered in her sleep a few nights ago.

Why did she say she was sorry that night to him while she was sleeping?

"So I saw that your company left you." Startled, I jump when I hear her voice. I turn to see Harlow sitting in a chair next to the door leading to her house. Her face is shadowed by the overhang of the tiny awning that covers the sliding door. She's wrapped up in a blanket, mimicking a cocoon, and all I can see are her toes peeking out from underneath it.

"Jesus, you scared the shit out of me."

I clench my chest with my hand, right over my heart. The beat of it is fast, and it takes me a moment to catch my breath.

"What the hell are you doing out here this late? Where is everybody?" I ignore her previous question. Maybe she'll forget she asked me, and I can pretend like it never happened.

I slowly make my way over to where she is, but I stop, turn and lean my back against the railing.

"Bed," she plainly replies.

An awkward moment of silence comes between us, and I really don't know what to say. Wait, scratch that... I have plenty to say. A million questions fill my head, but I am deciding not to ask them now. I'm trying to avoid looking in her direction, although I'm curious to know what time it is, and why while everyone else is sleeping, she's awake and out here.

"So why are you out here?" I ask.

She sighs and rises from her chair. The light of the moon and one streetlight brings her face into view. Her hair is twisted upwards on top of her head, tendrils touching the sides of her face. She's wearing her glasses, her hot-for-teacher glasses.

Sexy as shit glasses.

When she steps closer, more into the light, I see her eyes. They're red. Her cheeks are tear streaked, and I want to grab her and ask what the fuck is wrong with her. What went down tonight? Why did she kiss me? I'm playing a role, the role of the uncaring person who doesn't give a fuck. I need to keep my questions to a minimum.

"I couldn't sleep," she says as she ironically yawns.

"Oh, yea, why's that?"

She wraps the blanket around her a bit more and comes to lean herself next to me.

"It was too noisy to sleep."

I'm not following her. It's as quiet as a church mouse out here. The streets are empty and everyone else is asleep. Do I ask what was so noisy that it kept her awake? Another moment of silence blankets us until I realize what may have kept her awake.

Aw, shit.

"The noises coming from the other side of my wall in my bedroom kept me up. A picture fell off my wall actually. Hit me right here."

She points to her forehead, and I see a tiny red bump that has formed on it. My face heats red.

"I met your friend... Leilani is it? I ran into her as she was leaving your house."

I knew it. The girl was insatiable and fucking loud. Harlow's room and my room are right next to each other. Her bed and my bed on the same walls in two different houses, and I made that picture fall and hit her. Well, not me, but the chick.

Now play it cool, man. Don't give her any other information. Not any more than she needs to know. Don't fuck it up.

Do not fuck this up.

"Oh, yea. She's a fucking mad woman in the sack."

Too late.

She's laughs in a cynical way. "Oh, I bet. You should be exhausted right now after the sex Olympics you just performed."

Damn it, she heard us. That just solidified that. It wasn't

even me making all that noise. I just kept my eyes closed the whole time, thinking about Harlow.

I mean... I... I was thinking about what happened tonight and how upset she looked. That's all it was. I was distracted by that. Harlow's becoming a friend to me, like Porter and Max. I'd be concerned about them too if I noticed something odd.

Concern. That's a new feeling for me. Nonetheless, I start to feel it.

I'm not going to apologize for keeping her awake, so I'm just going to ignore her statement.

"Well since we are both wide awake at... I don't know what time it is, but want to go down to the dock?"

She pushes her glasses up on her nose a bit more, and shuffles her slippered feet towards the deck steps. She stands there.

"What are you waiting for, come on. It's almost four, so the sun should be up in a little while."

See how this girl confuses me? I can't figure her out.

I follow her down to the dock where we take our usual seats. The air is cool, feeling good on my face. It's so quiet here. Almost eerie. She pulls her blanket closer to her and snuggles down into the chair. No words are spoken, and I get the feeling she wants me to say the first word... but I won't. We just sit and stare at the calm waters of the bay, the outside light from another house reflecting on it.

This silence is killing me, I mean killing me. If she doesn't say something soon, I'm going to jump in that water and drown myself.

This is agonizing. I should have just gone to bed.

Another minute, another second, another millisecond and I'm going to fucking scream.

Fuck it.

"Ok, fine. You want me to ask? I'm going to ask. What the fuck was that tonight, Harlow? That guy, Chad, the ex. Why in all things sacred and holy did you look like he just stole your favorite toy or killed your dog? Get on with it."

She turns, surprised by my sudden outburst, and her mouth opens to speak, but her expression tells me she doesn't want to. Her head turns back towards the water.

Another awkward display of silence.

"Jesus, Turnip. What the hell? I can't figure you out to save my life."

I don't do this. I don't spend time trying to figure chicks out, what eats at them, what crawls under their skin to make them act the way she did tonight. This is not me. That's why I have no girls who are friends, except for my sister in law, Bella. Too much drama, too much to try to decipher. I just fuck them and leave them. That's what I know. Not this senseless bullshit. I'm about to get my ass up, and call it a night. Whether sleep invades or not.

"Fine, you don't want to talk. I'll go sit in silence by myself. I'm not here to piece you, the puzzle, together."

I get up and push back my chair a little too aggressively in the process. I decide to pause and give her one last chance to spill her guts. This woman is a tough nut to crack.

Her and those God damn glasses and... And lips and fingers in my God damn hair.

God damn it.

I realize I curse way too much, even if it's not out loud.

"Chad and I dated from sophomore year in high school till about two years ago, give or take a month or two. He was my first boyfriend, my first... Well you know, before, well..."

Let me make this easy for her.

"Before me?"

She turns her head finally and flashes me a smile.

"Yes, before you." She buries her face in her hands, embarrassed. I figure from the memory of us being together. She lets out a soft laugh.

"My first heartache."

I swallow hard because her tone is mournful. Her voice small when she says the words.

"Ok, so I get you guys dated for a long time, probably compared trust funds and ate caviar and shit like that, but what I don't get is, why did you have the reaction you did when he walked into the room? It's like you were there one minute and then gone the next, without even moving out of your chair."

She begins to rock a little in her chair, swaying in a way that makes her look like she's trying to get comfortable. It's almost as though she's thinking of a way to escape this, but the more she does it, the more it entices me to know what happened between them and for fucks sake, I have no idea why I care to know.

"It's complicated, Cruz. You've never been in a relationship. You've never been in love, so you don't know what it's like to have a broken heart."

She's right. Ab-so-fucking-lutely right.

"No, you're right. I don't know what that's like, but I'd figure after two years, you'd let it go, move on."

She turns completely around in her chair, a full view of her in front of my face, and she points to me with attitude. "Ah, see there's where you're wrong, Officer. I've tried, almost succeeding a few times. I am over him, believe me, but you see, we grew up in the same town, and we were raised in the same crowd. Our grandparents are old country club friends. Our dads, golf buddies. So it's hard to shut the memories of a relationship completely out of your mind when they are constantly around."

I knew there was more to it. You don't look or act the way she did over some high school first love, bullshit, douche bag, rich shit head, dumb mother fucker.

See, I curse in my head way too much.

"Ok, but did he break it off with you or you him? Did he cheat on you? Hurt you?"

She pulls off her glasses swiftly, her death glare ready to strike at a moment's notice.

"What's this the Spanish Inquisition? What's with all the questions? He fucking broke up with me, ok? Got it? It was messy, deceitful, gut wrenching, and I will not go into details, so don't ask for any more than I'm willing to say to you, ok?"

And she's right back to being the good old Harlow. I was waiting for her to show up, and here she is. All that's missing is a knee to my balls.

She shifts in her chair, pinching her fingers at the bridge of her nose, and I feel bad for pushing the issue.

She looks up at me with her big eyes, so full of sadness, and I feel responsible for it, even though I know I'm not the cause of it.

"I'm sorry, Cruz. It's a very touchy subject with me. Our breakup did some major damage to me, my self-esteem, my… My whole life. I'm getting better at forgetting. Love is complicated."

Just another reason why I don't do it. I don't fall in love. I don't even think I know the meaning of the word. I never had it in my life, and it's not like I missed out on it. You don't miss out on something you never had in the first place. It's not like when my bike got stolen in 5th grade, the one I rode to school everyday. The only present my crack-head mother ever gave me, granted, it was stolen by her on the way home from scoring a bag. I knew what it was like to lose something, but then after time, you forget about it and move on. I can't imagine love being like that. I need to understand it more, from Harlow's point of view. If I ask, will she explain it to me? Do I even dare? I go back and forth in my head, contemplating whether or not to ask her opinion, what her thoughts are on the subject. My mind wanders to what their relationship was like. How he treated her, if he cheated on her, why he broke up with her in the first place.

"Tell me, then," I say the words and they just literally flew out of my mouth, and I immediately want to take them back. I mean, my God, have I no self-control? What the hell am I getting myself into? I bet she uses her big words, says shit I don't understand, and I'll be making mental notes, so I can look it up on the Internet later.

Her face scrunches up in that adorable way she does when we have one of our conversations, and she can't believe some of the things that come out of my mouth. Like right now, for instance.

"You want to know about love? About being in love?" I nod, yes. "Oh, come on, now Cruz. Are you serious?"

"Yes, I'm serious. Since I've never been and will continue not to be, I'll think of it as a lesson. You have to practice being a teacher anyway, so… Teach. I'm all ears." I turn my chair a little closer to hers, and she does the same. I bet from where my face is angled to hers, I can count the little freckles on her tiny nose. I tuck my long legs under me and settle in for my lesson on love. Oh, and I prepare myself for the big words. Wish I had a pad of paper and a pen with me. It would make my life so much easier right now.

"Ok, here goes." Her eyes go all dreamily, if that's even a word. She sighs. The wind blows her hair a bit, giving me a shot at smelling her shampoo.

Damn, that smells good.

She begins her lesson.

"Love is the only thing that you can't fake, no matter what. It's when you look into the eyes of the person meant for you, you can see into their soul. I'm pretty sure you can't lie when you truly look into the depths of them. There's a resemblance there, like home, a place where you can put your trust into. Someone you can tell your deepest, darkest fears to, and no matter their opinion of them, it doesn't matter, they will be beside you. They will watch you succeed, and they will watch you fail, but the love is so strong, they can see past it. They can see past all the bad and take a good, hard look at the good."

Speech doesn't exist right now for me, because this girl's definition of love just blew me away. I remember that old movie Mask, about the kid whose face is deformed. He goes to some camp, falls in love with a blind girl, and shows her what color is for a person with sight. He uses a hot rock to describe the color red and a piece of ice to describe the color blue. What Harlow just said, the way she phrased everything, kind of made me see a little. It kind of took my blindness of the subject away. She described to me what love for her is like, what love is like in general. She remains still, just giving me a tight-lipped smile. I feel the sudden urge to know more. But I have to keep up my act of not really caring or being over interested.

I need to know, so my mind over takes my ability to have a filter, so I ask the question, "Was that what it was like for you and Chad?"

Harlow turns her head to the side, avoiding my question

momentarily, and the yearning to touch her face, overwhelms my common sense.

I take my index finger, touch her chin and turn it to me. Tears have formed in her eyes.

"Turnip? Look at me."

That face, full of sadness, and I only met him for a minute, but I hate that mother fucker for hurting her.

"I'm guessing by the look on your face that it didn't go that route. Am I right?"

She nods. No explanation needs to be given to me. That was her perception of it, of love.

As I still touch her cheek with my finger, the thought of her kissing me tonight comes into play. She hasn't explained to me why she did it, nor has she even attempted to tell me, so I'll go with my theory. She wanted to make him jealous. It's obvious. People play games. I get it. I'm not angry about it. It is what it is.

I release her chin and settle back in my chair. The sun is coming up, and I can hear the seagulls waking up in the distance. There's still a calmness on the water. No boats going by, no people awake at this ungodly hour to disturb it. Just Harlow and me doing what we do best on this dock. I think I learned a lot tonight, not just in the last hour or so, but earlier at the bar, last week, three weeks ago. Last year in that bathroom even. Harlow gave me a lesson tonight, and for whatever reason, I think it's one I'm not going to forget anytime soon.

CHAPTER 9

The best surprises

come in all shapes, sizes, and tattoos

Harlow~

The August sun is brutal already, and we are only in the first week of it. The heat should be measured by how many sticks of deodorant I have gone through in the past week. I'm a sweater. I'll admit it for the good of all womankind. It's only seven a.m., and it has to be eighty degrees already. The water on the bay is so still, and the smell of fish is fermenting in the air. Not a pleasant smell mind you.

There's only a few weeks left of summer, and I will admit it's been the best. Refreshing and relaxing… For the most part. I never did see Chad again, thank God. I think he knew to stay clear of me, which is unusually surprising. His relentlessness towards me when we are back in Princeton is immeasurable. Since his father and mine are golf buddies, when they all play together, he's always approaching my father about me. When he is questioned about our breakup from my father, his response was always that we were taking a break for a while. Break, my ass. Try broken, as in what it did to me. Dr. Goldberg and I still have our weekly conversations, but the more time passes, the more I find comfort in my other form of therapy, which, in fact, is coming down the dock as we speak. Well more like sprinting.

What the hell?

"Turnip, Turnip, it's Bella, she's… She's in labor."

The look of sheer panic is displayed on Cruz's face, so I stand up to greet him.

"Wait, what? She's not due for another month, Cruz. What's going on?"

He's panting and running his fingers through his hair fiercely.

"My brother called and he said something about her bag breaking and then the water came out of it and I was like what the fuck is that, then he said she was having contradictions and shit, and oh, God, I don't know."

I grab his shoulders and caress them and then I run my hands down to his forearms, as I tell him to take a deep breath.

"Ok, sweetie, relax. First of all it was her water that broke. Her bag of water, not her purse or anything like that and she's having contractions. It's when the uterus contracts and pushes the baby down the birth canal. It happens during labor."

When I'm telling Cruz what Bella is going through and how it's perfectly normal, he relaxes.

"Listen to me, the baby is just a little early. That's all and everything will be fine."

I smile at him and stroke his cheek. He leans into my hand, and he closes his eyes.

"Are you going to go see her, be there for your brother?"

He hesitates and looks out onto the water. It appears he's struggling with some kind of decision, and I'm not really sure so I ask. I take my hand from his cheek and use one of my fingers to bring his attention to my face.

"Hey, what's the problem? This is a no-brainer. You need to go. You told me on more than one occasion that Bella is one of your best friends, so don't be so hesitant about going. She needs you to be there, Cruz. They both do."

The look in his eyes tells me he knows I'm right.

Cruz lets out a sigh, and I see his body appear to be less tense. He takes a seat on one of our chairs, clasping his hands together and resting his elbows on his knees. His head is down between his knees so I can only see the top of his brown waves.

I bend my knees and get down to his level. My hands encircling his.

"Hey pal. Look at me." He doesn't, so I use my teacher voice on him.

"Raphael Cruz, look at me right this instant." He peers up at me, shocked and horrified at my tone.

"You are an Officer of the law, an ex-Marine, and my favorite man-whore in the world. If you're afraid of what's happening, don't be. It's ok to be afraid, but you are by far the strongest person I know so failure in this situation is not an option. Bella will be fine, and so will the baby."

He looks at me with his piercing blue eyes and marvels at my words like they are scripture. He believes what I'm telling him. I like this vulnerable side of Cruz. Big, strong tattooed men don't always need to show their rough exterior. Sometimes showing the other side is quite… Sexy.

Surprise, surprise.

"Babies come into this world early everyday and medicine is so far advanced that God forbid if there is anything wrong with the baby…"

He gets a panicked look in his eyes.

"Cruz, I never said there was anything wrong with the baby, I'm just making a point that there are highly trained medical professionals who will make sure the baby will be ok."

He grins solemnly at me.

"Do you trust me?" I ask. He nods, looking directly into my eyes.

"Well then good." I stand up after being in the crouched position for more time than expected, but he pulls me back down towards him, and I'm taken aback.

"Come with me… Please?"

His question is a plea, almost sounding desperate, and if I didn't know better, I'd say it's one for help, but one that says 'don't let me do this alone.'

So I won't.

"Should I pack an overnight bag?" He smiles. That's all that's needed for me to get my answer.

An hour and a half later here we are at a hospital called St. Mary's, but I'm pretty sure we are nowhere near Cherry Hill where Cruz said he was from. Actually, it's a pretty run down area. I had dozed off for most of the ride so I didn't pay much attention. I yawn and stretch my arms up above my head.

"Mornin' sleepy head." I turn towards Cruz and smile.

"Did you just call me sleepyhead?" I laugh at him

because it's just not like him to use those terms of endearment.

He rolls his eyes at me and pulls into the parking garage of the hospital.

"Yes, I was referring to you. I have to get used to using words like that since I'll have a niece or nephew running around."

Who would have thought Raphael Cruz could be... Sweet.

Cruz shuts off the car, but remains with his hands tightly around the steering wheel, almost displaying white knuckles.

"You ready to go?" I ask.

"Um, yea, but there's something I need to tell you first, Turnip."

"Ok, shoot." I hear the sound of his phone ringing and see it's his brother Antonio on the caller ID. He keeps allowing it to ring, and ring again, until finally I hand it to him and tell him to answer it.

"Yea, Antonio. We just pulled in. Yes, we. My friend Harlow is here... Yes, that one." He shakes his head and covers his eyes. I feel my cheeks warm, and I don't know why.

"Yes, ok. How is she doing? Seven centimeters? What the hell does that mean? Ok fine, never mind. We'll see you in a sec." He hangs up and looks at me.

"Sorry about that."

Knowing exactly what he's apologizing for, I turn smart ass on him.

"Sorry for what? I have no idea what you're talking about, Officer." I wink at him and open my car door, dismissing the fact that he was about to tell me something. I'll remind him later to finish.

We leave our overnight bags in the car, but I grab my

canvas tote with my laptop in it. I have to register for my grad classes and what a better time to do it than sitting in a hospital waiting room. Baby's arrivals are very unpredictable. Just because she's seven centimeters, doesn't mean a damn thing. It could be hours.

Cruz is very quiet, which is odd. The man never shuts up, so when we get to the floor and the elevator doors open, he steps out, but I tug at his arm.

"Remember what I said. Don't be afraid. Everything is going to be perfect."

He takes my hand in his and we walk down a hallway towards a nurse's station.

He took my hand?

Cruz stops at a desk to ask a nurse where Bella is.

"Excuse me. I'm looking for Bella Cruz. She's been admitted with pre-term labor." The nurse looks at a whiteboard behind her and we see Bella's name.

"Yes. She's in room 222." The nurse points in the direction for which we need to go.

Cruz thanks her and tugs me along down to Bella's room. When we open the door, I see a man standing at the head of the bed, an almost replica of Cruz, but with much more bulk to him. In the bed is the prettiest and tiniest raven-haired, dark complected woman with the biggest belly I have ever seen.

Cruz let's go of my hand and swiftly walks towards his brother, engulfing him in a hug. They pat each other's backs and their foreheads pull together to rest on one another.

Cruz goes to the woman lying in the bed, who is obviously Bella. He kisses her head and strokes her hair.

"How you doing there, mama?"

"Well they gave me an epidural, so now I'm ok. I can't believe you came, Raph."

"I wouldn't miss it. But why did you go into labor so early? You're not due for another month."

"We are fine. The doctor did an ultrasound and the baby's lungs are fine. Strong and healthy. It may be a little smaller than we wanted, but when it's time, there's no stopping him or her from coming."

Cruz smiles at Bella, and I lean against the doorway to the room.

"And this must be Harlow." She motions for me to come forward, and I feel a bit awkward, but her smile says not to be. She extends her hand out, and I take it, a bit subdued.

"I'm Bella. It's so nice to meet you, Harlow. I've heard a lot about you."

"Bella!" Cruz's voice rings out in a warning.

"Oh, nevermind him." She shoos her hand at him and winks.

"Likewise. Congratulations. How are you feeling?"

"I'm very ready, in case you couldn't tell. Oh, and this is my husband Antonio. The more handsome of the Cruz men."

Cruz takes a seat next to Bella's bed.

"Ha, ha. Very funny." I like their banter.

"Harlow, nice to meet you. And I will also say we have heard a lot about you, so forget what my little brother says." I shake Antonio's hand, and then take a step back from Bella's bed, feeling a bit out of place even though they aren't making me feel that way. A nurse walks in, checks the monitors that are attached to Bella, and then asks all of us to leave the room, so they can check to see if she is any more dilated. We step out into the waiting room, Cruz looks nervous, his head turning to look over his shoulder every once in a while. I'm assuming it's because he's worried about

Bella. I sit across from him, checking my email and getting back to Willow via text with updates. Of course, the woman can even scold me through text about how could I have gone with him all the way here for someone I don't even know, especially for the reason we are here. I'm trying to keep that out of my head, but leave it to Willow to give me a subtle reminder of it.

I hate hospitals. I hate the smell. I hate the yellowed, peeling wallpaper. I hate the old, worn-out chairs in this waiting room. I can count the frayed threads on this chair I'm sitting in. I hate the muffled beheaded voices calling for doctors over the intercom systems. Code blue, code red, code whatever.

I hate watching the nurses and doctors walk around in their green, thinly-clad scrubs. What's the point of them anyway?

I hate this floor. The thought of a million shoes being walked on in the very spot my eyes are focused on now makes me shiver. The shine from the linoleum doesn't make a difference. I know what's there. Dried blood from the bottom of shoes, dirt, germs, pieces of life. It's worse in Bella's room. I guarantee that fact.

I need to breathe. I need to focus on something besides the dirt-ridden, germ-infested floor below my feet.

I raise my eyes to him. He stares in my direction, our eyes meeting for a moment, and a slight smile appears on his face. Not his normal smile. One of uneasiness. I look at him puzzled, but then my anxiousness is replaced with calmness because he now looks like how I feel. His eyes tell me he needs me. I don't know why I feel the pull of his stare. It confuses me that look in his eyes, so I throw caution to the wind and get up to sit beside him.

The elevator dings as I make my way to the seat. Before I

can even sit beside Cruz, he's up out of his seat, his face looking strained, and somewhat uneasy. The tapping of his foot tells me his anticipation as to whom is about to get off that elevator will not diminish until the doors open. I find myself doing exactly what Cruz is doing, staring at the elevator doors like a child waiting for the jack-in-box to spring free. I'm not sure why we are staring at it, but as I look at Cruz, I know there must be something to it. The doors finally open, a couple rushes out and into the arms of Antonio. The woman wraps her arms around him, her handbag flopping to the floor. She is crying, but it doesn't appear to be tears of sadness, possibly just worry, and that's when it hits me, this is Bella's mom.

"Oh, Antonio, how is my baby girl? What did the doctors say? How is the baby? Is she pushing yet, we tried to get here as fast as we could mijo, traffic was horrible."

The woman couldn't be more than five feet, beautiful dark hair, and a lovely complexion like Bella's. Her father, not much taller than his wife, hugs Antonio as well and apologizes for his wife's over exaggerated rant.

"Tony, please excuse Marcella, she is so nervous, first grandchild and all."

Antonio smiles at his father in law and assures him she is ok and the doctors were with her.

Bella's mom goes to Cruz and grabs him in the same loving way she did to his brother.

"Oh, Raphael, you look so tired. I can't believe you drove all this way to see her. How are you?" She pinches his cheek and looks at him adoringly. He gently takes her hands and holds them close to his chest.

"I'm fine, Marcella. I just got off my late shift and came here as soon as I got the call from Tony. She's in good hands. Don't worry."

She laughs at him and pats his face.

"Oh sweet boy, you tell me not to worry when I can clearly see the worry lines already starting to form on your face."

She pauses, and I hear her say to him, "Does Rae know? Did anyone tell her?" Cruz's eyes go from Marcella's straight to mine with a look of doom. He swallows hard and reverts back to introducing me to her.

"Marcella, I want you to meet my friend Harlow Hannum. We live next to each other at the shore for the summer. She came with me for the ride."

Marcella turns to me with the warmest smile and eyes glistening. She approaches me and engulfs me in a similar hug she gave to Cruz and Antonio.

"Oh, mija, you are even prettier than Raphael explained to me. Beautiful girl, for you to come all this way to be with him, on this important day, you must be someone special."

I have to bite my lip and turn my chin towards the ground for fear my cheeks will become so red with embarrassment. I'll look like I was slapped in the face. Cruz comes over to Marcella and pulls her from me.

"Ok, ok. That's enough, silly woman." Clearly embarrassed himself, he takes my hand and leads me away from Bella's mom. He introduces me to Bella's dad, Jorge. When I meet him, he shakes my hand, then kisses the top and thanks me for being here. I'm not doing anything really. I just came for the ride. Still, their family's warmth and acceptance of my friendship with Cruz is heartfelt.

"Raphael, you still did not answer my question. Do you know if Rae knows? Oh, God forbid if she does." The sound of panic in her voice is a bit disheartening, so I ask the question out loud.

"Who is Rae, Cruz?" He ignores me and pulls Marcella

to the other side of the room. They are huddled in a corner, and I can't hear. The confusion sets into me as I see Marcella look over Cruz's shoulder to glance my way. If it's a family thing, that's fine, but to me it seems a little more secretive than that, and I have to remind myself that I am only here for moral support, but in no way, shape or form will I let it go, and Cruz already knows that this is the way I operate.

As they continue to talk, a doctor comes out and asks Antonio to come with him. Cruz and Marcella come out of their respective corner and join myself and Jorge in the waiting room chairs.

The room is silent, and the nagging feeling that I need to ask Cruz who this Rae person is pulls at my brain.

Screw it.

I bend my ear to him and begin the question.

"Cruz, who is…" Before I can even answer, he holds his hand up to me, stopping me from going any further with my questioning.

"Not now, Harlow, ok?"

"Ok," I answer him quietly.

Marcella and Jorge hold hands while the room still remains silent. Cruz gets up every once in a while, clearly nervous and clearly uncomfortable. A little while later Antonio comes from behind a double door, dressed in those God awful green scrubs. Everyone stands up when he enters.

"What's going on mijo. How is my baby girl?"

He looks worried.

"The baby is stuck so they have to give her a C-section, but don't worry Marcella, she and the baby will be ok. I can't say I'm not worried, but I trust her doctor."

Marcella starts to cry and Jorge goes to wrap his arms around her shoulders.

"She will be fine, sweetheart. This happens all the time, I'm sure."

"All the time! Things like this happen all the time? How can this be an ok thing, Jorge? What if she, what if the baby…" Cruz yells and runs his hands fiercely through his hair. This makes Marcella cry harder, and Jorge gives Cruz a stern look. I step into his proximity, trying to calm him by taking his strong face in my hands, making him look directly in my eyes.

"Raphael… Yes, I called you by your name. You need to listen to me. This does happen everyday. The doctors know what's best for Bella and the baby, and they know what is safe. You need to trust them, and not upset her parents anymore." I give him a reassuring smile, and he's receptive to it. Taking in a few calming breaths and placing his hands on top of mine, he nods. He apologizes to Jorge and Marcella, and they hug him and tell him they understand why he's upset. Antonio tells us he needs to go back in to Bella in the operating room, and he will come out or have someone tell us if there is any news. Before going back in, Antonio and Cruz hug, tears welling up in Antonio's eyes while Cruz holds his brother's face in his hands and kisses his cheek before shoving him towards the large steel doors where his wife and unborn baby wait for him.

Cruz explained to me before how Bella was his first crush when they were kids, how she was the sequential 'older woman', the one he followed around like a puppy dog, the one who in those teenage years taught him the fundamentals of women. Their likes and dislikes. What not to say. What not to do. How to act in front of them, and how to play hard to get. She even taught him kissing techniques, all the while pining for Antonio. Many a fight broke out between the brothers. Cruz explained it was more of an infatuation with Bella rather than love. He didn't believe in it like Antonio did and turns out Antonio won her heart. He says he's not capable of it, but what I've seen today in the eyes of Raphael Cruz tells me otherwise.

We sit in this stuffy, smelly waiting room watching odd women with swollen bellies being transported via wheelchairs from elevators, beyond the big steel swinging doors only operated by medical staff. I'm not even sure how long we've been sitting here. I keep looking at Cruz, whose eyes are fixated on the elevator doors. It reminds me to ask him first who Rae is, and second what the fascination is with elevators? I feel my phone buzz in my pocket, and I excuse myself and go to another waiting room to take it because it's a number I'm not sure I recognize.

"Hello, Harlow Hannum speaking."

"Yes, good afternoon, Miss Hannum," it's a voice I don't know.

"My name is Greg Landberg and I'm the director of human resources for the Grayson Elders School District. We received your resume which indeed is outstanding and we would like you to come in for a formal interview tomorrow. We understand that it's short notice, but we have an immediate opening."

A job, this phone call is for a job. To teach. In a school. In a classroom. A teacher. I need to tell Cruz.

My thoughts get away from me, and I really don't know how long it's been since I muttered a word in response if at all any.

"Oh, yes. I... I um oh Mr. Landberg, thank you so very much. I would be more than pleased to come in for an interview."

My insides are dancing, strumming up all kinds of over-charged emotions, but I must calm myself. It's just an interview. But this is my dream. To teach. I have every right to be all piqued.

Then it hits me. Before I can even answer with an 'I'll be there tomorrow', I'm hit with the realization that if things don't go well in that operating room, I can't leave Cruz here. He needs me, and I can't let him down.

"Mr. Landberg, unfortunately I do have a problem coming in tomorrow."

"That's too bad, Miss Hannum, because your references from your professors as well as your former employers tends to make us believe that you would be such an asset to our schools, granted our panel of principals who will be conducting the interviews agree with what I have seen and heard."

"I'm not currently in the area, and I'm helping out a friend who has a family member in a medical crisis, and I'm not sure how things are going to turn out you see."

Damn it, damn it, damn it.

Hospitals, smelly floors, yellowing wallpaper, blood, heartache, pain, suffering, death. It's all here, and I'm trapped in it. Fuck.

"I understand, Miss Hannum, but unfortunately tomorrow is the only day we will be conducting interviews. The teachers need to report to their classrooms in preparation for the new school year within two weeks."

Saddened as I am that I may be making the biggest mistake of my life, I look around the corner of the room I'm in watching Cruz with his broadness and muscle rock back and forth in that damn fraying chair like a baby, biting his lip, blowing gusts of air from his lungs, and I know I can't do it. I can't leave Cruz.

"Mr. Landberg, I'm so sorry but I'm going to have to…" I hear a slam and a yell coming from the next waiting room, so I peek around the corner, and I see Antonio jumping up and down crying. "It's a boy, a beautiful boy. He's perfect. Bella's perfect. They are both perfect." The brothers hug and laugh. Bella's parents cry and hug, and it's jubilation amongst the tiny family. Cruz searches for me and when he finds me, he smiles broadly. His bright blue eyes shining like diamonds, and he motions for me to come to him.

My heart warms, I feel a single tear fill my eye, and the beat of my heart is steadfast. I feel peaceful in this place of death and destruction.

"Mr. Landberg, what time did you say you needed me there tomorrow?"

CHAPTER 10

Even the tiniest of things
can make you open your eyes

Cruz

I'm holding this little thing in my arms. He's so small, so fragile, so… Absolutely amazing. I can feel my hands shake as I cradle this, this person, yes, he's a person. Flesh and bone. Blood coursing through his veins. There are five little fingers wrapped around my one big finger, so pink, so warm, so real.

Matteo Cruz. My nephew.

I never believed in the good things that could happen in life. I never imagined in this mixed up, fucked up world something so miraculous could appear. He wasn't here an hour ago, and now here he is. All I've seen in my life is despair, death, sadness, but just holding him makes all that disappear. It's nothing short of amazing. I look around this room watching my brother and Bella staring at me holding him, ridiculous smiles on their faces. I know what's running through their heads. They have so much hope for Matteo, so much love for him already and they don't even know him. How is that possible? To be that in love with someone you don't even know. I smile when I hear his little coos and grunts. Damn, it's cute. I stand up to hand him over to my brother, but he stops me and turns to Harlow.

"Harlow, would you like to hold him?" She's silent, a little too silent with an unreadable expression on her face. She shakes her head no.

"No, Antonio, thank you, this is a family thing. You all enjoy him. I'm going to go make a phone call. He is beautiful though. Congratulations." She steps out of the room and Bella and the rest of my family look a bit confused at her reaction. I hand the baby over to Tony and tell them I'll be right back.

I walk out into the waiting room and she's not there. I look in the other waiting room, not there either. I head downstairs and outside of the entrance to the hospital. I can see her on the phone, but I can't make out what she's saying. As I step closer, I can hear her say words like I can do this. I am strong. I will get through this.

I interrupt her, startling her in the process.

"Who ya talking to Turnip?" She turns and pulls the phone away from her ear and presses end on the call.

"Oh, um… Willow. I was just checking in and I was telling her about the baby." I don't believe her, but now is not the time for questions. Maybe I'll confront her on the way home.

"He really is such a beautiful baby and Bella and Antonio look so happy."

I smile at the memory of the scene that was just played out in that hospital room. Their dreams come true. First falling in love, then getting married, and then the baby.

That's all my brother ever wanted. A stable life, love, and a family to call his own.

We just stand there on the front steps of the hospital, surveying each other, wondering what to say next. Her black rimmed glasses rest carefully on her nose, and she pushes them up further as she takes in a breathe, her long strawberry blonde strands blow wistfully around her, and I can smell the approaching rain. So I continue to stand, speechless. My mind, on the other hand, has plans of its own. I don't even think about it, or the consequences it may have, but something inside tells me to do it, a force that's uncontrolled by my brain, there's some kind of jedi-mind trick type force controlling it. I have no power over my muscles, over my nerves, so I step towards her as she tucks a strand of loose hair behind her ear and turns her head in a different direction.

So I do it.

Her face cradled in my hands, my thumbs grazing her cheeks, I feel her stiffen, and then, I touch my lips to hers.

She gasps, but doesn't pull away. I kiss her lips not like how I kiss the girls I bring home from the bars. I kiss her without opening my mouth, instead I feel like with this kiss. I'm opening up my soul to her, relinquishing my thanks to her for being with me today, feeling the air from her nostrils on my face, making the slightest of moans as my lips peck at her mouth smoothly. She doesn't protest. I feel her hands drop from their cross position on her chest to them inching their way to my waist. She grasps my shirt as I tilt my head to the left, so I can taste her lips and get a better feeling of the heat that radiates off of them.

My mind works in a mysterious way. I could care less if she pulled away from me right this second. I just needed, for some ungodly reason, to kiss her. I have never had a feeling or a desire to do something like that in my whole life.

What's happening to me? I'm the guy who picks them up, fucks them till their knees shake and sends them home. Sometimes not really kissing them. But in this strange and fucked up universe, this woman makes me do things, feel things, that aren't me.

As my body tends to get closer to hers, I feel her hardened nipples against my shirt, I smell her sugary vanilla scent. I wrap a strand of her soft hair around my hand as it leaves her cheek, and I snake it upwards into it. I deepen the kiss by parting her lips with my wanting tongue, and she lets me in. She fucking lets me in.

I feel like I'm falling, like I'm on one of those free fall roller coasters on the boardwalk. My stomach tightens and rises and falls with each stroke of her tongue against mine. Sinking deeper and submitting into the force. The force I call Harlow.

She breaks away from me, and it's the last thing I want her to do. I could go on kissing her like this for God knows how long, and the thought of fucking her doesn't even enter my brain. It's nothing but mush right now, so kissing her just overcompensates for that longing if it ever came to that.

She steps away from me, bringing the outside of her hand to her mouth, holding it there. I drop my arms to my side and close my eyes, hoping she doesn't run, that I didn't scare her.

Oh, God did I just do something stupid?

"Why did you do that?" She asks me in a small voice.

"I wanted to thank you for coming here and for being with me through this. You didn't have to. I'm not the nicest person to you sometimes, and I'm... Well I feel bad for that, and I'm sorry. So... Thank you."

Now I wait for a slap, or one of her infamous knee-to-ball contacts, but she doesn't. She smiles and that same drop I felt a few minutes ago, like being on the roller coaster returns, and it's not a bad feeling, just a confusing one.

She picks up the canvas bag she's been lugging around all day and flings it on her shoulder.

"I got a job interview tomorrow for a permanent position for this coming school year, so I have to go."

Wow, she skipped right over the part about our minute's long makeout session in front of this hospital, but ok.

"Well, that's great. I'm really happy for you. But, don't you have anything to say about what just happened?"

She shakes her head no.

"Listen, no big deal, you um, well you just experienced a great thing. A new baby came into the world. I'm sure you're full of emotions, but I was wondering if you could take me to the bus station. I need to get home and I'm sure you want to stay, so you need your car."

She wants me to take her to the bus station? What the hell is going on in that big brain of hers?

"You are not going back to Sandy Cove on a bus, Turnip. Take my car, and I'll take the bus back tomorrow, besides, I have a shift tomorrow night so I have to get back before three. I would normally call out, but I'm pretty sure I have a good chance at a position on the force, so I'll have to look good. Calling out sick won't make it look that way."

"Are you sure?" She asks, unsure of my request.

"Yes, I'm sure. Want to come up and say goodbye to Bella and Tony?"

She smiles. "Sure."

We make our way up to Bella's room and we explain about Harlow's interview. Baby Matteo is in Bella's arms and again she asks Harlow if she would like to hold him, and again she declines the offer. She strokes his little hand and gently lays a kiss on his knitted hat covered head.

"Goodbye little man. You are a very lucky little boy to be surrounded by so many people who love you." As she goes to move from the bed, Bella stills her hand.

"Harlow, thank you for being here for my brother in law. I know he's glad you were here. Please come back and visit us anytime."

She nods. "I will and it was such a pleasure to meet all of you, truly it was and congratulations."

Harlow makes her way to the door, and I follow her out. I need to grab my overnight bag from the car.

We walk in silence down the hall, into the elevator and all I want to do at this moment is take her in my arms and kiss her again, but it's not going to happen. I'm turning into the world's biggest pussy. First, I get all mushy from holding a stupid baby. Now, not only once, but twice, I want to kiss this girl who I, sometimes, can hardly stand.

We make it to my car. Harlow gets in and starts the engine. I grab my bag and lean down into the window.

"Now text me when you get in. You may hit some traffic on the turnpike this time of day."

She smiles. "Yes Dad, I'll be ok."

"Smart ass." She rolls up the window and starts to pull away and then I remember something I wanted to tell her so I yell out her name.

"Harlow!" She stops, rolls the window back down and peeks out.

"Yea?"

"Good luck tomorrow, Turnip."

Then she pulls away, and I'm stuck with all these emotions playing around in my head. She's so guarded such a tough nut to crack. That damn wall she has built up around herself is alarming. I mean, did that kiss mean nothing to her, 'cause she sure as hell acted like it didn't.

No time to think about it now.

Who the hell am I kidding?

I go back up to the maternity floor when I hear loud voices coming from the nurse's desk.

Fuck! Rae's here. She found them. Tony is yelling at her. Jorge is trying to calm him down, and I can't believe this woman has the balls to show up here. This is what I've been afraid of all damn day.

"Rae, what the hell are you doing here?"

The small, fragile woman, who, in fact, is my crack-head mother turns at the sound of my voice. I haven't seen her druggie ass in over a year. She's missing teeth. Her skin is ashen, and she must not weigh more than ninety pounds. Her clothes are ragged and mismatched.

"Now, now Raphael, is that any way to talk to your mother. I'm here to see my first grandchild. I have every right to, tell them Jorge." She turns to Jorge, and he shakes his head at her.

"Now come on, Rae, don't make a scene. This is a happy day for all of us. If Antonio and Bella want you to see the baby, they will let you know. Why don't you go home and we will be in touch."

He gently takes her arm and steers her in the direction of the elevators. She pulls away swiftly.

"Get the fuck off me, Jorge. These are my boys, not yours, and that new little baby in there is my grandchild as much as it is yours, so let me see him."

Tony is not as gentle or understanding as Jorge is.

"No way, Rae, maybe if you clean up a little we'll let you, but until then, stay away from my family and me."

She stumbles and slurs her words as she tries to talk. "You all thought you could keep it a secret from me. Well, people in the neighborhood talk, so fuck you all for trying to keep me away."

Her arms flail around and she almost falls, slurring her words. Just the sound of her scratchy, smoked-out voice sends shivers down my spine.

"Fuck you all, everyone of you. Mother fuckers. You have no right to keep me from the baby, you bastards. No good, unworthy bastards. I should have gotten rid of you myself with a wire hanger. Fuck the day you both were ever born."

Before Tony and I could react, security comes down the hall and seizes her and carries her off in the elevators. The whole time she curses and fights them, struggling in their arms. Before long, the doors close on the scene I prayed would not have taken place here today.

My first thought: thank God Harlow did not see this. She thinks my mother is some saint. Some June Cleaver who dotes on her son's. The perfect wife and mother. I shouldn't have lied to her, but when it comes to any type of situation with a girl, it's what I do best. I made Porter and Max swear to secrecy, they can never tell Harlow or the other girls in the house what my mother is really like. The epitome of embarrassment.

Jorge doesn't look as worried as Tony and I do, and we agree not to tell Marcella or Bella that Rae was here. This is supposed to be a happy time and bringing Rae into the mix will only cause tension and worry.

We go back into Bella's room. The nurses took the baby down to the nursery to clean him up and do some other shit I'm not sure of. Marcella and Jorge decide to go down to the cafeteria, so I stay with my brother and Bella.

The waiting doesn't take long. I can see Bella's smirk as soon as her parents leave the room, and I know without a shadow of a doubt what route the line of questioning is going to go.

She sits up in her bed, sipping on a cup of tea. The news is on the lowest volume possible, Tony texts his friend's pictures of Matteo, and I see the passive look on my sister-in-laws face.

"Freaking say what you're thinking Bella for Christ's sake."

She gives me the innocent doe eyes, and I know she's a crock of shit.

"Moi? Whatever are you talking about brother in law?" She winks at Tony as he glances up from his phone.

"You know I can persuade some of those pretty nurses out there to withhold any kind of pain medication from you, so you better watch it."

Tony laughs and Bella bats her eyelashes in a comical sort of way.

"Is that so? You're not a stud-muffin everywhere you go, you know."

But I do know that I am. True statement.

"Whatever. Just give me any of those chicks out there and a supply closet, and I'll show you a stud-muffin as you like to call it."

"Oh, yea, well what I call it is bullshit!" Bella gets a bit loud. The woman can have a temper. Tony calls her passionate.

Gross, but whatever.

"Care to explain mother of one?"

She shimmies up a bit up in her bed. Tony flies to her side to raise her up, and fluffs her pillows to make her more comfortable.

He kisses the top of her head gently.

"Thank you, my love." Her throat clears and the look in

her eyes means she's all business now.

Her index finger pointed at me, her foot tapping under the blanket and lips pursed.

"First of all, I talk to you once a week, maybe twice, same with your brother. When you first went to the shore it was all about banging the chicks, partying, who won at beer pong, whatever." She's flustered, and I think it's hysterical.

"But as the weeks went on, every phone call began with something about that girl and ended with something about that girl. You told us so much about her and her life. I feel like when she walked in here today, I've known her for a thousand years."

Now I think she's stretching the truth a bit.

"And if you think I'm stretching the truth a bit then you're the damn liar. How would I know she wears black rimmed reading glasses, and that she has freckles only on the bridge of her nose and they flow a bit outwards on her cheeks? Her life goal was to become a teacher? How do I know she's shy, but when she speaks to you she makes you feel like you're the most important person in the room?"

I shrug. "Fuck if I know."

Tony slaps the back of my head.

"Watch your mouth, she's a mom now, none of that language around her."

"Raph, I know these things because you told them to me. Maybe you said it without knowing you actually did, but you did. She stood in that doorway before you introduced us and I saw a light in your eyes that I've only seen once and I've known you since you were five."

I know the instance she's talking about.

"When you came back from your last tour and saw us waiting for you when you got off that plane. That same look appeared when that girl was in the closest range to you.

Then, by the grace of God, that look stayed with you, now it's gone because she just left."

Bella must still be on those pain meds because I'm pretty certain my facial expressions have not changed since I got here.

"You have problems, lady. She's just a friend. We hated each other at the beginning of the summer, but we've developed a friendship and things between us have changed."

"You're darn tootin' things have changed. That girl who just walked out of here changed you!"

I get up from my chair, scratch the stubble on my face and look out the window at the dreariness that is down below. I have been the same damn way for the past twenty four years and I'm not about to change. This is who I am. I'm someone who doesn't allow people to change me. The only person who has ever changed me was my mother, and I think I've come to accept the fact that it was a good change. It made me strong, built my defenses up. It made me less weak, and gave me the mindset that I'm the only person I can count on. Well, that's a lie. I'll always have Tony and Bella, and now I have Matteo.

"I'm going to go grab a coffee. Anyone want one?"

Antonio looks at me confused.

"Since when do you drink coffee?"

"Oh, he didn't tell you that part did he?" Bella chimes in.

She crosses her arms over her lap and gives Tony her 'I know something you don't know' look.

Frustrating woman.

"Well, he drinks coffee with Harlow every morning on the dock of the house they are renting. It's just them, and they talk about all sorts of things, like she's rich, he's not, but she doesn't know that. She doesn't know about Rae and where he lives. He told her he's from Cherry Hill."

"What the fuck, Raphael? Why are you lying to her? Your life; our lives are what they are. If she's your friend and you care about her then why lie?"

I really don't want to have to explain to him why I lie. It should be clear as day from the scene that just took place in that waiting room. Why would I tell a girl who was raised by two loving parents, in a big house, with a top notch education and a big bank account that my mother is a crack-head? She whored her body out for drugs and my brother and I had to fend for ourselves for most of our lives. She'd probably turn and run and never speak to me again.

And that would kill me.

"You know what you two, I'm going to the cafeteria and this conversation is over. Harlow is a friend. I don't do the girlfriend thing." I motion to them both. "And I certainly don't do what you two are doing. I don't want it."

With that I walk out of the room.

I went into the Marines to escape the life I had, which wasn't one. I know what it's like to starve, to be cold, to not have running water 'cause my mother didn't pay the bills. I know what it's like to wear shoes two sizes too small because there's no money to buy new ones and socks that were somehow chewed up by mice in the middle of the night. I know what it's like to be alone.

And I've learned to live with it. Harlow never had to deal with any of that. Just because her parents made her get a job and pay for some things on her own, doesn't mean she would have any clue as to what my life was like. She's so out of my league. It's almost comical. She's a pain in my ass with her big brain and her over-judging everything I do or say, down to the girls I bring home and fuck. Yes, I kissed her, which is still plaguing my mind as to why. Maybe it was because it was all those emotions that were built up over the day. I haven't slept. We came right here from my twelve hour shift because I was worried about Bella. Holding my nephew in my arms... And then Rae showing up was the cherry on top of the mother fucking sundae.

I'm so tired.

⟳

My phone buzzes in my pocket and startles me awake. I must have dozed off in Bella's room after I came back with my coffee. I look at my phone and it's a text from Harlow. The roller coaster in my belly suddenly rears its ugly head, and here I am fumbling to press the message button as quickly as these large fingers of mine can.

hey dickcop, lol, home safe. hows the little man?

if you are referring to my penis, I think you have the wrong man

Haha. very funny. how is everyone?

fine. you ready for tomorrow?

as ready as ill ever be

good. my bus is @ 8 so i'll be home in the early afternoon

ok. be safe.

good luck tomorrow. i know they are going to love you

lets hope. xx

"See what I mean Tony, look at his face. Since when does he get a look on his face like that from a text. It was her wasn't it?"

Oh, my God! Damn, this woman can see through me like a pair of titties on a wet t-shirt.

"Bella, what do you want me to tell you?"

"I want you to admit that you feel more than friendship for her."

Tucking my phone back into my shorts, I cross my arms in front of me. "You want me to admit that I'm feeling something other than friendship for her?"

She nods and I really struggle with what I feel. I struggle with what happened between us outside the hospital and about the feeling it left me with. This can't be happening to me. It can't be real. What I think I feel can't be. I don't feel this shit.

"Fine, Bella. Maybe I do, but I'm confused and I'm trying to figure it out. All I know is I feel different when she's here, and I'm feeling different when she's not here. I can't explain it, but I don't know how to remedy it either."

There. I was honest. I'm confused as to the way I feel. I know when I'm with her I feel something that I can't recognize, and I know when she's not with me... I want her to be.

"Don't even dare say I told you so. It's not a big deal. Nothing's going to happen anyway. She's way out of my league. She's not even on the same farm team as me."

I'm fucking McDonald's and she's Beef Wellington. Yea,

I felt something when I kissed her. I didn't know what I felt before I did that, but now I do. With my head running in a hundred different directions, is it that I just can't see what is in front of me. Eight and a half weeks worth of getting to know her. Realizing she's not the stuck up bitch I thought her to be. The spoiled, little, rich girl with the silver spoon in her mouth. The girl who always has the answers. But the truth is, most of the time she does.

She's my therapy.

I'm pacing around this room, pulling at my hair, my hands shaking from nerves and Bella and Tony must think I'm having some kind of post-traumatic episode or something. I think Bella knows better. I see the way they look at each other as I wander around, not being able to sit still. I look at Bella, who knows me all too well. I'm like a piece of glass she can look through. A kaleidoscope of emotions, and she sees every one of them, like Harlow does.

"Raph, sometimes what's right in front of us isn't as clear as we hope it could be. Our minds are asleep, and then we wake up, and the possibility of what the reality is, stares us in the face. It's scary, but the truth is, once it hits, we have to confront it head on and accept the reality."

Her words knock me down like a tornado, and I'm pretty sure that kiss hit me to realize what this really is.

Harlow is my reality.

Damn it! Why is it that I was so blind not to see it before. Too close-minded, too quick to shut it all down.

Harlow, Harlow… Harlow.

Harlow is my warmth from the cold, and the food when I'm hungry. She is the light in my dark, the patch to the hole that's inside my heart. In this crazy life I live, how can one person make me feel all the things I do? Before I met Harlow, I was a shell. I was just going through the motions for pleasure, not really feeling, just existing. Running through my life, or running from it, but when I see her on those mornings, by the dock so sweetly sitting there, waiting for me, her vulnerability slipping away day by day, I know that it's where I belong. In her presence. Anticipating the time when I can be near her, close to her, breathing in her smell, her touch mere inches from me, every morning, every day, working its way into my soul. A soul that really didn't work. A man on the outside. Inked flesh, wounded by so much, but she heals that. She believes in me, she believes I have a soul, she believes I'm worth something. To me, that's more pleasure than I could never get from some random fuck I bring home from a bar. A year ago, she showed me pleasure, made me come so hard and fast, wanting that again in my mind a thousand times over after that night, but not realizing that the feeling she gave me was what I wanted again from her and more.

Was I trying my damnedest to fill that void over the course of the past year with other women because what I felt for her that night in that bathroom bar was something more that sex? Was there something deeper in those eyes when I looked into them? I played that night over and over again in my head, just thinking I'm a young guy who scored one night, experimenting with some uninhibited nature.

No, God damn it. That's not it. It's not that. If it was, I would have just forgotten all the details that made it real. I remember her soft skin, the way her thighs felt against my hand, the silkiness of her hair. She smelled like sugar, all sweet and tasted like it just as much. The way her lips felt on mine, not caring who was beyond that door. How her body reacted as I made her come, the pulsating way she trembled, the warmth that I felt all over my body when she did. I didn't fucking forget it like I did with who knows how many others I've had between that night and now.

And I know that there's something real I'm feeling. I knew it when I kissed her today. That feeling returned. I was just too caught up in the whole excitement of it all last year to truly know, to truly figure out that she's what I want, what I need. I lied to Bella and Tony back in that room when I said I didn't want what they have, 'cause guess what, I do. I want Harlow. I want her like I want my next breath.

How the fuck did I come to this conclusion?

But how do I convince her that that night was more than sex, more than just some hookup. How do I convince her to give in to it? Give into the feelings, 'cause God knows she's the one who has made me give in. Harlow. She cracked this shell that's been around me for so long. I've fought in wars, faced death, seen death, built up a wall of hardness around myself, and she broke it. Crushed it to the ground. I'm not the man I was, and she's the reason. I feel safe and secure around her. Two things I've never had in my life. I've never given in to the whole soulmate thing. To me, it was nonexistent. A fable, something made up in a fairytale. I'm still not one hundred percent convinced of it, but I don't think I can go on another second without finding out the truth behind it. I wonder if she felt something when we kissed. Did she feel that electric spark, the current running through us? How her body molded into mine. She couldn't deny that... Right?

I've never done this before. Try and figure out if someone feels the way I do. Girls fall in love with me all the time.

See, that's a lie. They fall in love with my body, my face, the way I make them feel. I'm a puppet on a string, dancing around for their entertainment, fulfilling their pleasure, while I mask mine with some fucked up fantasy of the way things should be when you're with someone.

I have to tell her. I have to convince her that it's more than friendship, more than just sitting on a dock telling each other about our life's worries and war stories. It's more than sexual innuendoes and drinking games. There's some other kind of deeper meaning behind all of it and for the first time in my life, I'm going to find out what everyone else in my life is talking about.

My heart is not the cold sheet of ice I thought it was because Harlow Hannum melted that away. I'm not letting another moment go by without telling her, without trying to convince her to give in… To me… To us.

CHAPTER 11

And the teacher is the one being taught

Harlow~

I can still feel his lips on mine, even after being home, showered, dressed and asked a million and one questions by Willow, I can still feel them. As I laid in bed last night, constantly tossing and turning and unable to sleep due to the memory of Cruz kissing me, I have forced myself to believe that kiss must have been from pure adrenaline on his part. Lack of sleep, the rush of excitement, the new life he held in his hands, yep, that's what I chalked it up to, pure adrenaline. That kiss was nothing more than a thank you for being there for him, he even said so himself. I know he asked me afterwards what I thought of it, why he had done so, but I was so taken aback, even I didn't have an answer for once, so I used my interview as a distraction.

The interview.

My future rests in the hands of three men and two

women. Throughout my interview, his lips had the advantage over my concentration. When the panel of principals and the head of the school's administration looked over my credentials, my letters of recommendation, a mock up lesson plan I had to come up with in well... Less than a day's notice, the feeling of his lips on mine still lingered. The whole drive home was difficult in weighing out the reasons why I felt some kind of unnatural reaction to it. Or was it natural and I was so caught up in the moment to even know the difference. Still the fact remains, and the one I lost sleep over is his happiness, his passion, the excitement made him do what he did. He's Cruz for God's sake. Someone who I've come to admire. We have bonded over this summer. We tell each other almost everything, except I don't care to know who his flavor of the evening is. We kid. We joke. It's almost like hanging with Craw... Almost. He's a force to be reckoned with when it comes to women. We've had lengthy conversations regarding his take on relationships and sex. Numerous times. His comfortable way of talking to me about those things is a red flag in my brain right now.

It was just a kiss between friends. He fucks them and leaves them. Famous last words by him: 'Get in and get out'.

But why for the love of God does this plague my mind? Why is it taking up every corner of my thoughts and yielding them into some kind of twisted thought process? We need to talk when he gets back. I need to answer his question from before, at the hospital. What did I think about what happened between us? What did I think about the kiss, and I'm fully prepared to tell him exactly what I think? Or at least what I talked myself into thinking.

Before he came outside the hospital to see me, I knew I had to try to talk to Dr. Goldberg. Just being there made me panic and I'm pretty sure I did a good job of hiding it. I haven't spoken to Dr. Goldberg, or at least needed to speak with him in a few weeks. Cruz was there to talk to me, to listen, but in this particular situation, he's unavailable to help me under the circumstances, I had no choice but to call Dr. Goldberg. He instructed me to repeat my mantra, so I did. I'm not sure, but I think Cruz bought the whole Willow being on the phone story.

So when he gets back, we will go to the dock and talk. That's what's going to happen. I tried to call him to tell him how my interview was but his voicemail just keeps coming on. Come to think of it, the bus ride should have only taken him two hours to get home. There must be delays. It did wind up raining last night, so maybe that's what the problem is.

My interview went great, in spite of it being done at such an accelerated speed. They need someone, and they need someone… yesterday. They said they would get back to me by weeks end. That's two days. My whole future could be planned in two days.

I walk down to the dock to relax and read and wait to hear from Cruz. I hear Max call my name.

"Harlow! You down there?" I see him hang over the top deck, and I turn in my chair to wave to him. He disappears and runs down to meet me. He looks frazzled.

"Max, what's wrong?"

"Have you heard from Cruz since you've been back?"

"No, why? Is something wrong?" My stomach drops from the tone of his voice.

"His Captain called. He's been trying to get a hold of him for a few hours now, but he says his phone is going straight to voicemail."

"Max, why weren't his parents there?"

He runs a hand through his mohawk and sighs.

"Harlow, ask Cruz. I gotta run to Jax for a sound check, so as soon as you hear from him, call me. I'll leave him a note at the house just in case."

Ask Cruz. The words run through my head. Did he get in an argument with them, or are they away on a vacation or something like that? I could ask Bella or Tony, but maybe it's best if I just ask Cruz myself.

My mind goes to everything that could possibly be going on and why Cruz hasn't called or what has happened. I don't think I can stand it, so I'm going to call Bella. I have to be cautious when asking so I don't upset them and make them worry.

I call the hospital and ask for Bella Cruz's room. They connect me and Bella picks up on the second ring.

"Hello?"

"Bella, hi this is Harlow Hannum."

"Harlow, hi sweetie. How are things? Did your interview go well?"

I can hear the little stirring and cooing sounds of baby Matteo close to my ear.

"Great, actually, but I should be asking how you guys are."

"We are doing great. Matteo's feeding well and we can go home tomorrow. Did Raph make it home ok?"

Shit!

"Well, that's really why I'm calling. I haven't heard from him and he told me he would be home early afternoon and it's almost five, so I'm a little worried."

"You're just a little worried?" Her tone isn't accusatory, but it's questionable.

"Yes, I am. Actually, I'm a lot worried. He always picks up when I call and usually gets back to me through text within a minute and now it's going straight to voicemail."

"Harlow, maybe his bus is running late and he forgot to charge his phone or something like that. He's a big boy, I'm sure he's fine. The man has fought in wars, so don't worry too much."

"I'll try, it's just, well I'm just… Well, it's just not like him not to answer or at least try to contact me."

"Give me your number and if by some chance he calls me or Tony, I'll tell him how worried you are and for him to call you."

I give her my number and say, "Thank you."

"And Harlow, just so you know, and if I'm crossing a line here, I'm sorry, but he cares a lot about you and worries for you as well, so thank you, for feeling the same about him."

"Thank you, Bella. Take care of that new little man, and I'm so glad I got a chance to meet you and Tony."

"Me too, Harlow and hopefully we'll see a lot more of you sooner than later."

The line goes dead, and I stare at the phone.

My phone starts to buzz. I fumble with it, hoping it's Cruz, praying that it's him, telling me he's ok, but it's a number I don't recognize.

"Cruz?" But it's not.

"Miss Hannum, this is Greg Landberg from Grayson Elders School District."

Great, I guess he's calling to tell me they hired someone more qualified.

"Mr. Landberg, so nice to hear from you. What do I owe the pleasure of this call?"

He laughs, but in a friendly way.

"Well, the pleasure is all mine, believe me Miss Hannum. We would like to offer you the position of seventh grade

English teacher for this coming year at Grayson Elders Middle School."

No, he did not just offer me a job. I pinch myself. I mean I just pinched my arm.

"Mr. Landberg, I... I don't know what to say."

"Well we were hoping you'd say yes, and that you can report for duty by next Wednesday, so you can get acclimated with the school and the curriculum for the coming year."

Here is my future. I have a job, and it's all I ever wanted. This is happening so fast.

"Mr. Landberg, thank you so very much and I accept. I can be there next week. Just tell me what time and where."

"We were so very impressed by your interview and we know that you will be a wonderful asset to our school. My secretary will send you more information and a copy of the contract for you to look over. You already submitted to us all the necessary paperwork on background checks and so forth, so that's taken care of."

I thank him for the opportunity, and that I will see him then. I try to dial Cruz again, but it still goes straight to voicemail. Wait till he hears. Wait till he finds out he got a job as well. Wait till I get my hands on him for making me worry the way I am.

I run up to the house to tell the girls. Willow is going to teach sixth grade Spanish at the school, so we will be together.

"Well, girls I think this calls for a celebration. A night out tonight for one last hurrah before we have to head back next week," Willow says. She'll head back with me on Monday so we can prepare for Wednesday. Only four more days here. I'll have to say goodbye to Sandy Cove, among other things.

That reality sets in. I only have a few days left here. My time is being cut short at the shore, but my dream is coming true. I'll be a teacher, and I'll be happy… Finally… Maybe.

CHAPTER 12

*Don't expect too much
like in those cheesy romance novels*

Cruz~

Can someone please tell me how much worse the past six hours can get? First, I get on the wrong bus and wind up in bumble-fuck who the hell knows where and why? Because I fell asleep on the damn bus, and I'm at least three hours away from home, not stopping anytime soon mind you. Then I lost my phone. I lost my fucking phone in the bus terminal. How could I be so stupid? Where is my freaking head? Lack of sleep, thoughts of the girl I need to get home to so I can tell her how I feel about her. That's where it is. This whole bus ride I've been trying to figure out what to say to her, how to tell her. I wrote it down on the back of a paper towel from the men's room in the bus terminal. I don't know how to write shit, I can't even form the right words to express myself half the time. I fight. I fuck. I work hard. I've never had to tell a girl I think about her all the time. When she's not around, I miss her, and I look forward to seeing her every morning. When I'm at work, she's on my mind. How her scent stays with me all day after she's been near me. All those things I never really even realized I was thinking of until now. It just seemed like second nature to me to think about her. We spend so much time together, I'd have to say that's normal.

Right?

I think I've read what I wrote a hundred times on this trip, and I have more crossed off and written over than I care to share. The old lady next to me smells like moth balls and scotch. The rain hasn't stopped. I can't find a working pay phone anywhere to call Harlow.

But what if she's not even caring that I said I'd be home in the early afternoon. Maybe she could care less. Maybe she met up with her ex, and he took her to some country club for dinner, buying her diamonds and is sweeping her off her feet and crap like that.

What if I tell her I want her and it turns out she doesn't want me. Then what?

I'm scared, and I don't want to be.

In my mind, I'm just as scared as I was in Iraq and that was scared shitless. I remember we had to convoy from Kuwait to a base in Iraq. It was a mile long. We didn't have armored vehicles like the military does now, and all the roadside bombs that were set up were destroying ours. The sick feeling in the pit of my stomach now is like the feeling I had that day. Not knowing what the outcome is going to be, but I've taken rejection my whole life, and I've dealt, so what the hell. Just get me off this bus, so I can see if a bomb is going to go off or not.

The houses are dark, but the cars are still here when the cab drops me off. I go inside, and I see a note from Max telling me they're all at Jax. I smell like that old lady who sat next to me on the bus, and I'm in desperate need of a shower.

You know what? Fuck it. I'll run the twelve blocks to Jax. I already stink so what's the sense of even bothering with a shower.

I run as fast as my legs can take me. It's dark and there are plenty of people hanging outside on the sidewalks near all the local hangouts. I push my way through, my heart racing. Although I'm running my knees are shaking. The crumbled up paper towel with all my thoughts are in my pocket. I get to Jax. I'm sweating, panting, nervous as all hell. I say hi to the bouncer and make my way in. I swim through the crowd, searching for her, that mane of strawberry blonde that I just want to run my hands through. I feel a pull on my arm, and as I look down to see whose hand is on me. I realize it's that girl I took home a few weeks ago. The one Harlow ran into after she left my room.

"Hey, Cruz. Long time no see. Where you off to so quickly?"

I really don't have time for this. I didn't want to talk to her when she was naked and wanton in my bed, and I certainly don't want to talk to her now.

"I'm kind of in a hurry, so I'll see you around."

But she doesn't let go, only tugs my arm stronger.

"I don't get what's got you in such a rush, but if you stick around, I can certainly make staying worth your while."

I take her hand, which is now squeezing my bicep, off of

me. I don't want to be mean, but I need to be blunt.

"Listen, I'm here for a girl, not just 'some girl', but 'the girl'. You and I had a fun night, one night, but that's as far as I wanted it to go."

If I didn't know better, I'd think her eyes turned a shade of black, rage sending a clear path my way. I walk away from her, not looking back, but I can feel her burning a hole right through me with her stare.

I go towards the stage, not seeing a soul I know until I see Max and his band enter the stage. I yell for him, and he hops down.

"Where the hell have you been? We kept calling and calling and you were nowhere to be found. You gave us a freaking heart attack, man."

I grab his shoulders. "Who did I give a heart attack to?" Hoping with all I have that he gives me the answer I want.

But he doesn't.

He looks over my shoulder and shakes his head.

"What are you looking at?" He points, and I turn my head just in time to see the roadside bomb go off.

No. God, no.

She's with him. Close, with his arm around her waist.

Knox.

"That's not a good scene, Cruz," Max snaps at me.

"That's why I'm here, to make it better."

I leave Max and go to her, bomb or no bomb, I have to know. I have to let her know that this is more than friendship.

I stalk over to them. His eyes catch mine and his smirk tells me he knows I came for her. His cocky grin, his name-brand shirt, his perfect gelled-up hair.

No games, just her.

I didn't come here to get into a pissing match with him, I

came for her. The only one that matters.

I tap her shoulder. She turns around, with tears in her eyes, and suddenly my heart hurts.

Why is she crying?

She takes one look at me and goes to say something, "Cruz, where have you…"

But I interrupt.

I spin her away from him, and my lips are the only things that silence her as I pull her against my chest and kiss her. Her body molds to mine as she doesn't protest the kiss, only throwing her arms around my neck, and I lift her tiny body. I could care less that there's a hundred people in this room, that Knox is here watching us. I kiss this girl because she's the only thing in this room right now. All that matters, all that I think ever will be.

The way her tongue lashes around mine, her nails digging into my hair as she holds on for dear life, her sweet lips, her sweet scent. The scent of my Turnip.

I place her back down on the floor and immediately she goes to speak, "I don't know… I don't under…"

I place my finger on her lips telling her softly to shhh… I go into my pocket and pull out the paper towel. The words are smudged, but these are my thoughts. I won't let some smeared ink ruin what I have to say to her.

"Let me talk first since you usually have the first and final words." She rolls her eyes at me and it's adorable.

"I wrote this on the bus on the way home. And before you say anything, I got on the wrong bus, lost my phone, fell asleep and missed one of the stops, but here I am, and I'm sorry I worried you." I clear my throat as I begin to read the words that are meant for her.

"I'm not a man of many words, let me rephrase that, I am a man of many words, but usually not the right ones, but here goes. A year and a half ago right across that dance floor, right to where that door is, I met a girl who knocked me for a loop, except I didn't know it then. You took me under your spell, and it had nothing to do with what went on behind that door. It had everything to do with the way you made me feel. I felt. I actually felt." She looks confused.

"Do you understand where I'm going with this?"

She bites her bottom lip and wipes a tear falling down over her adorable freckled cheek.

Knox interrupts, his cronies gathering around him, watching me, waiting to see what I'm going to say next.

"No one knows where you're going with this, asshole, so why don't you shove off and let Harlow and me finish our conversation."

He steps a bit closer, puffing out his chest. I'll give him credit, he's got balls to stand up to me like this. I look dead on in his eyes, and I'm not about to let him ruin what I came here to say to her. So even if what I'm about to say isn't directly to her face, I bear my soul with my words. I'm looking at him, so he understands that I'm not fucking around. I'm here to let this girl know I want her, and he can't have her, again, ever again.

"So why don't I tell you where I'm going with this Chad. See that girl next to you?" I point to Harlow, and then I stuff the paper towel with the words back in my jeans. I don't need it. Whatever comes out of my mouth is what it is.

"She just turned my world upside down. She makes it chaotic with her big words and over-opinionated attitude. But you see, I like that. It means, if she feels the same way about me that I feel about her, our life won't be boring. Now you see where I'm going with this?"

Chad bursts out with laughter.

"Oh, come on Harlow. Are you really going to fall for this shit? Look at him. I know what he is. He's a fucking rent-a-cop. Please. What can he really give you?"

He backs up, and I push up my sleeves in an attempt to let him know to back the fuck up.

"See those tears in her eyes, they're not there because I caused them and never will be. That's what I'll give to her."

I think I've wasted enough words on him, so I turn my body towards her. Her eyes are bright blue, dark smudges from her mascara circle under them, so I take my fingers and wipe any traces of tears of darkness away. If it's the last thing I do, I'll never have to do it again.

"I can't promise you the world, 'cause I don't have it. I can't promise you I'll give you flowers, or take you dancing. I'm not the person who talks all mushy like in those silly books you read, or like those guys in the old movies you make me watch with you. I'm honest to a fault so when you ask me if your ass looks big in a pair of jeans and they do, I'm going to say yea, go change them. When you have a big zit on your face and you ask me if I can see it, I'll say yes, go put some girly stuff on it and cover the damn thing 'cause I won't lie. I can't promise we won't fight, because let's face it, it's what we do best. We don't agree half the time, but it's what makes us... Well us."

I pause and wait for her to slap me, kick me in the balls, or just walk away, but all she says is, "Continue." So I do.

"If you don't feel the same, let me know. If there's doubt in there..." I point to her heart. "Walk away, and if you just want to be friends, well, I'll have to learn to live with that part, but I won't live without you in my life."

She's silent and I'm not sure where this is going to go. Time seems to stand still as I wait for her to say something, anything. Max's band starts to play and it's suddenly deafening loud in here. She goes on her tippy-toes and whispers in my ear.

"You think it would be appropriate if we go in the bathroom and finish where we left off a year and a half ago?"

That's my girl.

I caress her hair, the softness making my fingers tingle.

"Nah, let's start by introducing ourselves, last names included." I extend out my hand. "Hi, I'm Raphael Cruz, but you can call me Cruz." She takes my hand and laughs.

"Harlow Hannum, damn glad to meet you, Cruz."

I'll admit, keeping my hands to myself on the walk home is difficult, but I do it, and don't think for one minute I don't have a million dirty thoughts about what I want to do to her when we get home. I just want to be close to her, so here's my arm around her shoulders, her arm around my waist, and the two of us are as giddy as kids at a carnival. The last few blocks we sprint. We race to the top of the wooden steps, into the house, and as soon as I fling open the door, I grab her and thrust my tongue in her mouth, devouring, tasting her. Hands are in hair, tugging. My hands fly to touch her breasts. I touch them slowly, and then pick up my pace. I can feel her nipples harden beneath my thumb. Her hands are caressing the crotch of my jeans, which quickly turns rugged, dredging on God damn obscene.

But this isn't what I want. It's how we got here in the first place.

I take a step back from her, and I notice the confused look on her face.

"Turnip, this isn't what I want."

The confused look is now replaced with one of dread and sadness, and I think I just said the wrong thing. Well, I said the right thing, I just said it the wrong way.

Am I already on my way to fucking this up?

Grabbing her sweet face in my hands, I pull her body closer to mine. She's a bit frigid, so I rest my forehead against hers.

"I didn't mean it that way. I mean I want to slow this down, not rush it, although I want nothing more than to rip off your clothes and devour you, but not here, not like this."

And I mean it. She's too special just to throw on my bed and fuck.

She relaxes, her body softening, and I feel the relief release from her. I bring my lips to hers, taking them softly, and placing kisses across her jaw to her neck, concentrating on a spot behind one of her ears. I grab her lobe and nibble on it, sending chills throughout her body. She shudders and sighs.

"I want you so much it hurts."

When I tell her that, she moans softly and her hands roam my body, making me so much harder than I already am.

"I have to tell you something, Cruz."

I continue my assault on her neck, and whisper in her ear, "Tell me."

"I got a job." I don't stop what I'm doing because I'm so consumed with her taste, her smell, her warmth.

"That's great... So proud of you."

I reach her lips and peck gently on them, as I place my hands on her hips.

"There's something else." She dips her face and begins to mirror what I just did to her neck, her jaw, her ear.

"What's that?" I say back.

"You did too."

I pop my head up, not really understanding or hearing what she just said.

I pull away from her, but just enough to still be looking at her face.

"What do you mean I got a job too?"

She smiles, and she grazes my jaw bone with her fingers.

"Your Captain called Max when he couldn't get a hold of you and told him there's an immediate opening for a full time position on Sandy Cove's force. You, Officer, are no longer a rent-a-cop."

Well, I'll be damned.

I pick up her tiny body and swing her around, making her laugh and squeal.

"I got a job and you... You got a job, and we can..."

Wait. I got a job here and she got a job...

"Where did you get a job at Turnip?"

Her eyes turn down so her focus is on the floor. I lift her chin with my finger so she's looking at me. Those adorable freckles in my full view.

"Home."

She got a job at home. Of course, she did. I didn't expect her to get one here. It's not her home. Just her summer home. My happiness for her finally getting her dream is replaced with gloom. I just got her, now I have to let her go. I can't give up this opportunity. Full-time positions are few and far between, and I worked so hard for it, but I worked so hard to let her know my feelings too. I stroke those tiny specks on her cheeks and grin, but it's not my megawatt one.

"I know that face, Cruz, and believe me, I'm feeling it too. I realize what this means as well, but I'm not worried.

For once, I'm not."

"How's this going to work?"

She gives me a reassuring smile, kisses my lips with sincerity and tells me, "Because we care about each other, and it's strong and distance is just going to make us stronger. Then when we do see each other, we'll savor it. It'll be like we never left each other's sides."

This woman is so sure of herself, so sure about us, and that's just another reason why she owns me.

She fucking owns me.

"I can hardly stand being away from you for a day, how are we going to make this work? I've never done this before."

She doesn't speak. She takes my hand and leads me to the back door, down the steps towards out dock.

Our place, our sanctuary. It's where we belong.

She forces my shoulders down to sit on one of our special chairs, and she slips off her shoes one by one... Slowly. Her legs straddle mine, and I can feel the heat between her legs on my jeans, and it's amazing. Her vanilla scent engulfing my senses, the way her hair feels as it grazes my arm, tickling my flesh. She begins to rub herself on my lap, wrapping her hands around my neck, biting and licking the skin on it. Her faint breath in my ear as she reassures me there's nothing to worry about.

"I need you to listen to me, Cruz. I think I know you better than you know yourself, and you will be fine. Trust me, trust in us, and let's make the most out of what time we'll have out of this. Let's let it all fall into place and see where the rest goes. I'm going to be the risk taker this time, you've taught me that. I knew it from the first time you made me stick my toe in the water."

Her words melt into me, and already she's turning me

into something I'd never thought I'd be: a pussy.

"I'm going to give as much of myself as I can for now, Turnip. This is so new for me, but this feeling is addictive, and I don't want it to end, so yea, let's just dive in, and see what happens."

She kisses my lips and nods. "Agreed," she whispers against my mouth.

The tension rolls off of me, and we go back to kissing… A lot. Her hand wanders across my stomach, lifting my shirt, touching my skin, and it feels so good. I can hardly stand it. Just her touch can send a million, tiny electrical waves through me, one inch at a time.

The friction of her middle rubbing against the crotch of my jeans is painful, but pleasurable, and I want her. I need to take her.

Now.

I inch up her shirt, feeling the smoothness of her belly on my fingertips as I lift the shirt and pull it over her head. I throw it to the side as her tits practically pour out of the black lace bra that holds them against her. I give her a look as to say if it's ok if I continue, so I unhook it from behind. Her gorgeous nipples exposed to me, erect, almost begging for my mouth on them, and that's what I do. One at a time, suckling on each one, stroking them with my tongue while I hear her subtle moans. Her hands still linked behind my head, but her head is thrown back, exposing her long neck to me. I release a nipple and attack her neck, licking the salt from it, tasting her, feeding on her, wanting more.

"I've waited so long for this, Turnip. A year and a half is a long time to go without having you."

She looks into my eyes, and says with the seductive look of probably the sexiest woman I have ever seen, "Well then what are you waiting for?"

And that's all the ammo I need to take her, and finally be inside of what's mine. The one thing that has turned my calm little world upside down in a matter of months.

I lift her up, cupping her ass in my hands, and with one of them, I tug down her shorts, exposing her black panties. Underneath is my heaven. I've had it before, but now it's different. It's not a stranger I'm about to fuck, it's the girl who rules my world.

I don't know how I do it, but I manage to keep her up with my one arm and slowly trace the outline of her already wet panties with the other. Anticipating what's beneath them.

"Touch me, Cruz. I can't take it anymore. I need you to touch me."

I slip my fingers along the hem and feel her wetness there, begging for me, so I give her what she wants, what she needs, what I need.

"Oh, God." She moans as my fingers invade her. Her grip on me is strong, and for being so small, it surprises me. I watch her face as my fingers dip in and out of her, picking up my pace as I watch her fly over the edge, and it's fucking gorgeous, and she's mine.

Her breathing is rapid, and my fingers wet with her release, and now I need to feel her all over me.

I sit back down in the chair, leaving her standing there naked, the moonlight reflecting off the bay's water, and I don't think I've ever seen anything so beautiful in my life. Her perfect face. Her long hair hanging over her shoulders just touching the outline of her gorgeous tits. I slowly pull down my pants, my cock springing out. I reach for a condom, slide it on and pull her onto me without warning. I impale her, getting the feel of her around me. The heat coming off her pussy, her skin against mine, making me hotter than I think I've ever been, feeling so much, almost to the point where I want to weep, and why do I feel this way?

Because I feel. I feel something this time. Not just to get off like my normal ways, but I feel things inside for her, I never knew I was capable of. I try to take my time, her body rising and falling onto my cock. Slowly, she takes me in, inch by inch, but the feeling is so magnificent that I'm not so sure I'll hold out much longer. Our lips hardly move from one another and the sounds of flesh against flesh are savored, because it feels too damn good, and I don't want it to end.

"I'm going to come, Turnip, hold on to me ok?"

She nods, unable to speak, and that's something I find most sexy. She can't even speak.

I raise her up and down on me a few more times, gripping her hips and kneading my fingertips into her skin. I can feel the corners of her bones under my palms as I come like I think I never have before.

That's a lie. If memory serves, I did, a year and a half ago. You don't forget something like that. Her body falls against mine, and there are no words, only pants and breathy sounds coming from both of us. I hold her close to me, not wanting to let her go… Never.

"I leave Monday." She tells me, making me want to hold her closer than I already am.

"Tomorrow is Sunday already."

Silence. Only silence. Harlow climbs off of me and dresses. She tells me not to worry, but her lack of words makes me think otherwise. I get dressed and stand beside her. I wrap my arms around her waist, and we look out on the moonlit bay.

"Come on." I nudge her. Let's get some sleep.

We make our way back to the house and to my room.

We don't bother to undress. We just crawl under the sheets, and I put my chest against her back. Our legs are tangled together at the ankles, knees twisted and locked between one another, and it's the most unusual, but most satisfying feeling I think I've ever felt. I'm liking this. As I wrap my arms around her shoulders and gently rub the silk-like strands of her hair that fall on them, I hear the change of her breathing, and I know she's fast asleep.

But as tired as I am, I don't want to waste any time sleeping when I have her with me now, because I know in twenty four hours, she'll be gone.

And it's not fair, but I have to believe this will work. It has to, because if I lose her like I have lost so much in my life, this time I don't think I'll recover.

CHAPTER 13

Believe

Harlow~

As I stand on this dock, knowing that I won't be back anytime soon, I think about the last twenty four hours and all that has taken place, actually the past eight weeks. I have the heart of a man who I despised at one time, almost to the point of making me physically ill. But that's in the past because here we are hugging and kissing like it's the end of the world, and it will be the last thing we ever do. How did I not see this coming before? Dr. Goldberg tried to tell me. Craw tried to tell me. Was I that close-minded that I didn't realize my feelings? Yes... Yes, I was, but now that's unimportant. He has me. I'm his. He is mine.

Yesterday was a blur, well a good blur. The majority was spent in his bed, (I'm not complaining because there was no place else I wanted to be) with the exception of a walk on the beach, and dinner with the gang before Willow and I leave Sandy Cove and head back to Princeton to start our new jobs. Exciting as it is, the bittersweetness of it all has replaced that. Leaving me with a feeling I have had in the past. One I'm not a fan of.

Dread.

Even when I was with Chad, and he would go away on his trips with his buddies to Cabo, or on a golf trip with his dad, I knew what was going to happen once he left, he'd cheat. For some odd reason beyond anything I can comprehend, I don't feel that way leaving here and leaving Cruz. He asked why I was crying at Jax the other night when I was talking to Chad. I told Cruz how Chad wanted me back, and he kept telling me over and over again how no one else would love me. How there was no one else who could make me feel the way he does. How no one would ever want me like he does. When I told Cruz our conversation, he was angry, but told me these exact words: Chad's words couldn't be farther from the truth.

He starts his new job with the Sandy Cove Police tonight. Four, twelve hour shifts with three days off. He will have some weekends off, if he's lucky, but for the most part, weekends off are a thing of the past at least for now. Him being the low man on the totem pole and all.

We discussed that night in the bathroom of Jax last summer. We laughed as he told me when he saw me throw down a few shots of tequila like a drunken sailor, he knew he had to have me. That in turn left butterflies in my belly. He told me he watched me from the time I entered the bar, until we left, even after I rejoined my friends that night of our lovers tryst. Cruz told me he replayed that night over and over again in his head, and when he saw me the night he pulled me over when I arrived here. The whole time he gave me that fake sobriety test, all he thought about was how I made him feel that night, twelve months prior. The pleasure and the sheer rawness of it all.

I did that to him. I made him feel something. Me. Not the other way around. I've never made anyone want me, or need me like Cruz needs and wants me. A temporary distraction inside a bar bathroom has brought us to this. I never want to let him go. I know I have to start my future, but I feel like Cruz may be a part of that future, that's how much I care for him. I've soaked his shirt with my tears. I've lost so much and leaving him now scares me, but I have to believe that this will work. I can't say the words I love him to him, not just yet. I'm pretty sure I do love him, actually there's no doubt, because the dread I feel leaving him is overwhelming and you just don't feel the way I do when you just 'like' someone. I haven't been in love for so long, and I'm not sure I was ever in love with Chad. He ruled me with an iron fist, and not in a good way. He ruled me by telling me what to wear, how to style my hair, what color it should be, not to be a teacher because I wasn't smart enough, never good enough.

I was just never enough for him, but I kept going back for more, and it ended with me almost ending my life.

I love how strong Cruz is. How he calms the raging sea of emotions I constantly have, but how is he going to do that almost three hours away? We will video chat, it's been discussed. He will check his schedule and the first weekend he has off, he'll come to Princeton to see me. It won't be for a while, but I'm hoping how the old saying goes 'absence makes the heart grow fonder' is true to life. This will be an unexpected journey, one I'm willing to take with him, because like he said to me a few days ago, he needs me in his life, and he doesn't want to live it without me in it. I believe him because I feel the same way.

We walk to my already packed car after I hug the guys and Thea goodbye. I'll see the girls and Porter more than I'll see Max. Willow is M.I.A. and I'm wondering where she ran off to.

"So I'll check tonight and see when my next days off are. Even if it's a Sunday, I'll drive to see you and spend as much time with you as I can. Every chance I get I'll come to see you, but absolutely I'll be there for Greta's wedding on New Years Eve.

It's hard to fight back the tears as he tells me these things, 'cause for a while it will be hard, but I've had to deal with worse.

A lie I'll keep telling myself until we are together again.

Willow comes out of the house, followed by Max.

Max?

Yea, ok, whatever.

I reluctantly pull away from Cruz after a long, searing kiss that I'll not soon forget. I know as I drive away, I'll still be able to taste him on my lips and feel his fingertips weaved in my hair.

"Trust in us, Turnip, believe in us and everything will be ok." He points to his heart. "You're in here, and there's no way you're getting out."

I swipe at my tears and laugh. "I thought you weren't going to be mushy and stuff."

He chuckles against my ear. "I'm not 'cause I think your ass looks big in those shorts. Happy now?" I smack his arm, trying to quickly end this torturous goodbye.

I get into my car, and Willow goes in hers. My tears are like a river, uncontrolled and raging, and I shake as slip into the driver's seat. I grip the wheel, resting my head on it, and he dips his head in the window.

"You call me from a rest stop. You call me when you

want. Hell, call me when you get to the end of the street." He smiles at me, but I can see the pain in his eyes. This hurts him too, but the big baby won't admit it. This is the truth of Cruz. Strong like the Marine he is. Soft on the inside where no one else but me can see past the built up wall and the Broadway show he constantly stars in.

I start the car, and he hangs on my lips as I slowly start to drive away, pecking at them, once, twice, three, four times, not wanting him to part my mouth, but knowing I have to say goodbye, so I gun it, looking at him through my rear-view mirror, and before long he's a speck of a reflection, and so is my heart. I feel the pain. I feel the emptiness, and I tell myself to believe.

Just believe.

Of course, I've talked to the man a million times in the past month. I can't text at work, but when I leave school for the day there has to be no less than I'd say oh… about twenty texts from him. Always joking, always telling me he misses me. The video chat thing is doing ok, but he does mostly night duty, so it's hard. He'll text me a picture of himself, of the stars on his hips and joke about how when he sees me he fully expects me to give them a lick.

The man is insatiable.

I love my new job. Seventh graders are funny with all their raging hormones and know it all attitudes. My mom tells me we were the same growing up. We thought we had all the answers. The staff at the school is great. I feel comfortable, and it was an easy transition from student to teacher.

As much as I love my parents, even though they have been so wonderful to me, I needed to be on my own. I needed to move out and get my own place, which I did. I bought a small condo about ten minutes from their house, and I'm in absolute love with it. Of course, in the grand fashion of my parental units, I put the down payment on it myself, but they bought me some of my furniture. Sometimes Craw stays with me, and Greta, well Greta is too busy being Bridezilla at the moment. The wedding is a short three months away. New Years Eve, figures, even Greta could take the spotlight off the new year. Cruz is coming to the wedding, which I'm so excited for. Unfortunately, he has to work Christmas Eve and day, but is off for New Years. He's staying for four whole days.

Oh, the possibilities.

I make myself blush when thoughts of him, his rock hard abs, and his sexy tattoos appear in my head.

I can't wait for him to meet my parents. They say they feel like they practically know him from the way I'm always talking about him. My mom says I have twinkling stars in my eyes when I mention his name, the same ones she says she had and still does for my dad.

That's true love.

Somedays when I come home to the empty house I occupy, I get sad. Not that I don't like being alone, I just well… I'm not used to it. My phone buzzes in my pocket on my way home from work and it's Cruz. I can't help to smile when I see his name on the caller ID.

"Hi there, dickcop. What are you up to?"

"Hi there, yourself, Turnip. What are you up to?"

I pull into my driveway and turn off the ignition.

"Just getting home from work. You have the day off today, don't you?"

"Yep. I'm just driving around, doing some much needed errands."

"Well at least you're being productive and using your time well."

"Hopefully."

I tell him to hold on while I get my work bag and the bag of groceries I picked up on my way home. I dig out my keys and walk towards my front door. I can see something sitting in front of it, not close enough yet to see exactly what it is, and I immediately try to think back if I ordered anything that would be delivered. And I can't.

"You there?" He asks.

"Yes, yes I'm here. I'm getting ready to walk in my door."

I get closer and see that whatever it is, it's wrapped in green paper, so I tuck the phone under my chin, and bend over to pick it up.

Well, I'll be damned.

A bouquet of turnips.

I look around, onto the street, to the neighbor's door that's next to mine.

"Cruz?"

"Yea, Turnip?"

"What errands are you running?"

My heart accelerates, palms sweating when he doesn't answer. I put the key in and turn the lock and there's my answer, standing in my foyer.

Looking at his baby blues, his broad shoulders, and his smile is like I just stepped right into heaven. I drop everything I have in my hands to run to him. Jumping on him, wrapping my legs around his waist and kissing him like it's the first time.

As soon as I touch his sweet lips and run my hands through his unruly hair, I feel truly home, not with bricks and mortar, but in his arms.

His kisses are fierce, red hot, and it makes my blood course through my veins at speeds of those of the greatest of forces.

He backs me up against one of the walls, tugging at my clothes, and me at his. Not being able to get them off fast enough, we cut through the red tape, no talking, just living, breathing, sharing the desire we both feel for... Each other.

When he enters my body, the pleasure I feel is immeasurable, leaving me in a dazed frenzy of emotions. The feel of his hands on my body, the softness and hardness of the way he takes me, letting my body give into him, sending me over the edge over and over again. I try to speak, the words coming from me are in spurts and interrupted sounds.

"How'd... You... Oh God, yes, don't stop... Did you get in my house?"

He grunts and moans and he continues to impale me, my back banging against the drywall behind me.

"Oh, Christ... I... I called Craw. He had a key. I met him over... Jesus, Turnip... My God you feel so fucking good."

I claw his shoulders, trying to steady myself as I ride him with all the power and energy I have.

"Over what?" My breathing heavy and labored as I ask the question.

"Cof... Cof... Coffee. Oh God here I come. Hold on, sweetheart."

He pours into me, still pumping away, as I'm sent hurling into space, seeing stars, colors bursting, air changing, the universe spinning out of my control.

Cruz pulls out of me and we slide carefully beside each other down the wall.

Panting, sweating, smiling, and sated.

I turn to him.

"Well you were right, you did spend your time off productively." He reaches for my hand and kisses it.

"I missed you so much I didn't think I could go another day without seeing you. It's been a month you know?"

"I'm well aware, trust me. What's with the bouquet of turnips though?"

He shrugs at me. "I told you I don't do flowers."

Typical Cruz.

"How long are you staying?"

He stands, pulling up his pants, but keeping them unbuckled so I have a great view of the stars that touch each of his hips. I trace them with my fingertips, studying them and the intricate detail on them. He rolls his head back at my touch. I lean in a bit closer, my face only centimeters from the ink that's embedded in his smooth skin. I dart my tongue out to taste him, his skin still warm from our friction. The edge of my tongue skimming the outline of the stars, as I place kisses along the perimeter.

"What are you doing to me, Turnip?" I look up at him underneath my lashes and smile.

"You told me you couldn't wait for me to lick them, so I'm taking full advantage of your day off."

He kneads his fingers in my hair, and I work my way up his body, putting my lips on his flesh. His hard, hot skin almost burning my lips.

When I reach his lips, I kiss him differently, there's something else I feel in this kiss and the way he responds back to it solidifies the fact I have come to terms with: I'm in love with Raphael Cruz.

As much as I would like to spend the next few hours in bed with Cruz, and never let him out of my sight, I want him to meet my mom and dad. Craw called, and he said he told Mom Cruz came to surprise me, so she wanted to meet the young man who swept me off my feet. Cruz said he was looking forward to it. At six, we make our way to my parent's house, kissing at every stop light, every stop sign, our fingers intertwined the whole way. When we pull up to my parents, Cruz's eyes are wide with surprise at the size of it. I look over at him and reassure him it's just a house.

We enter the house and my ten year old yellow lab, Sadie, greets us, jumping on Cruz and making him laugh.

"Down girl, get down," I tell her while giving her a nice rub of the ears.

"Hey sweetie," my mom says as she rounds the corner, apron fixed across her chest and tied.

"Hi, Mom. I want you to meet… Um…" I don't know what to say or to call him. Cruz, Raphael, but he takes care of it for me.

He extends his hand to take hers. "Harlow's boyfriend, Raphael, very nice to meet you finally, Mrs. Hannum."

My boyfriend.

Hot damn!

"Well, Raphael, or is it ok to call you Cruz?"

My mom winks at me and Cruz chuckles.

"Yes, ma'am, that's fine."

"Then Cruz, it's very nice to meet you as well. I've heard a lot about the man who makes my Harlow happy."

I blush and Cruz takes my hand and squeezes it, taking it up to his lips to kiss it.

"That's the goal, Mrs. Hannum, and I plan to keep it that way." He pulls from behind his back the small bouquet of daisies he made me stop for on the way here. They're my mom's favorite.

"These are for you. Thank you for having me in your home."

My mom gasps and I roll my eyes as he gives me a cocky grin.

"Oh, they're my favorite. I used to grow them on my parent's farm. Thank you so much, Cruz. Come in the kitchen and sit while I finish dinner."

We follow my mom through the foyer into our kitchen, and I step up on my tippy toes and whisper in his ear, "I thought you didn't do flowers." He kisses my forehead and replies, "I do for moms, not for you. For you, it's turnips, Turnip." I smack his arm.

Craw comes home from campus and sits for dinner with us. Dad is still at the office, but will be home soon. Mom asks Cruz about his new job and how we met. We both laugh at the question, and she doesn't get it, but Craw does, so he gestures with a finger down his throat when Mom's not looking. We hear Dad come in.

"Hey, crew, I'm home." He goes right to my mom and plants one on her, and strokes her hair, kind of like what Cruz always does to me.

"How was your day, love?"

"Great, two of the three spawn are here and we have a guest, Joe."

My dad doesn't notice Cruz sitting next to me in Greta's chair. He was too consumed with greeting my mom. God, their love amazes me.

Cruz stands up even before my dad has a chance to come to the end of the table where we sit. Just like with my mom, he extends his hand.

"Mr. Hannum, nice to meet you. Raphael Cruz."

Dad shakes his hand, thoroughly, eyeing Cruz in a dad sort of way.

"The Marine, correct?"

"Yes, sir. MWSS."

"Marine Wing Support Squadron. Very impressive, Mr. Cruz. Thank you for your service."

"It was my honor, sir."

I think my face hurts from smiling so much. All this is so unexpected. Craw looks at me from across the table, giving me a thumbs up.

During dinner, Dad asks Cruz about where he served and a few things about his service I had already known. Mom is impressed. Dad is impressed and Cruz is relaxed, grabbing my hand under the table, giving me glances during dessert and asking Dad about being a lawyer. They do the small talk thing while I help Mom with the dishes. Cruz asks my mom if she needs help, but she tells him he is a guest, and guests don't clean up. Now if Grandmother were here, she'd stick a butler's uniform on him and tell him to get to work. She won't be as impressed with him as my parents are, and that worries me a bit.

I look at my watch and realize it's almost nine and Cruz has a three hour drive back to Sandy Cove. My stomach sinks and I feel sick because our time is up.

We say goodbye to my parents. They tell him they look forward to seeing him at Greta's wedding.

The car ride back to my house is silent. I hate this. I really do.

"Holy fuck!" He yells and pulls to the side of the road. His hands fly to his hair and he looks ashen.

"What the hell is wrong with you!" I yell at him.

"We had sex three times today and we didn't use condoms. How did I let this happen? Please tell me you're on the pill or something?"

I'm a bit taken aback by his words, but he doesn't know the truth. Is it a good time to tell him? Do I allow him into the darkness that has plagued my life for almost the last two years?

Yes, because I love him, and he has the right to know.

"No, I'm not on the pill," I snap, but immediately regret saying it in that tone.

Running his hands thoroughly through his hair, his jaw opens and shuts as he tried to process what had happened. "Oh, my God, Harlow. We could be in big trouble here."

My mind suddenly goes to the place where I don't want it to go. I've been doing a really good job at hiding it, but he looks so worried. I need to emerge from the dark place before it grips me and pulls me in further. I have to remember to be strong, not to let it bring me to where I so seldom go anymore. That was before Dr. Goldberg, that was before Cruz, my therapy, my only hope.

"No, we can't 'cause I can't be pregnant."

"Yes, yes you can be. Christ, Turnip, I came in you three times and you never know. You very well could have just gotten pregnant."

I feel the strain of his words, and they aren't true. The impossibility of them makes me panic, bringing me further down, sinking deeper and deeper. I rock back and forth in my seat, biting my lip, holding back the tears, ready to implode. So I do.

I can't hear myself scream the words, but I know I am. It's the only time in a very long time I say the words out loud.

"I can't ever be pregnant! Never, ever. It will never happen. I had a fucking abortion and I almost bled to death so I had to have a partial hysterectomy. I'm almost twenty three years old and I will go through my whole life knowing what I did will directly affect me for as long as I live. Are you fucking happy now that you know?! Are you fucking happy?"

My tears turn into sobs, and I'm so afraid to look at him, so ashamed of the consequences that have brought me here. I lean my head against the coolness of the window and between my muffled cries I tell him to take me home. He doesn't say a word, just pulls away from the side of the road. When we get to the front of my house, I feel a little calmer, but not enough not to let him know the rest of the story if he wants to. I'm in love with him, and he either needs to accept what has happened to me, or leave me. Either way, I'm afraid of losing.

I sigh and look over at him. His eyes stare at the street in front of him, hands resting in his lap.

"I didn't want you to leave here tonight like this, with this between us. If you want to know the story, I'll tell you, and you can form your own opinion. It is what it is, Cruz, and I can't go back and change what happened. It's taken me such a long time to get through it."

He turns to me with solemn eyes.

"Can we go inside and you can tell me?" His words are quiet, but not harsh or angry, just soft.

We go into the house and I make us some coffee. We sit across from each other at my breakfast bar. The seeping hot liquid's scent creeping through my nose, and I take a much needed sip.

"I'm going to tell you the whole story, Cruz, some stuff will make you angry, you may even hate me for it, but if we are going to be together, I need to be honest with you."

He reaches for my hand, and I'm grateful for it.

"I could never hate you, Turnip. I… Go ahead."

"In February of last year, I found out I was pregnant. It was Chad's baby, and I wanted to keep it. He, of course, didn't. See that would have ruined his dating life."

Cruz grins sadly at me, and I shrug my shoulders.

"I was still away at school, and when I told Chad I wanted to keep the baby he gave me a million and one reasons not to. It wouldn't look good for such prominent families in our society to have a child out of wedlock. His parents would disown him, even though our dads are golf buddies. He convinced me I planned it, I trapped him, and he told me that the whole town would look at me as a whore if I trapped Chad Knox into having a child."

Cruz shakes his head, and his eyes grow dark.

"When I stood up for myself and told him I wanted to have the baby, that's really when things got ugly."

He told me I wasn't worthy of carrying his child. I was worthless, and I believed it. He twisted my thoughts and my feelings, and that's when I knew that the only way out of this was to do what he said and get rid of it."

"And you believed all that?"

I nod. "At the time, yes." Cruz's stare bores into me, his nostrils flaring. His hands are flat against the top of the bar, but I know him and I can tell his anger is building.

"Just get rid of it? Those were his words?"

Ashamed, I nod, looking down at my hands tangled together and sweaty from nerves.

He adjusts himself in his chair, finding a more comfortable position, probably to tell me he wants nothing to do with me, and that I'm a disgrace.

But again, he surprises me with his actions.

He stands and comes over to where I'm sitting. He places his arm underneath my body and lifts me up, cradling me in his arms, and takes me into the living room. He sits on the sofa as I sit in his lap, forcing my head to rest on the broadness of his shoulder. I feel so safe with him, like nothing in the world could ever harm me again.

"Tell me the rest," he whispers to me softly.

"He didn't go with me to the clinic. Willow took me to one near school. I wanted it done there so the risk of my parents finding out would not be a possibility. So we went and after it was done, Willow took me back to our apartment and within an hour I started not to feel right, and all the... All the blood started to pour out of my body. Clumps."

Cruz senses my panic, so he strokes my hair and tells me to relax.

"Willow called Craw and he came right over. He was at the same school as us, and they took me to the hospital where they performed surgery. They told me that I could have bled to death because the clinic I went to was not sanitary even though it looked it."

Kissing my ear, then my temple, he asks, "So is that why you looked so uncomfortable when we went to the hospital for Baby Matteo?"

I look up at him confused. "How did you know?"

"Well for starters, you were dangerously pale the whole time and I caught you several times counting the tiles on the waiting room floor. You must have done it a half dozen times."

"That's how I calmed myself."

He smiles at me. "That must have been really hard for you to see Bella in that room, and I'm guessing that's why you wouldn't hold the baby."

I touch the tip of his nose. "Score one for the big guy."

"So I was in the hospital for a few days, telling my parents I went to Florida for Spring Break with the girls.

Willow paid for the whole hospital stay in cash from her trust fund so we didn't have to use my parent's insurance so they wouldn't know."

He brings me in closer to him, holding onto me for dear life. I hear him say against my ear, "My God what you must have been through."

"They only left my ovaries. Apparently they work just fine. I'm in therapy. Have been for a while now. His name is Dr. Goldberg. He knows all about you. He even told me once he thought I had feelings for you."

He brings my face up towards him and looks in my eyes.

"Really? Well I'll have to meet him someday, won't I?"

He kisses the tip of my nose. Such a simple gesture, but one that I adore.

"Turnip, your parents seem to be incredible people who I think would have helped you and understood. Fuck Knox and whomever else."

I agree with him.

"But that's not all there is."

He looks startled. "There's more?"

"Yes. When I came home I told Chad what happened and here I found out he was with someone, and he didn't want her to find out about me. That's why he wanted me to get rid of the baby. I didn't see him again until a few weeks later at the country club with his face bashed in."

"Why was his face bashed in? Not that I'm opposed to having his face bashed in, but continue."

"Craw did it after I tried to kill myself."

He quickly moves me off his lap and rests me on the couch, pacing in front of me. His hands go immediately to his hair, tugging it like he does when he's upset or nervous.

"I don't understand how and why you could do that to yourself. Out of all this, Turnip. You... You are so smart and so caring and so fucking beautiful, why you would want to end it all over some mother fucker like Knox. And I'll fucking kill him, Harlow. I swear it."

I stand up and take his face in my hands. Willing him to look at me.

"I'm fine. I took pills. Craw found me. They pumped my stomach. I didn't take enough to kill myself anyway. I can't even do that right."

That's when he walks away from me. Going into the bathroom and slamming the door. It seems like he's in there forever. I knock on the door.

"Cruz. Are you ok?" The door swings open and he engulfs me in an embrace, squeezing the air from my lungs.

"Don't you ever joke about something like that, don't you ever think you're not worthy of anything, cause you are, you're everything. Do you hear me? You. Are. Everything."

I cry on his shoulder, relinquishing so many pent up emotions, months of anguish, but yet a sense of relief.

"Oh, baby, don't cry. Please, it's ok. I'm so glad you told me. Please baby, look at me."

He brings our faces close together, leaving his eyes closed, running his thumbs over my freckles.

"I know. I'm sorry I kept it from you. I should have told you sooner."

We stand here like this for what seems like forever. He lifts his head and looks at me with such amazement in his eyes.

"You let me call you baby. And you did it without telling me not to." I smile.

"Want to know why I hated it?"

"Pftt, you might as well. I know everything else right?"

"Chad called me it, and every time he did it made me sick to my stomach. Every time he tried to get me back, even the night I met you last summer, he said it. He was there that night with another girl, but he still cornered me when she wasn't around. Every time he tried to convince me that he was the only one who would love me, he called me baby."

Cruz steps away from me, megawatt smile present and accounted for.

"Good, I'm glad you told me, 'cause I like Turnip so much better anyway."

CHAPTER 14

When the truth slaps you in the face, make sure you turn your head and take it like a man

Cruz

I'll kill that mother fucker. I've killed people in battle before, I don't think I'd have problems killing Chad Knox. As much as it pains me to say, and as much as I hate what Knox did to her, Harlow's smarter than that. What kind of hold did this asshole of all assholes have on her?

She appears on the outside to be so strong. See, she has this way about her, the kind that makes you feel like you're the most important person in the world. No one has ever made me feel like that. Only her and that's why she's mine.

It's not easy being away from her, especially after the last visit when she told me about what happened to her, and the reason why I want to kill Chad Knox.

When I'm on duty, I dig out my phone constantly, so I can look at a picture of her. I miss seeing her face. I'm pretty sure I'm bordering on stalker because I sleep with her pillow from Willow's parent's house next door. I stole it once she left for her new job in August.

Huge. Pussy.

Yea, well the girl does stuff like that to me. It smells of her. Even, after all this time, it has a few stray strands of her hair still on it. Before I drift off to sleep, I inhale the scent that lingers, and I feel close to her.

Unbelievable, right?

Renting the house from Porter's parents is great, but lonely. Max will come down sometimes to hang, or play a gig at Jax when he has a break from school, but mostly it's just me. On my days off I work out, run on the beach, which is as cold as a witch's tit. November isn't kind to Sandy Cove. I pick up overtime when it's available, just so I have something to do, so that I'm not constantly thinking of her. On my not so consecutive days off, I go see my nephew. He's got to be the cutest damn thing I've ever seen. Before, he was just this blob, eating and shitting, sleeping and shitting again. Now he actually smiles at me, even blows those silly raspberries out of his mouth everyone gushes over. I have to be the constant joke between Bella and Tony about Harlow.

Bella knew how I felt about her, that I better not fuck it up, be good to her, and Bella is constantly saying, "See Antonio, I knew it, that girl changed him."

Truth is, yes, she did. And that fact continues to make me a pussy. Do I care? Do I mind? Abso-fucking-lutely not!

As I sit here in my patrol car in front of Jax, I think back to the night I told her how I felt about her. I would have never pictured us being together. I mean she hated me at one time. Crushing my balls, punching me, and thinking I was a man-whore. Which I was. I was the biggest man-whore known to man, but things change.

Harlow's ring tone sounds in my ear and it's freaking one a.m. on a Wednesday. I can't imagine why she's awake, but I just have to smile, knowing when I answer it will be her voice.

"Hey there, Turnip. Why up so late? You o.k.?"

"Hey baby. Yes, I'm fine. I just missed talking to you today and I couldn't sleep. How are you?"

When she calls me baby, I think it's the sweetest fucking thing that comes out of her mouth. That and that tongue of hers when she's kissing me.

"I'm bored out of my mind. Did you have a good day at school?"

"Yes. It was great. Those kids are cool."

"I can't wait to meet them someday."

She's silent, and I can hear the rustling of the sheets beneath her, and fuck me, but I wish I were between those sheets with her.

"Turnip? What's going on?" The tone of my voice goes up an octave when I ask.

"Well… How about that someday being sooner than later?"

"What do you mean?"

"Can you come to career day on the twenty forth? It's the week before Thanksgiving."

I tell her to hold on and I dig out my schedule for that week. I don't have off, but I tell her that I can try and switch with someone. She sounds disappointed, and I am too, but I'm still going to try.

"Babe, I know this is hard and it's not the ideal situation, but I'm trying here."

I can tell she's crying.

"I know, I know. I just… I just miss you so much, and

even though I'm not alone, I feel like that."

She hurts my heart, and I want nothing more than to be with her, right now.

"Me too, sweetheart. Me too." I hear a sob escape her.

I need to lighten the mood a little and quick.

"Wanna have phone sex?"

She laughs. "You're insatiable, you know that?"

"Yes ma'am, I do."

So I let the game begin, but as much as I'd love to pull out Morty and give him some exercise, I'm working and that would be illegal, so this will be all about Harlow.

"So what are you wearing?" I whisper to her.

In a seductive voice she tells me, "My plaid, flannel pajama pants, and my dad's old college t-shirt."

"Ohhh, that's so hot, babe. Tell me more. Are you wearing granny panties too?"

She laughs, then moans, playing along well.

"Oh, yea. They are two sizes too big and ivory cotton. They even have worn patches on the ass. You like that?"

"Yea, I do. Are you wearing fuzzy socks too?"

"You know it, and my favorite sports bra with the sweat stains."

"Oh, God Turnip, are you trying to make me come right here in my patrol car?"

"I'm also wearing zit cream and my eyebrows and upper lip need to be waxed." Her voice, breathy like Marilyn Monroe or something like that.

"Oh, when you talk about facial hair, it's the fucking sexiest thing ever."

I continue to hear the sounds of her either snuggling further down in her sheets, or she's sticking her hands down those flannel pants she's wearing.

"Talk to me, Cruz. I need for it to be like you're right

here with me. I'm touching myself, but I want it to be like it's your hand."

I have zero problem with her request, but I have to keep myself under control. I can always take care of business when I get off duty.

"Ok, babe. Think it's my hand, touching you, softly, stroking your thighs, my fingers inching towards the middle, and I can feel how wet you are already."

She whispers, "Oh, yea."

This is going to be harder than I thought.

"Now I know what you like, you like to be teased, so I will tease you. I'm lightly running my thumb across your clit. Do you feel that?"

Breathlessly she says, "Yes… Yes I do. Keep going."

"Now I do it a few more times, in constant circles, just to get you heated up. I'm reaching up and I'm rubbing my hands all over those gorgeous tits of yours. You like?"

"I like, a lot."

"Good, Babe. Now I'm going to put my fingers inside you, then I'm going to lick you there. My hot tongue is tasting you. You are so fucking perfect, and I love hearing you moan as I suck on you. Can you moan for me?"

"Yes, Cruz. Oh, God… Don't stop. Keep it up. I'm almost there."

Harlow's voice cracks and her breathing is heavier than before. I know this is how she gets when she's almost there.

"You taste so fucking good, but I need to be inside you. Imagine me inside you. I can feel you all around me, your sweetness, your wetness. I'm not going to be nice babe. I'm going to keep pounding into you, licking your neck, biting your ear like you like. I want you to touch yourself while I'm fucking you."

I'm so hard right now, it's uncomfortable, and I still have

another five hours to go before I can let the beast out of his cage. This girl makes it impossible for me to think straight. My head is cloudy. I close my eyes and imagine her lying in her bed with her fingers covering every inch of her sweet pussy, wishing it was really me doing all the things I'm saying to her.

"Keep going Cruz. Tell me more."

"You like it hard and fast sometimes so that's how I'm giving it to you. Hard, fast, harder, faster. In and out, my cock rubbing against your clit. Oh, God Turnip, I can't... I can't."

I can't even form a sentence right now, but I have to hear her go over the edge.

"Faster, Harlow. I'm fucking you faster. Feel me, baby. Feel Me."

"I feel you. I feel you! Here I come..." She cries out in ecstasy, and I'm really afraid I'm going to come right in my uniform. I had to quicken this one, and I know I will do anything I have to do in order to go to that career day next week. I have to see her. It's not an option.

So, somehow I lucked out. Got a guy at work to switch days off with me, so here I am, almost to Harlow's school, and I can't wait to see my Turnip. It's been way too long. I never thought I'd grow to depend on her, how she makes me feel, how our distance only makes us stronger.

So I have three whole days with my Turnip. My normal day off, today and the next two. Thursday is Thanksgiving and me being the new guy, well, I have to work most holidays, but I don't have to work New Year's. I'll be back in Princeton for a few days for Harlow's sister's wedding.

I pull up to Grayson Elders Middle School. It's really a beautiful school. Most of the buildings here are. Old and rich, like the men who built them. I go up to the office, and I'm buzzed in. I head to the office, fully clothed in uniform for the kids. My badge on, and my gun and holster locked and not loaded.

The women in the office see me approach and flock to the front desk.

"C-can I help you, Officer?" One of the women asks me. Stars in her eyes and I'm assuming wet panties.

"Yes, ma'am. I'm Officer Raphael Cruz of the Sandy Cove Police Department and I'm here to give a lecture to Miss Hannum's seventh grade class for career day."

Pink heats up her cheeks, and she blushes.

"Oh, yes, um, you are Miss Hannum's, her um, her…" Her voice trails off.

"Her boyfriend, yes ma'am." I wink at her which immediately makes her blush, again.

"I'll escort you to Miss Hannum's room."

Another lady flies around the desk and pushes the one I have been speaking to away.

"No, no Cathy, I have this. I can take him."

"Oh no, that won't be necessary, Rose. I can take him."

They give each other the evil eye and go back and forth with one another. Obviously, there's going to be an older women cat fight in about a minute if I don't stop it myself.

"Ladies, if you just point me in the right direction and tell me the room number, I'm sure I can find it."

They look up at me and smile their fake smiles, but they do and tell me her room number is two hundred. I thank them and leave the office with the two of them still in a heated disagreement.

When I reach Harlow's room, I stop when I hear her voice. So sweet and gentle and just loving. There's a glass window in the closed door, and I can see her in the front of the room, near the blackboard, and she turns to write something, then back around to address the class. I can see her hair is up in a high ponytail, (perfect for grabbing onto later) and she's wearing her hot-for-teacher glasses.

Fuck me!

I'm not even in the same room with her, and she's killing me.

I better get this over with, so I can get her back to her place and not out of her bed for a few days. I hope she gave Willow and her family warning not to call a search party when she is M.I.A. for a few days.

Harlow Hannum is all mine.

I knock on the door of her room, and she turns and comes towards it, opening it slowly. She smiles, sending goosebumps down my bare arms.

What an affect she has on me just from a single smile.

"Officer Cruz, how lovely it is for you to join us. Please come in." She winks at me before turning back to the class.

"Boys and girls, let me introduce a friend of mine. This is Officer Cruz of the Sandy Cove Police Department. He is here to speak with you all about his career on the police force."

I hear some gasps when I enter the room. Twenty faces look at me and half of them are girls. Can you guess which ones gasped?

"Hello everyone. Thank you for having me today. Miss Hannum was kind enough to ask me to come speak with you about my job. Does anyone have any questions for me?"

I hear whispers among the kids, and I turn to Harlow, who gives me a grin.

"Boys and girls, settle down please."

I see a girl in the front raise her hand delicately, and I point to her. Her head raised, but her eyes are down, not making eye contact with me, and I see her cheeks are pink.

"Um, Officer Cruz, I... Um want to know what you think is the best part of your job?"

I don't think anyone has ever asked me that, so I have to make my answer a good one.

"Well, I would have to say the best part of my job is helping people."

She doesn't look satisfied with my answer.

"Like how do you help people?"

Ok, so I have a feeling this kid is going to give me a run for my money.

"Lots of ways."

"In what ways?"

Oh, Jesus. I look to Harlow, who is trying to mask a smile. Just looking at her makes this line of questioning worth it. Her eyes light up my soul.

"I help people who are lost, who need to find their way home, some people who are injured and need the assistance of an officer. I also take care of the bad guys, and there are some out there."

"What do the bad guys do?"

"They hurt other people, steal from other people, make life difficult for other people. But sometimes when the bad guy is caught, it makes me feel good I have the kind of job that I do. I think it's the best job around."

Harlow is now standing beside me and gives me a look that tells me I did good.

After a while and some more questioning, I show them

my gun and my badge. Most of the girls in the class, well all of them really take pictures of me with them with their phones like little paparazzi.

Harlow tells the class to thank me for coming in today. I tell them thanks for having me and give them a wave.

"Boys and girls, I'm going to walk Officer Cruz out and I'll be right back. Take out your Intro to English Lit books and continue on chapter ten."

We exit her classroom and she walks me down the hall, the only noise I hear are the sounds of her sexy heels hitting the floor. I'm suddenly pulled into some kind of dark alcove, and before I know it, Harlow's hands are in my hair, hat tossed off, of course, and her lips are on me. Her tongue searching mine. No other woman with a lip between their teeth can make me burn throughout my body like she can. I'm lost in my own erotic bliss. I'm addicted to her.

She releases me and smiles.

"I missed you like crazy, Officer. You did really well in there."

I trace her bottom lip with my thumb.

"Well they gave me a run for my money."

"I think the girls have crushes on you."

She pouts, and I know she's kidding.

"Maybe… but I only have eyes for you."

She sighs and touches my chest.

"I'm halfway through the day, so are you going to go straight to my house?"

"Yep, got my key. You know where to find me."

She gets a devilish look in her eyes.

"It better be in my bed with nothing on except a full view of those hip stars."

I laugh. She calls me insatiable.

"You got that right. Promise you'll wear those sexy

teacher glasses for me the whole time I'm worshiping your body?"

"I'm pretty sure you can bet on that."

She gives me a swift kiss, and I walk back down towards the office. I spot the two secretaries who come out into the lobby to say goodbye. A little too urgently I might add.

"Bye, Officer Cruz. Thank you so much for coming," one of them says to me.

I tip my hat. "Thank you ladies, the pleasure was all mine." And the blushing continues.

I get back to Harlow's house. She's done a great job of making this place her own. The last time I was here she didn't have any pictures hanging or trinkets or doilies or whatever chicks have lying around. Now when I walk around I see photographs of her and her family, and her and her girlfriends, but my heart stills when I see a long table leading to her upstairs lined with pictures of her and I. One from earlier in the summer and one with us fishing. There is one on the boardwalk when we all decided to act like kids and ride all the roller coasters. But the one that gets to me, that steals my breath, that makes my heart pang loudly, is the selfie we took of ourselves in her car on the way to her parents when I met them for the first time. Her eyes, big and blue and bright. Under them so much pain that I want to take away. I want to rescue her from it all. Make it so she never has to feel pain again. I look at us. Her and I.

Us.

There's an us, and I don't ever want there not to be an us. Then there's the thing that's been staring me in the face for the past few months, it's been gnawing at me like a toothache. The one thing that I swore I'd never do… Well, I did it.

I've fallen in love with her.

Damn, it.

I'm so fucking screwed.

"Honey, I'm home," I hear Harlow say in a singsong tune as I'm preparing to knock her socks off with my culinary expertise.

Not really, it's tacos, but she's a simple woman, easy to please. She walks into the kitchen and drops her bag suddenly at her feet, clearly surprised at what she sees.

"Um, where are your clothes?" She asks, placing her hands on her hips and using her authoritative teacher voice.

I continue to stir the meat in the pan, and I turn to her and address her over my shoulder.

"What do you mean? I have clothes on?"

She saunters up behind me placing her hands on my abdomen and placing a trail of kisses along my back.

"Not really, dear. An apron does not qualify as clothing. It's more of a cover up." She snakes her hands to cup my ass, and I lean my head back against her. I shut the pilot light on the stove burner off. I can't concentrate when her hands are on me.

"Why'd you stop cooking? I'm starving." I turn to face her and kiss the tip of her nose.

"I'm hungry too, but I'm pretty sure dinner can wait."

I attack her lips, just like she did in her school. When my lips touch hers, I feel like I never want them to come apart from hers again. Now that I know I'm in love with her this kiss is different. The way I even touch her feels different. I can't explain it, I'm not good at the words like she is. I just know it's different.

It really doesn't take long before she is kneeling before me, and I know she wants to do something to me she hasn't done yet. When the first lick happens, I'm out of my mind already. She takes the head of my dick in her mouth, licking it like a lollipop. I've never pressured her to give me head before, I just didn't care if or when it happened, but now that I'm in her mouth… Well, let's just say I didn't know what I was missing. She's phenomenal at this, taking me in, then pulling me out. She licks the edges of my length, and I weave my hands into her hair, holding her head as she bobs forward, then pulls back. It's not that this isn't hot, because it is, but something about this moment is more intimate than the sex we have. This is just another thing that she surprises me with, that she was willing to do this for me even though I never asked for it. I like her spontaneity, the way she's aggressive, but yet her mouth is graceful and loving. This woman could bring a grown man to his knees with her tongue and soft lips. I feel high. I literally feel like I'm floating above my body, looking down on the way she sucks me, makes love to me with her hot mouth. It's fucking insane. I don't want to come this way. I just want to be with her, be inside her.

"Baby, please, it feels so good but I need to have you, and I don't want to come this way. I want to be inside you when I come."

Shit. That just shocked me. I can't believe I would even say such a thing.

She looks up at me, still on her knees. Her long lashes and baby blues looking in shock.

"You…you sure you want that? You're ok with it?"

I suddenly feel nervous, so I place my hands under her armpits and raise her up to me, and I gently place her on the breakfast bar that's behind her.

"No, no please don't freak out sweetie. I just thought, well… I… I, um, I." I stutter 'cause I want to tell her I love her first. I want to scream it on top of a mountain, and I know I sound like a pussy, but this is momentous. Me, I mean me, I love someone. I love Harlow. This is the most special day of my life. I never thought it was possible, that I could love anyone but myself. I mean I love Antonio and Bella and Matteo, but this is being in love. Shit people do everyday, but not me, and here I am. I'm in fucking love.

"What is it you wanted to say to me, babe?" She strokes my face, searches my eyes and tries to communicate with me with only a look. I want to say it, and I go to, but my fear holds me back. So I chicken out like an asshole.

"Nothing baby. I just thought about it, but if you're not comfortable, it's ok."

She smiles and keeps touching my face, drawing an invisible line with her finger across my stubble.

"I don't care, Cruz. I can't get pregnant, and I feel so close to you and trust you, that I think it's fine." She continues to talk as I carefully, and methodically slide my hands up the sides of her legs, searching for the seam of her panties to bring them down. She keeps her sexy glasses on, which I asked her to do.

I go back to giving her soft kisses, slipping my tongue in and out of her mouth, and blazing a trail along the outline of her lower lip.

"Babe, I'll do whatever you want me to do. I just want to make you happy." Her panties dangle from one of her ankles, and she keeps her fuck me hot heels on.

"You being here with me, like this, makes me happy. I didn't think I would ever be this happy again."

I ease my cock into her, because my want and need to take her and always have her as mine consumes me. She hisses when I push into her. Her nails dig into my shoulder as I stand and control myself as I step into the bliss I call Harlow.

I love the way her arms wrap around me, holding me, as though she couldn't get any closer, even if she tried. If I could crawl into her and stay there where I'm bathed in her warmth, then that's where I'd live, with her, inside. Inside her heart, inside her soul.

The sound of our body's slapping together, her tongue licking my neck and ear, and the faint sounds she makes when she's about to come, is my undoing. My need to satisfy her, to pleasure her, is all I want. Fuck me and my pleasure, for once. Just the thoughts of what I can do to her is enough pleasure for me. I feel how responsive Harlow is to me, how her wetness surrounds me, and I don't hold back anymore. I come in her body, and all sense of reality is gone. With the exception of loving her being my actual reality. The reason for me to exist. The heat between us bounces off into the room, giving the air the scent of sex, lust and love.

I love her.

I love her.

I fucking love her.

We sit on the floor, exhausted, and we pant. I take her hand and kiss it gently, looking at her hurts so good. Her cheeks are pink, and her complexion is dewy. Her hair, well that ponytail she wore is now halfway down with tendrils all over the place. She looks like she's just been through a war, and I like it. She snuggles down into my chest and holds on to my waist with her arm. She places her ear over where my heart is and I hear her hum.

"Why are you humming, babe?"

"Because sometimes I feel the need to remind myself that you are real, that this is real, and I hum to the beat of your heart. I do it all the time, you just don't know it." I kiss the top of her head and stroke that beautiful hair of hers, wondering how this person floated into my life and how I let her.

"It's not a dream. This is happening. You and me."

I suddenly feel wetness on my chest, and I think she's crying. I sit up a bit more and adjust my body to look at her.

She is crying.

I wipe away her tears. My chest feels like it's caving in just from the look on her face.

"What's wrong, Turnip? Talk to me."

Her sobs come out in spurts, and her breathing is hitched.

"I... I don't know how we can keep on doing this. I miss you so much when you're not here. I... I thought the skyping and the phone calls were going to make it all ok, but I know I can't stand being away from you. I'm sorry if I'm acting like a baby, but I'm always honest with you and I want you to know how I've been feeling." She swipes at her eyes and looks down, linking her fingers nervously together.

"I want more, Cruz."

She has more. She has me. Every part of me and it kills me to see her like this and to know that there's nothing we can do about it right now. I have to try to make it seem better and put my best effort forward in making sure that being apart isn't a permanent thing.

"Turnip, right now, honestly this is how it has to be. It's not ideal. We both know that, but how about we wait till after next summer. You'll be back in Sandy Cove at Willow's and I'll be at Porter's. In the meantime how would you like it if while I'm here in Princeton, I submit an application to their police department, and if it happens now, then I'll move? I'll quit Sandy Cove's force and start over here, and if not, at least they have my name and application, and hopefully something in the next nine months opens up."

Before I know it, she's on top of me kissing me from the top of my head to my cheeks, my eyes, my ears, my neck. Little kisses and screams of joy fill my ears.

I laugh. "I guess you like that idea, huh, Turnip."

She wraps her hands around my neck and sits on my lap. Her smile is so bright and beaming I have to squint.

"That sounds like the most perfect idea I have ever heard." She stares at me. I take in the lines of her face, the curvature of it, the freckles that drive me insane, and the look in her eyes... That damn loving look in her eyes can make me beg, make me forget all the bad in my life. When she pulls my lips to her and kisses me, I hear the sound of my internal bell ringing that we're about to go for round two.

I'll do whatever I have to do to make her happy. I'll leave Sandy Cove. I'll leave a good job and get another just to be with her. It's a relief that she feels the same way I do. I'd move to the ends of the earth to be with her. I love her that much.

CHAPTER 15

Auld Lang Syne

Harlow~

Cruz did what he promised. He submitted an application to the Princeton police department and two other precincts in two neighboring towns. I'm going to pray with all I that have he will get hired sooner than later.

I still can't believe I cried to him the way I did, but the truth is I can't stand it. I hate being this far from him. I never felt this way, not even with Chad. I was used to him coming and going, but with Cruz that's something I'll never get used to. The warmth his body gives, the light he gives my heart, the pleasure he gives my body, mind, and soul. If I were a betting woman, I'd toss all the chips down on the table and say that last month in my kitchen, he was going to tell me he loved me. I saw it in his eyes. I felt it with every fiber of my being. I know that I'm in love with him, but for Cruz, that's a newfound emotion and an envelope I'm not going to push. Just feeling it in my heart is enough… For now.

I hear the sounds he makes when he sleeps. Soft breathing, stilling my heart when he turns over to wrap an arm around me, pulling me closer to him when he realizes I'm too far away from him in this bed. I want to see this everyday of my life. I want to wake up with him beside me, touch him, revel in this bliss. I know I'm young and twenty-four is knocking on my door, but I see myself with him for the rest of my life. It's not that farfetched. My parents were married by the time they were twenty-four and Greta was on her way. Against my grandmother's wishes, but she's a different story.

Thanksgiving came and went. We did the normal feed the homeless at a shelter, then had dinner at my parents. Grandmother wanted us to go to the club for dinner, but my parents do not believe in making people work on a holiday and missing dinner with their family. Cruz worked, but spent the morning with Bella, Tony and the baby, so I'm glad he got to see them. He mentioned his parents were on a cruise for the holiday.

Odd.

Who leaves their first grandchild on his first holiday? I didn't question it because I didn't want to upset Cruz if he already was upset about it.

The Christmas season has always been my favorite. The hustle and bustle of it. I love the lights, the music, the people pushing each other around in the malls. It's magical. This year, it's a little different. I have Cruz in my life, but he won't be here for Christmas. He's working. That low man on the totem pole thing again. It stinks. I won't see him again till a few days before Greta's wedding.

The kids in this school are crazy around the holidays. I guess they need a break as much as the teachers do, so they are getting a bit antsy, which in turn... So am I. Grading finals for this semester is exhausting. I'm looking forward to saying bye to Grayson-Elders for a whole ten days.

Willow breezes into my classroom after a brief little knock.

"Hey. You up for some drinks after here at The Barn? My treat."

She plops down in one of the desks across from me and kicks her heels off.

I tap my red pen on my desk.

"You better stick those back on. My next class will be here any minute and aren't you supposed to be at lunch?"

She lets out a breath making her straight blonde bangs fly up off her forehead.

"I suppose but I really need to get out tonight. C'mon. What do you say?"

Her whiny tone makes me roll my eyes. I know she's going to keep at me about this no matter what, but I still try.

"Wills, I haven't bought a present yet. I still have to go pick up my shoes for Greta's wedding, and I have not had a chance to get a Christmas tree or even hang a wreath on my door. The rest of my neighbors are all decorated outside with lights and those silly blowup Santa's and my house looks like Scrooge lives there."

She crinkles up her nose.

"Oh for the love of Pete! Why would you want one of those smelly things in your new place anyway. They're messy and sticky, and… Well messy. Let's just go get a few beers. I will go with you this weekend to get a tree and we can go shopping too."

See, the woman will badger me and give me every reason in the book why or why not I should do something. I could go for a few cold ones though.

"Pleeaaseee, Harlow…" Again with the whining.

I put down the red pen, even though I have to finish these grades by the end of the day. I shake my head at Willow as she clasps her hands together, pleading with me to go to damn happy hour.

"You're not going to give up are you?"

"Nope."

"I figured as much."

I stack my papers and rise out of my chair.

"Will you leave now if I say yes?"

She pops up from her seat, a huge smile plastered on her face.

"Abso-fuckin-lutely."

I point at the door as she sticks her shoes back on.

"Fine. I'll meet you at your car at four p.m. Now get out and go eat the mystery meat in the cafeteria."

She practically skips out the door after blowing me a kiss.

The Barn is a bar in Princeton we've been coming to for years. Porter used to work here and still does when he's home on break. Willow and I settle in a booth hidden from the bar area. I don't intend on staying late. I just need to unwind.

I sip on my beer and Willow and I share some fries.

"So, how's it going with the big guy?"

Obviously, talking about Cruz, I can't help but to beam at her.

"Awesome. Just simply awesome."

"I'm guessing all around. You know like side to side, up and down. Lots of up and down."

She winks at me, and I choke a bit on my sip and laugh at her bluntness.

"Oh, come on, Har. It's gotta be good right? I mean looking the way he does and the way you do. I'm sorry but I wouldn't mind being a fly on the wall to see some good old-fashioned hot fucking."

"Willow Taylor. My God, do you have no shame?"

She ponders the question and munches on a fry.

"Um… Actually, no, I don't."

We laugh together and I ease back into the booth, kicking my heels off under the table.

"He's fantastic, I will say that. But that's all I'm going to say. Somethings have to be left up to the imagination."

She closes her eyes, sighs and rests her head in her hand as her elbow holds it up.

"Yea, imagination is good." She looks dreamily, at me and I do feel myself blush as I think about Cruz and what it feels like to make love to him. Passion is his middle name. It should be on his birth certificate or something.

"Wills? Are you ever not horned-up?"

She shakes her head. "No, not really. I'm in my sexual prime. Down there is buzzing twenty-four seven." She points to her lady parts.

"Are you happy, Har?"

I nod, agreeing with her, but feeling the loneliness seep in.

"I am very happy. I miss him though. I didn't think it would be this hard to be away from him. To have this long distance thing going on. I mean we talk everyday and skype all the time, but it's not the same."

Willow finishes her beer and motions for the waitress to bring her another. She points to me as to ask if I need one.

"I'm good for now."

"Do you love him, Har?"

"Yes. I do. I think I really do."

"Do you think he loves you?"

Now there's the question of the century. Does Raphael Cruz love me? Is he capable? Will he ever be capable?

"Does it feel the same with Cruz as it did with Knox?"

I chuckle at that thought.

"Not by a long shot. I was dumb and naïve. I'm wiser to it now. With Chad, I was in a constant state of worry. I knew that when he dropped me off for curfew he went off to some other girl. It happened all the time. I was just blind and didn't see it for what it was."

She points to me with a fry dangling from her fingers.

"Bullshit is what it was. He had you wrapped around his finger for so long. It was like you were in a trance or something. I tried to pull you out, but you weren't having it."

I know all this. She did try. She would tell me about his 'extra curricular activities', but I just didn't listen or rather didn't want to. We were the golden couple. The one that people envied. All the while it was a sham and I was the joke.

Hardy, har.

"Well, it's all in the past. It is what it is. Telling Cruz

what happened between us has helped me a lot. I'm only seeing Dr. Goldberg once a week now."

She reaches over and pats my hand.

"I'm proud of you, Har. I really am. I have to give the dickcop some credit."

"Oh, yea? What's that?"

"He brought my best friend back to me, and for that I'll be forever grateful."

I was lost for a while, a long while. Withdrawing from my friends and pretending everything was fine on the outside with my family after it all happened. Willow stuck by me though. Good times or bad times I know she'll always be there.

We finish another beer and polish off the fries. We walk to our cars and before I get into mine Willow grabs me and hugs me.

"Har, you're a lucky girl, you know that?"

I hug back not really understanding what she means. I look at her and search her face for the meaning of her statement.

"I mean, Har, you have finally found someone who makes you feel special, wanted and needed. Therefore you're a lucky girl." She releases me and smacks my butt as I get into my car.

"I'll see you in the morning, unless you're up late and can't get up. You know you haven't taken a sick day yet. Typical."

She winks at me, gets in her car and drives away.

Why on earth would I take a sick day? I feel fine.

Driving home from The Barn through the streets of Princeton, I wonder what life would be like for me if I had gone through with my pregnancy. I'd have a baby to buy presents for, take him or her to see Santa and to wake up with on Christmas morning. Would Chad even have had anything to do with it? I'm guessing not. I've never really thought about what my life would have been like, especially this time of year. I really don't want to think about it. I don't want to be sad. What's done is done and I'll live with that guilt forever.

I turn down my street, my very festively decorated street and I'm searching for my dark, non-festive house... But I don't see it. I drive a little farther down, slowly, and I stop in front of mine.

Lights.

Everywhere.

My whole house is outlined in bright colorful lights. The roof line, my windows, my tiny front porch. They're everywhere. Plastic lit candy canes align my driveway and the small Japanese maple tree that sits in front of my house is adorned in the magical lights and decorated with the biggest Christmas balls I have ever seen. The four windows in the front have lighted wreaths hanging outside of them too. All I can do is stare at it. My jaw is actually dropped to the floor.

My dad sent someone over to do this, or maybe it was Craw.

I dial Daddy first. Picking up on the second ring he sounds so happy that it's me calling.

"Hey, Dad."

"Hi, Har! How are you sweetheart? So good to hear from you. What's up?"

"Dad, did you send someone over to hang Christmas lights on my house?"

"No, honey I'm sorry I didn't, but I feel bad now I hadn't thought about that sooner."

"No problem. Maybe Craw did it. I'll give him a call."

"Sweetie, you ok?"

"I'm fine, Dad." He always knows when I'm a little down from the sound of my voice.

"Harlow Jeanne Hannum? Dad knows you all too well."

I roll my eyes, but smile because he does know his daughter.

"I just miss Cruz, Dad. It'll be another few weeks until we see each other. It's hard."

Dad sighs into the phone. "Sweetie, in all the years you were with Chad, you appeared happy... On the outside, but Mom and I knew you weren't. I don't really know what transpired between you two in order for you guys to breakup, nor do I want to know, that's your business."

Oh, Dad, if you only knew. You'd probably hate me, but you'll never know.

"What I do know is that I've seen the light in your eyes return since you've been with Cruz. It's a different look than you had with Chad. Maybe it has to do with the fact that you're older, or maybe... No definitely, it's because you're in love with him."

I blush because my dad is on the phone with me, and we are discussing my love life. Crazy, but sweet all at the same time. The most significant thing about this whole conversation is... He's right. Cruz brought me back to life, albeit there may be some who tend to disagree. I am happy because he's my savior.

"Wow. You've been doing your homework, haven't you, Dad?"

He laughs in the phone. "No, it's just a sharp observation that parents make. I created you my dear and I know more than you think. You'll see someday when you have kids of your own."

I bite my lip and hold back the tears because that is a reality that will never be.

"Maybe someday, Dad. Well, I'm going to go and find out who my Christmas fairy is."

"Ok, sweetie. I'll let you go. Oh and Har?"

"Yea, Dad?"

"I just wanted to say that I think Cruz is a lucky guy."

I grin. "And why's that?"

"He has you. I'll talk to you later. I love you."

Too late for holding back the tears. My dad's words seem to have brought them out.

"I love you too, Daddy."

I hang up and shut my car off. I get out and my foot immediately goes into a pile of slushy snow. I should've worn my boots, damn it.

I close the car door and marvel at the spectacular light show that's before me. Someone actually took the time to do this for me.

It couldn't be. He's working a twelve hour shift.

Approaching my house slowly, I don't see his car as I look around my street. It would be impossible for him to be here, right? I stick my key in the front door and turn the lock and walk into a winter wonderland and a hot cop.

"Merry two weeks before Christmas, Turnip."

I wish someone was here to take a picture of my face. Because I never would want to forget the way I look right now.

"How'd you... When did you... What are you doing..." The rest of my sentence goes out the window because Cruz engulfs me in a hug and plants his sweet and sexy lips on mine.

He smells like peppermint and chocolate chip cookies, and so does my house for that matter. When he pulls away from me, he strokes my freckles and smiles.

"Thank God you didn't come home earlier. Willow did a good job."

"Wait, what!?"

"I called Willow a few days ago. She told me you were a little sad and stressed about the holidays, so right now my Sergeant thinks I'm raging mad with the stomach flu and I can't get my face out of the toilet."

Willow's a sneaky bitch, but I love her anyway.

"So that's why she got me out tonight. What time did you get here?"

He takes my hand and leads me into my living room. Before me stands the grandest of Christmas trees decorated with Christmas balls in the colors of red, green and silver. It's magnificent.

I really don't know what to say. I just stare at it and it's beautiful display of lights and pine smelling branches.

"I got here right before you left for the day. I just parked down the street away from the direction you take from work and went to work like the busy little elf I am."

Cruz comes up behind me and wraps his large, strong arms around my body and places soft kisses from my earlobe down my neck.

"Do you like it, Turnip?"

I stammer for words because there aren't enough to express to him how thankful and grateful I am for this.

"I… I just don't know what to say. It's so beautiful. I've never seen anything more beautiful."

Cruz turns me around as we stand in front of his masterpiece. The glow from the tree lights illuminates his face, and I silently thank God for this, for him.

"See that's where you're wrong."

He cups my face, strokes his thumb over my lips, across my chin and to the bridge of my nose. He lightly kisses both my eyes, then the tip of my nose before meeting back to my eyes.

"What I'm holding in my hands is the most beautiful thing I've ever seen."

I feel the pink creep into my cheeks, and the tears drift down my face.

I look up at him adoringly.

"You make me so happy. Thank you."

He pulls my body closer to his own, and he feels warm and safe to me. He's just home to me.

His lips graze my earlobe and he whispers seductively, "Have you ever had sex under a Christmas tree before?"

I giggle as his stubbly chin tickles me while nuzzling my neck.

"I don't believe I have but there's a first time for everything, right?"

Everything about this man makes me feel like I'm on fire, especially the way he eases into my body like he's savoring every inch of me. The glow from the tree lights makes the sweat from our body's sparkle, and that's how I feel inside, sparkly. It may sound a bit immature, but it's the truth. My body reacts to his in ways I've only read about or dreamt about.

When he suckles my nipples and palms my breasts as they heave from the relentless pleasure, he surges into me and I swear if I didn't hold back my orgasm would take over, and I'd be lost and upset that it was over. With Cruz though, there's no holding back. His tenderness and forcefulness is unlike anything I could have ever imagined. I never thought being with someone like this could do the things his body does to me. His lips heighten my release when he goes down on me, tasting me like I'm his last meal. Licking me, sucking me and his fingers invading all the sensitive areas he's become so familiar with. He brings me to the hilt of pleasure over and over again. The way he grips my ass just to pull my center closer to his mouth, it would honestly take no more than that to make me come. Just seeing the top of his head, gripping onto his thick waves and watching him, watching me as he eats at me makes me feel like I could drift into another world, and sometimes I feel like I actually do. When he comes up for air and kisses me, I can taste myself on his lips and the thought of that used to make me feel uncomfortable, but with this man, there's nothing hotter, nothing more erotic than the fact that my taste remains on the tongue of the man I love. God, the things he can do with that mouth of his.

It's so intimate and hot all wrapped up in the only package I need this Christmas, and it's him. Our bodies slap together with the cries and moans that I'm sure my neighbors can hear, but I don't care. My wish is for it to always be like this. When we fuck, we fuck and I discover things I like more and more when we do. Cruz likes to experiment, and I'm opening up to the fact that I do too. When we make love, that's a different story. Our high is being with each other, wrapped up in a tangled mess of lips, arms, legs and tongues.

Yes, when I come with him I see stars. I bask in the glory of our bodies intermittently coming to life. The desire when we are with each other is beyond any words I could possibly speak. People in movies make it look glamorous and dramatic and sometimes with the two of us, it is. Other times it's nothing but sheer, mind-blowing, hot as fucking hell, stick-a-cherry-on-top-of-the sundae and fuck me into next week kind of experience.

When we finish, Cruz reaches back and grabs a blanket off the sofa. He nestles his front against my back and wraps us up in it, and we revel in the beauty of the twinkling lights.

"That was unbelievable."

"I'll say," he whispers as his big arms surround me.

"It's been almost a month, baby." He beams up at me.

I'm very aware of how long it's been. Phone sex only takes you so far. Nothing compares to the real thing.

"Thank you for this, Cruz. It's so wonderful and special. My first Christmas tree in my very first home. I don't know how to thank you."

He kisses my cheek and sits up.

"No need to thank me, Turnip. But there's more."

I sit up clutching the blanket to my body.

"More? What more could you possibly do?"

He goes under the tree and retrieves two small boxes, and I look at his fine as all hell naked ass.

Oh, sweet lord, I only need that under my tree.

He turns to me smiling.

"Well presents of course and stop looking at my ass."

Busted.

I'm shocked and giddy all at the same time. I didn't get a chance to get him anything yet, and now I feel embarrassed because of it.

"Oh, babe, I haven't gotten you anything yet. I wasn't expecting you till the twenty eighth." Cruz hands me the first box, and I hesitate with it in my hands.

"Open it, Turnip. It doesn't bite."

I rip open the shiny paper to reveal a white, square box. I pop open the lid and take out the tissue paper on top, tossing it aside.

I pull out… A mug. Yes, a mug. It says 'I heart cops'. I laugh.

"Oh, honey you shouldn't have."

He smiles at me. "Smart ass."

"Look inside."

I pull out a t-shirt that's stuffed inside it.

Baby blue, like his eyes and I unroll it.

It says 'Property of Sandy Cove Police Force'.

"You like it?" I hold it to my chest. I beam at him. My smile is so big. My cop. I'm property of Cruz.

"Of course I love it. It came from you."

With a devilish grin and a raise of his eyebrows he tells me, "Now this is to be worn to bed every night by you when I'm not here, but when I am here I expect it to be worn sans panties. Got it?"

I nod. "Got it."

I lean over and give him a lingering kiss.

"So perfect," he whispers against my lips.

"Open the other one."

It's a smaller box, long and rectangular in shape. I rip open the paper and inside is some kind of gift certificate.

"YMCA?"

He shakes his head and points to it.

"It's for swim lessons."

I'm amazed at his gift. It's not diamonds. It's not pearls. It's not airline tickets for some exotic island destination. It's something from the heart. Something I need, not what I want, and I think it's the most thoughtful gift I've ever received.

"It means a lot to you that I do this, huh." He takes my hand and puts it to his lips. Kissing each finger, then reaching the palm of my hand.

"You are precious cargo my dear, and I want you safe.

You mentioned it to me after the whole dipping the toes in the water thing so I thought it would be perfect."

I reach up to stroke his perfect face, looking into his perfect eyes, feeling his perfect skin.

"It's perfect. Like you."

Our lips meet and Cruz gives me a kiss that should be in the Guiness Book of World Records for the hottest, most loving kiss.

That kiss sounds the bell for round two with my perfect man.

Christmas was wonderful. Craw, Greta and I spent the night at my parents, waking up to Mom's French Toast, and Dad making us open presents one at a time. Mom was a bit melancholy knowing that this would be the last time all three of her children would ever be under her roof on Christmas morning.

And I'll never have that. I mean I could adopt. I can't see myself going through life without children. If I end up with Cruz, who has made it clear to me in the past that he doesn't want children, that is either something I'll have to deal with in order to be with him, or something we must discuss. I'm getting way ahead of myself. I mean the man can't even tell me he loves me, even though I know he does.

Greta's wedding is tonight. My sister is getting married, and as happy as I am for her, I can't wait for it to be over. She's a pain in the ass, to put it lightly.

Grandmother had Christmas Day at her house. It's cold in there. No pictures of family, only old portraits of strangers. Like the ones you see on the Antique Road Show.

She really doesn't engage in any conversations with me. Mostly Greta. Craw and I stick together because we were cut from the same cloth.

The only time she actually asked me a question that day was if Chad was looking forward to the wedding. Now she damn well knows we aren't together, so I don't follow what kind of game she's playing. Then Greta lets out of the bag that I have a boyfriend, and he will be my date. Grandmother's only reply was "Oh."

So much for a delightfully stimulating conversation between the two of us.

I wake Cruz up by doing none other than sticking my hands down his boxer briefs.

Don't judge.

Cruz groans, but has a smile on his face at the same time.

"Woman, didn't you get enough the last few nights and days for that matter." I remove my hand from his hardness, and I straddle him.

"Nope. I can never get enough of you. In the kitchen, on the stairs, on the sofa, under the Christmas tree, on the bathroom sink, in the shower. Would you like me to go on?"

He laughs and pulls my body down onto his.

"I'm pretty sure we've covered every inch of this place."

I kiss both his cheeks and his nose, and my hand goes back to where it previously was.

"I think we have time to check out a new location? You game?"

He sends a fiery kiss to my lips, and I'm lost, as usual.

"I could never deprive you, but look what time it is. You don't want your sister going crazy 'cause you're late for your hair appointment."

I groan. "Ugh, I guess not, but you could always join me in a location we have already visited."

He looks at me with the devil in his eye. Yes, he is the devil, my devil, and if this is the way I'm going to hell, I'm fully prepared.

"And where is that?"

"Care for a shower?"

I can't think straight walking down this aisle. I hate that there are three hundred people staring at me, but my eye catches only one person. His blue eyes brazen, dressed in a tux, looking like sin on a shingle, and he's all mine. Cruz looks at me as I take each step slowly as instructed by my sister. The organ and trumpets make their sounds reverberate throughout the church. Cruz winks at me as I try to be as steady on my heels as I can. I wear heels all the time, but today I'm nervous for some odd reason. Could it be that all eyes are on me right now, or someone in my grandmother's circle is thinking 'oh, there's the granddaughter who doesn't like money,' or is it that I know Chad is going to be here and so is Cruz, and I do not want any trouble? Maybe a bit of all of the above. I take my place in one of the aisles with the rest of the bridesmaids and wait for my Cinderella looking sister to come down the aisle. She is breathtaking and looks so happy. Her fiancé, Jeff, stands in front of the altar, beaming from ear to ear. In spite of all my sister misgivings, and her unreasonable ability to make a simple situation all about her, when it doesn't, I love her very much and am so happy for her. I know she's going to have a beautiful life.

We arrive at the reception venue, which is my grandmother's country club, well my dads too. She is an owner of it, and my dad has a piece of the pie even though he doesn't have anything to do with it. Grandmother insisted he have some. Mom told him just to go along with it for argument's sake. So he's been a silent partner, only golfing there on an occasion with Mr. Knox and clients. Dad could care less about the social aspect of it, as well as the monetary part of it.

I can't find Cruz. I know he's here because I see his car in the lot. I dash around the room, trying to avoid 'hellos' from my parent's friends and my family. I ask Craw, but he hasn't seen him. I step through a set of French doors that lead onto the patio that overlooks the golf course. White lights and green garland go beyond as far as the eye can see. The smell of balsam and pine invade my senses, and I remember it's New Years Eve, still the Christmas season. The country club is most spectacular during the holidays, but the patio is a sight to be seen, especially this night as I see the one I love standing by the main fountain that has been transformed into a winter scene just for Greta. The lights dance off the water and extravagant icicles form around the edge of the fountain. The water almost looks silver against the lights and ice sculptures of snowflakes and ice skates shine in colorful prisms in front of bright lights. It is a sight to behold, except for the man who stands in front of it.

"Hey, Dickcop. Wanna do the Macerena?"

He turns around at the sound of my voice and steals my breath. I mean literally extracts air from my lungs.

"Here? Now? Or should we wait to request the band play it. It is our song ya know." I laugh and step closer to him.

"This place is magical, Turnip. Just look at it. I know that sounds weird but I have never seen anything like it before."

It's no big deal to me because I see it every year, but here's the thing, he's the one that's magical.

"Glad you like it. I'll let my grandmother know."

He looks confused, and it's because I didn't tell him she owns the joint.

"My Grandmother is an owner here, so she does this every year with the other existing owners."

He shakes his head. "I knew your family had money, but you never told me she owns part of this place. Wow."

"Yes, and so does my dad." I interrupt him before he can say anything else. "But he has nothing to do with it. He goes to a few of the board meetings and that's really it."

Cruz says nothing more, just steps towards me and wraps his arms around me. Not kissing me, just holding me, and in this moment, I want to tell him all the things I'm feeling. How the love I have for him is beyond any comprehendible word I can properly use. But not now. It's time for us to go in and have dinner. I can be patient, and I can worry about what his response will be. This is more than a fling. This is more than sex. This is my destiny we're talking about here, and I feel as though Cruz is it.

He is my destiny.

The wedding was so lovely, and Greta is so beautiful. She takes her first dance with her husband, and they look like they are floating on air. Cruz stands beside me, holding my hand, and I can feel him looking at me. Mom and Dad are so happy. I scan the crowd looking at all the guests, and I see the one person, or make that two people I was trying to avoid all night.

Grandmother and Chad.

What a lovely couple they make. Her arm is wrapped around his. He whispers something in her ear, and she laughs like he's a comedian or something. He spots me and raises his glass, Grandmother looking anywhere but in my direction.

I roll my eyes and hang on Cruz's arm a little tighter. I'm actually calm seeing him, the hunter. I'm no longer his prey, his sacrifice. He will never again rule anything that has to do with my life.

When the song ends I excuse myself from Cruz, who is now standing talking with my brother. Thank God Craw likes Cruz and is just happy that I'm happy in the process. I give them both a kiss on the cheek and scurry off to the ladies room.

I exit and run right into the chest of Chad.

"Hey baby. Lookin' good in that dress. Not that you don't always look good, plus I know what you look out of it, too." He tries his best to pull me closer to him and he reeks of scotch.

"Oh, for the love of Pete, Chad, you're drunk. Leave me alone."

He releases me when I go and push him away.

He places his hand on his heart. "Aw, baby, that hurts. Why so cold?"

I try and dodge around him several times and this little game is over.

"Get out of my way, Chad. My boyfriend and Craw are right out that door and you do not want to mess with them. You've already seen what Craw can do to you. I don't even want to think about what kind of damage my boyfriend could do to you."

He straightens out his tie and sniffs.

"Well listen, sweetheart. When you're finished playing cops and robbers with that punk out there and you wise up to the fact that he doesn't fit with you, or your family, call me. You know I always have time for you, baby."

He kisses me on the cheek, and I suddenly feel dirty. I swipe at my cheek, getting rid of the feeling of his lips on me. He disgusts me.

I walk back into the grand ballroom, and I realize it's almost midnight. I search the crowd for my piece of magic. I spot him, and he spots me. Yes, it's like those trashy romance novels or the old time black and white movies I make Cruz watch with me. Here we are in the middle of the dance floor. Midnight is fifteen seconds away, and as the seconds tick by, I'm not going another moment without telling him how I feel. I mentally prepared for it to flow out of my mouth, no questions asked, just the plain old truth.

He greets me, "Hi."

"Hi."

He grabs me and our foreheads touch as he sways my body along with his slightly.

"Cruz, I have to tell you something."

His eyes remain closed. "What is it my Turnip? Tell me."

5,4,3,2,1…

"I love you."

The swaying between us stops and he pulls his face forward looking right into my eyes. This is it, the moment of truth. He's going to say it back. I know it.

But the moment never comes. Just a tender kiss with hidden meaning. He loves me, he just can't say the words.

I should have prepared better for this. Thinking it was the most romantic time to tell the person you're in love with the fact that did indeed you love them, guess it was the wrong one.

I'll go on believing it's just that he doesn't know how to say it to a girl because he never really had to say it to someone or wanted to. But a slight amount of doubt lingers in the back of my mind. Is this all just fun for him, or does what I felt in his kiss gives me the answers I need?

CHAPTER 16

I've met the devil
and her name is Evelyn Hannum
Cruz

She told me she loved me, and I can't say it back. What the fuck is my problem?! I must be missing some sort of function in my brain. Maybe Rae did drugs when she was pregnant with me, and I have a birth defect. She stood there looking so fucking gorgeous that it stole my breath. Her eyes reflecting off the bright fireworks that danced outside the glass enclosed room we were just in. The look of love and disappointment were both reflected in them, and I feel like a total shit. Of course, I love her. Doesn't she see that? Does she actually need to hear the words? She pulls her arms around me and whispers, "Happy New Year, Babe." She gently kisses my cheek, and I whisper, "Happy New Year, Turnip."

We dance to a slow song. I inhale the scent of vanilla in her hair, the shimmer of her dewy skin, and just being with her in this moment, is one I will never forget.

"Hey, you want a drink? I'm going to go up to the bar."

She pulls away and smiles at me. "Sneak me a beer, ok? I'm going to go talk with my family."

Ha, she makes me laugh. She's a beer drinker, but at a shindig like this, no beer for girls allowed. I give her a chaste kiss and make my way to the bar.

The line is pretty long, so I pull out my phone and see I have a few texts from Max, Porter and Coop wishing Harlow and me a Happy New Year. Then my brother sent me a picture of Matteo dressed as baby New Year. I can't wait to show Turnip. She's going to love it.

I feel a tap on my shoulder.

"Mr. Cruz I presume?" I turn around to see who the disembodied person was who just spoke.

"Yes, ma'am. You must be Mrs. Hannum, Harlow's grandmother? Pleased to meet you." I stick my hand out to shake hers, but she looks at it like it's road kill.

Ok.

"Mr. Cruz, may I please have a word with you?"

This lady is scary. Silvery hair, pulled back tightly against her already surgically tightened skin, she's tall like her son and thin.

"Yes, ma'am, of course. What can I help you with?" We remain in line for the bar as she graciously waves hello to passers by, giving some of them strange kisses that only involve air.

"What you can help me with? It's what I can help you with. Mr. Cruz you are an officer of the law, correct?"

"Yes, ma'am and a Marine."

She looks at me surprised.

"Oh, a Marine."

I think I've really impressed her so far.

I nod.

"Well then, you have fought in wars I presume?"

"Yes, I have been on three active tours in Afghanistan and Iraq."

"Well then you know all about battle." She receives a glass of champagne from a white-gloved waiter, sipping it while waiting for my answer.

"Unfortunately, yes. I know all too well."

"So since you are so familiar with battle then you won't care that my granddaughter is a battle you will not win."

I am not following Granny one bit.

"Pardon me?"

She finishes the rest of her drink and gives a wave to someone calling her name to say hello. A smile proudly shown on her face as she continues to talk.

"Mr. Cruz, I know all about you. Your drug-addict, whore of a mother, your daddy gone by the time you were two, where you come from, what kind of people you associate with. You lived in filth, came from filth. And please don't bother to ask me where I got my information from. Only know that it is accurate and correct because I have power and wealth, Mr. Cruz and I have my ways. And by the look on your face, I can tell that my granddaughter is not aware of any of this, am I right?"

I nod, trying to raise my head to look for Harlow. I wish she could read minds, and I can tell her to come rescue me from this woman.

"So what would you like me to?" I say through gritted teeth.

"I'd like you to stay as far away as possible from my granddaughter. She's different from you in case you have not taken notice. We are a different breed than you, she is terribly… How do I put this… Out of your league so to speak."

I feel a sudden drop in my stomach. I've only felt this way a few times in my life. When my mother didn't come home for days when I was about eight, and when I watched some of my men blown to bits when I was at war. She knows all about me, about my life, and damn it, I should've told Harlow the truth about me, about Rae, but I was too scared. Knowing her now the way I do and loving her so much, I should've been honest with her.

I'm a coward. Add that to the growing list of things I am becoming. Good or bad.

"See, Mr. Cruz, my granddaughter was brought up with class, with money, with the finer things, things you would have no idea about. I mean did you really think a mug and a t-shirt would possibly be well suited gifts for a woman like Harlow?"

How the hell did she know about the gifts?

"Oh Mr. Cruz, your facial expressions are quite revealing. My Greta told me about the gifts. Harlow told her. Cute Mr. Cruz, cute and oh so sincere, but when is my granddaughter going to grow tired of the cuteness? Certainly not a lifetime. She is different, our Harlow, doesn't care about money or power but deep down she is a lot like my people, my class of people, and well… You just don't belong in that class."

I keep my head turned straight ahead, finding Harlow and she waves to me when she sees me.

"How could you possibly provide for her? On a police officers salary? She may act and think that money doesn't matter, but Harlow is young, naïve, and you could never give her what she really wants and needs."

"What do you suggest I do?" I ask solemnly.

"End it, now. Before she gets hurt. You don't belong together. She belongs with Chad, always has, since they were children."

Evelyn's voice isn't so warm and fake-friendly now. There's a sternness to it.

"Harlow and Chad, they fit together perfectly. You are what I call a temporary distraction until she opens her eyes and sees the truth. Chad can give her all she needs, everything her heart desires."

I swallow hard thinking about what she's saying. I feel drunk, even though I'm not, and the room is suddenly spinning out of control.

"Truth is, Mrs. Hannum, we love each other and I know Harlow. She isn't about the glam and the glitz and the things you talk about."

She throws her head back and laughs, keeping it classy, but still she mocks me.

"Oh my dear boy, you sound just like my Joseph did when he met Harlow's tramp of a mother."

"But her parents have been married for years and seem very happy. I've been in their company."

"Yes, well Joseph has always been a rebel of sorts. Harlow is a lot like her father. I couldn't stop him from making a mistake, he got her pregnant, and well… Greta came along and I know she's not a mistake but then I didn't know better. You are a mistake, Mr. Cruz. I refuse to allow my granddaughter to follow in her father's footsteps."

I've had enough of this bullshit. I become hotter and agitated, and I won't allow her to bully me.

"You are one sick and twisted old bitch, aren't you lady?" I turn and look at her, my eyes blazed with fury.

"Tsk, tsk, temper, temper, Mr. Cruz. I'm neither of those things. I am a woman who simply won't allow anymore trash into my family. Leave her. Do her and yourself a favor. If not I'll be forced to tell Harlow the truth about you, show her the evidence, then she will hate you even more. And I really would not want you to get fired from Sandy Cove's Police Department because of a positive drug test, now would I?"

She's a certifiable nut job.

"What?" I ask her confused.

"I know a lot of people, Officer, especially in Sandy Cove, so I would hate if you took your annual urine test and it came back positive for opiates. Or even if drugs were found in the McMillian's vacation house. That would simply be a tragedy. I mean what would poor Porter think of his friend then? You can't risk it. You already have a record."

She gets closer to me, invading my personal space, and I can smell the stench of her perfume, and it nauseates me. She bends into my ear. "I have my ways, Mr. Cruz. You can't fuck with Granny."

The woman is pure evil. I mean she must bleed it, but I wouldn't put it past her to do all the things she said she'd do. I could care less if I got fired from Sandy Cove, but a drug conviction I can't. I just can't.

I shut my eyes tight, thinking if I open them, she would be just a bad dream, but as I do, she's still here, smiling. Her bright red lips looking like she just tasted my blood, stole it from me like a Vampire.

"Don't say I didn't warn you, Mr. Cruz. I told you, I'm a powerful woman."

She walks away, and I'm left with the afterthoughts of everything she says.

I'm a stupid man. I should have told Harlow the truth. Not that the truth would matter anyway. Granny would go to extremes to try to keep us apart. My life, my job, my past, my… future hangs like a set of balls in Evelyn Hannum's hands.

Oh, my God, Harlow.

Now she's going to hate me. Either way she's going to hate me, and it will kill me if she does. No matter how I look at it and no matter which road I choose… I'm fucked.

CHAPTER 17

The Road to Happiness is not Paved in Gold

Harlow~

12,096,00 seconds

20,160 minutes

336 hours

14 days

That's two weeks broken down. Two whole weeks since Cruz has left, and I have actually spoken to him. Spoken with words. This does not include texts. I get answers back from those. Two word answers, but it's something.

It doesn't seem right that most of the time his phone goes straight to voicemail. His excuse: Sergeant is cracking down on phone use during shifts. Plus, he tells me he has taken on different shifts for extra money so that's why he hasn't physically called.

And I call that bullshit.

If I don't hear from him by week's end, I'm getting to

the bottom of it and quick.

I've bitten my nails down to the skin, I'm not eating like I should be from lack of appetite, and my concentration is damn near nonexistent. I don't understand it. Why isn't he calling me back? All I need is to hear him say, 'I'm ok baby. Just real busy.' That's all I need. Listening to his voice on his voicemail is not cutting it.

Willow strolls in the breakroom during our lunch time here at Grayson Elders.

Great.

Here we go with the twenty questions.

"He call yet?" Apple in hand, taking a bite of it and crunching in my face as she speaks.

"No."

"That's it? That's all you have to say?"

I look up at her, willing myself not to tear up, fearful of the truth that may lie ahead for me.

"What do you want me to tell you, Willow? No. I've left voicemail after voicemail, and he texts me back with the same old excuse. He was sleeping now he's at work and can't talk. I told you something is wrong and I can feel it in my bones."

Willow sits down and takes my hand, which only makes me want to cry.

"He's been so distant since the wedding."

"Har, let me ask you a question. Did you notice a change in him after New Years Eve when you told him you loved him?"

I think about that night. How he held me on the dance floor. How when we went back to my condo we made love. We didn't fuck, it was passionate and loving. He held me all night, never letting me go. And yes, I kept telling him I loved him, and he didn't say it back, but I felt it. I felt the love. When we were at his car when he was leaving, I could have sworn I saw a tear in his eye when we said goodbye. He almost crushed me when he held onto me so tight. So I answer Willow truthfully.

"Yes."

She stands up abruptly, pushes her chair in and pulls me up out of my seat.

"Well my friend. Hope you don't have any plans this weekend, 'cause we are making a trip to Sandy Cove."

The ride to Sandy Cove was nothing but me tapping my already chewed fingernails down to the skin. The nauseous feeling still remains in my belly even though I took one of my anxiety pills. I can feel the difference in my body from not eating. My clothes feel larger, my stomach slowly shrinking. I don't know what to say to him once I see him. Maybe it's just that he is busy, maybe he's taken all the overtime because he wants to save enough money for when he gets a job in Princeton and we can get a bigger place. Maybe he wants a new car. There very well could be an explanation to it all. I use my logic because I am a logical thinker. I don't always use it in situations, but I'm smart. Think with both things. My head and my heart. That could quite possibly be my problem.

We love each other is the mantra I keep chanting in my head.

He loves me.

I know he loves me.

We love each other.

This constant gnawing in my stomach keeps me up at night. Toys with my emotions. I can't sit still. I lash out at my students for the tiniest of things. They all guessed Cruz was my boyfriend from when he came for career day. I heard them whispering about me, saying I'm not the same and that my boyfriend must have dumped me.

Little bitches.

"We're only a mile out from Sandy Cove. Do you know where he's going to be?" I don't turn to Willow when she asks me. I stare blankly out the window, looking at how desolate this shore town looks in January. So very different from summer. The reeds of grass along the edge of the water as we cross the bridge come in to sight. Swaying in the cold winter breeze, they look brown and not the mossy green color they were a few months ago. They look how I feel.

"He doesn't go in till four, but who knows now if he's working overtime or not."

We pull through the stoplight, the sign for Sandy Cove to my left. The weathered sign brings back so many memories. Good ones. I met the love of my life here. I can admit that. Cruz is the love of my life. When you feel love in every fiber of your being, when it curls your toes, takes away your sense of direction, normalcy, steals your breath just from a touch, that's when you've known you have found him. Even just a glance from across a crowded room. That second your eyes meet. Only people who are truly in love know what that's like.

We turn down Barnacle Lane. I can feel the bile start to rise up into my throat, praying in a way that he isn't here.

Too late.

"I can't do this, Willow. I can't. I can't." I begin to hyperventilate, my breathing increasing in speed. The dizziness overrides any sense of clear thinking I had just moments ago.

Willow grabs my shoulders, the sharp feeling of her nails digging into my skin alerts me to breathe. She turns my body towards her.

"Stop this shit right now, Harlow. This is crazy. You have no idea what's going on, so stop making yourself nuts wondering. That's why you're here. To find out the answers."

I do my deep cleansing breaths and take control of the way I'm feeling. I need to be strong because when I walk through his door, there could be absolutely nothing wrong. He could sweep me up in his arms and kiss the top of my head and say, 'Hey, Turnip. I missed you so much.' That's the positive way I need to think.

I get a grip on my bearings and with Willow holding my hand, I walk up the wooden steps to Porter's house. I can hardly hold on to the wooden railing my hands are shaking so badly. My legs, well… I consider them jello. The blinds to the slider are shut, his car is here, so I know he's here and not at the station. So many times on just the flight up the stairs, I contemplated running the opposite way, but I won't run. This is my soulmate I'm here to see, to find out why he's so distant. I came here for answers.

I lean my hand against the cold glass of the slider, forgetting my gloves in the car, and the ice that has formed on it stings my perspiring hand.

"Harlow, just knock on the door. I'll be right here."

I knock once. Gently.

No answer.

"Ok, he's not here. Let's go."

Willow rolls her eyes at me and shoves me aside as she proceeds to bang on the door.

The blinds open and Cruz stands there not looking the least bit surprised to see me. He hesitates and slowly pulls open the slider, sans shirt.

"Um, hey." He pauses, not meeting my eyes directly. "What are you doing here?"

He looks funny. The brightness of his beautiful baby blues is replaced with a darkness I have never seen. His hair is way overgrown. His bare chest and arms look thinner to me in just a few short weeks.

I bite my lip, willing myself not to scream, but I answer casually.

"I haven't heard from you in weeks. I was concerned."

Still standing at the door not inviting us in, he runs his hand through his hair and looks over his shoulder into the living room.

"Harlow, now's really not a good time."

Now's not a good time?

The words bite at me.

"No, I think now is a great time. Invite me in."

When I try and nudge myself through the door, he stops me, putting his hand up, and he touches my chest. His touch… I haven't felt it in so long, and I've missed it, but his actions keep me on high alert. This is the man I love who is acting like some stranger. It's like I'm not standing before the same person. Willow steps to my side.

"What the fuck is your problem, Cruz. This is your girlfriend whom you have not spoken to in weeks. We drove all this way so she can have an explanation as to why you're being a dick."

"I told you, I've been busy. I'm working a ton of overtime and I'm tired. What do you want from me?"

I step away trying to get a good look at the person who stands before me, still not meeting my gaze.

"What do I want from you? I want to know why you're avoiding me. You don't take my calls, or answer my messages. You give me one or two word answers in a text, and you know what, it's bullshit. I want answers and I'm not leaving here until I have them." I stand my ground. I won't allow myself to be the girl who curls up and hides away from all her problems. I'm here to face whatever it is I need to deal with and if my heart breaks in the process, then so be it, but at least I'll have answers.

He slams the slider closed. The blinds flap from the strength of it, and I'm not hesitating. I'm going in.

I push open the slider and Cruz grabs his shirt from the arm of the sofa as I trail behind him. As he slips it on over his shoulders, I grab his strong arm and pull him around so he's looking at me.

"God, damn it, Raphael. Look at me!"

He shrugs off my hand, running his hands through his hair, pulling at it with force.

"Why, Harlow? Don't you get the hint?" He steps away from me, smugly adjusting his shirt and smoothing his unruly hair.

"I mean seriously, this whole thing was fun, but… Well…"

He paces around, acting anxious, and it infuriates me because he's not making sense. I move closer to him, but he steps away, almost like a game of cat and mouse. I step around the sofa towards him. He goes to the other side, like he's afraid for me to get too close.

"Hint? I can't take a hint. What are you trying to say, Cruz?" My heart accelerates. I can feel the beat of it inside my head, through my ears. I swallow hard trying to get rid of the lump that has formed in my throat. Searching inside my heart for a reason he's being like this.

He throws his arms up towards me in desperation.

"Oh, for Christ's sake, Harlow. Let me get it into that big brain of yours." Finally, he steps to the other side of the sofa, meeting me, looking at me, but not really looking at me.

"You knew what you were getting when we started this whole thing."

"What the hell are you talking about?" Tears threaten to spill, but I hold back. I'm waiting for the validation. The words that will make me walk away. He's silent. Maybe thinking of the next bullshit excuse to give me.

"No, apparently I didn't. So tell me, be the tough, macho guy you are, and just tell me. And don't you dare fucking hold back on me, Cruz. That's not who you are. Just say it."

My tone is still calm as the words leave my lips.

"Just say what?" His tone the opposite of mine, and I'm startled by the rage that's obvious in his voice.

"Just say what you really are. What this all was. I need to hear you say it. I'm not answering what your perception was of what I was getting when we got together."

He smirks, arrogantly.

"Oh, please. Like you don't know. I'm exactly the same person I was when you met me last year."

I yell. My arms folded over my chest because he's lying.

"Bullshit."

"Bullshit?" He questions back at me.

I nod.

"Fine. You think that all you want, but the truth is you were just a fuck. I didn't have time to go out and explore my options, so I thought you'd be a willing and able candidate. I mean really, how convenient, living next door to me."

Self-righteous is the only description I can decipher his words. I don't believe him, not a word. This can't actually be how he's thinking. Maybe he's drunk, maybe he's high. That's not possible. It can't be possible. I talk myself out of every scenario. I observe every part of his body language, and I know he's neither one of those things.

I lean against the wall near the sofa, crossing my feet and arms. "I think you're a liar." I chuckle as the words come out.

He looks at me confused, dipping his head towards the side and bracing himself on the back of the sofa.

"Excuse me?" He asks.

"You heard me." I uncross my feet and make my way towards him step by step.

"You. Heard. Me. There's no way in hell that this was just some fling for you. I'm not just a fuck. We both know that." As I keep up my movements, languidly towards him, he backs up, not meeting my eyes but his feet move backing up against my steps until he hits the counter of the kitchen.

"I love you and you're scared because you love me. You're just too afraid to admit it. I feel your love everywhere, even when we're not together." I grab his hand and place it over my heart. He hesitates and I can feel it warily, but I don't give up. My strength overpowers his for a change.

"That's my heart. You feel it? It doesn't belong to me anymore... It's yours. You replaced all the sadness I've felt. You made me feel things again. You made me feel whole."

His eyes finally meet mine, his mouth agape. I see a bit of the sparkle in his eyes and the tension in his hand subsides, and I think he's coming back to me. He's out of the trance, and now he won't be afraid to love me, to tell me.

He closes his eyes, feeling my heartbeat beneath his hand.

I whisper to him, "I know you love me."

His relaxation is temporary, because now I see the darkness return as his eyes open.

He winces and pulls his hand back.

"Woman, you are delusional. I don't love you, Harlow. Fucking is not love. You must be confused with someone else. See that's what I do, I fuck, then I leave."

I shake my head. "No, you don't mean that. I changed you. You changed me. There's no way you mean what you say. You do love me. You don't do the things you do to someone whom you don't love. You don't surprise them with visits, or Christmas winter wonderlands, or come to family weddings with them and say the things you said if you didn't love them." I wish I could step into his brain and permanently implant my words into his brain.

He goes to the refrigerator, pulls out a beer and flips off the cap, tossing it into the sink.

"No. I don't. God damn it! What does it take or what do I have to do to convince you?" He steps into my line of sight, almost touching his nose to mine. My breathing falters. I inhale taking in every scent of the man I love.

"You did change me in a way. See, I never go back for seconds. You were my first, but then I came to realize that your pussy isn't golden and it sure ain't worth a two and a half hour drive. If I want some, I can get it at any place, at any time, at my immediate disposal." Stepping away, he chugs the rest of his beer, and Willow makes her way to him, fists clenched, and ready to strike.

"You no good ass. I warned her about you. Porter told me your deal and I warned her. Who the hell would even allow you to fuck them with that probably diseased dick of yours?" She turns to me. "Sorry, Har. I really didn't mean you."

Before he has a chance to answer her, I hear something come from his bedroom. Something dropped, and then I wait and hear it again.

He has someone here. He's with someone else, they're in his room. I caught him. This is what this is all about. When he realizes I heard what I heard, he shrugs. The look of total satisfaction on his face. But it's not his face.

"What did I tell you, any place at anytime." He smugly smiles. "I'll give you credit for a few things, Harlow. You are one fantastic lay. You're hot, but way too damaged for me. The baggage you have well exceeds what I can handle. You told me yourself you're crazy. I've had my share of nutty women, but oh… Man, you take the cake."

I don't even think the words leave his mouth fully before I lunge my body at his.

I punch. I slap, and claw at him, not giving him time to react because my movements are swift.

I scream at him not really hearing myself, but I know the words that implode.

"I can take you not wanting to be with me 'cause you think I'm crazy, but I won't allow myself to be cheated on again. I put up with it for years and years and I fought to be first when I wasn't. I want to be first. I'm tired of being second choice. I don't care who… who is in there. All I know is I'm second choice again and I hate you for it. I really ha… ha… hate you."

There's no more strength left in my body to fight anymore.

All I can get out is about a thousand more 'I hate you's'. He stands there taking it until Willow pulls me away. I fight her when she grabs my upper arms to get me away from him. I really can't make out his face through my tears.

He pushes off the counter.

"That's right. Solidify how crazy you are. Keep it up. Gives me all the more reason to be happy that this is over. You just love to be in love, don't you? Well, I don't do love and the quicker you get the fuck out of here and out of my life, the better."

I can't breathe.

No air.

There's no air.

There's nothing.

Oh, God help me. Please someone, help me.

Willow pulls at me to the door, as sweat pours from my face. I will go. I'll leave, but I have one last question for him as I feel my heart shatter like a glass globe crashing to the floor. I turn looking at him for the last time. He seems unaffected, just standing there with his arms folded across his chest, feet spread apart in a defensive stance. I swallow my tears hard, tasting the salt.

"Why?" I question him barely getting the word out.

He pauses, looking at me, well really through me, through my soul and answers. Finally.

"Because I can."

CHAPTER 18

Can't Turn Back Time

Cruz

"You know that I really wanted no part of this collaboration, right?"

I nod my head at Max, who exits my bedroom.

"And you know that as soon as Harlow and Willow go back home, Willow will tell Porter everything and he will kick you out of here?"

Again, I nod.

"And you know that everything you just said to her, you can never take back? She's going to hate you."

I exhale and look out the window to our dock, and I know that everything Max just said is true.

"Cruz? You gonna talk, or are we just going to stand here and wait for the apocalypse? " Looking over at Max, the sick feeling in the pit of my stomach returns.

"I've already packed most of my shit. I fully expect to

hear from Porter first thing tomorrow. I'm surprised Craw didn't call him in the first place after he left me that message that Harlow was on her way here and I…"

I pause, thinking of the words I said to her. How I just destroyed her. I destroyed the only thing in my life I ever loved, that I was ever sure of. The one thing that loved me back without thinking of the person I actually am.

"I want her to hate me. It's the only way."

Max sits next to me on the couch after grabbing the bottle of Jack out of the cabinet and a few shot glasses. I can't stop shaking. It's like I'm outside the door in the twenty degree weather, but I'm sitting here on this sofa not fully comprehending what I just did. My knees shake so bad I can here the bones clang together.

"What did Craw's message say?"

I lean back on the sofa and scratch my two day old unshaven face.

"Called me a mother fucker and that I better not be playing games with his sister or else he'll kill me."

Max shakes his head to agree.

"Craw's pretty tough. Surprisingly, I wouldn't put it past him. I heard what he did to that asshole Knox."

That asshole Knox ruined her, then she found me, now she's right back where she was and it's going to kill me.

He pours two shots. "I'm pretty sure she bought the fact that there was a girl in your room." We don't clink glasses. We don't cheer to the fact I just broke someone's heart. We just chase down the amber liquid hoping it warms my body and stops it from shivering, but see I'm cold, everywhere. In my heart and in my fucking soul.

"I know you feel as though you had to do what you had to do, but she loved you man, and I'm betting if you told her about her Wicked Witch of the West Grandmother, she would have put her foot down. I mean her mom went through something almost similar, right? That's what you told me."

I nod, throwing back another shot. It burns. It burns so bad.

"It's better this way. I could never give her what she wants, what she needs. I'm poor. I'm a cop, and I have a record from when I was eighteen. I'm lucky I'm even a cop."

Max looks at me confused and I remember he doesn't know.

"Oh that's right. You don't know the story. Tony and I were busted when he was twenty and I was eighteen. Cops came looking for my mom, they found her stash of weed. We told them it was ours, so she wouldn't get thrown in jail."

"But you fucking hate your mom. Jail would've been the best place for her. She could've sobered up there."

Max is naïve.

"No, man, she'd be worse off. Drugs are so easily accessible in there." I've always felt the need to protect that woman, as much as I despise her.

"I still have it on my record. That's why I went into the Marines."

"I see." He pours another shot. "So what now?"

I close my eyes and imagine a future without Harlow in it, and I hate it. It's bleak and dark, like my heart.

I take a letter out of my pocket and hand it to Max.

He reads it, looks to me, then back to the letter.

"You were hired by the North Ridge Police Department? That's like the next town over from Harlow. What the fuck man. When did you find out?"

I take it back from him and crumple it, tossing it over my shoulder.

"I found out last week. I drove down there two weeks ago for the interview without letting Harlow know. Then I got the letter, which made me decide to do what I just did. We would never be happy. Her grandmother would've crushed me and made our lives miserable."

"So your plan was to crush Harlow instead? You love her, dude."

I do love her, with my whole fucked up self.

"She's better off without me. She'll be happier. I'm not good enough for her. I know it, and she'll come to know it."

Max stands up and grabs his coat from the hook in the hallway.

"I gotta go man. I know you have your reasons but I wish you'd at least given her the chance to make the decision for herself. I think she would have understood the truth about the way you grew up, about your mom… About everything. Truth is a powerful thing, and you know what man, love… It's the only truth. Truth is love." He gives me a pat on the shoulder and makes his way out my door.

I can't go back and change what I did. I'll live my life without her. Yea, a piece of me died, true, but I'd rather live with the burden of my broken heart, than her having a lifetime of hers broken because I couldn't give her the life she deserves. Our lives are so different, and mine would only wind up damaging hers in the end.

She'll be ok. She'll move on, and it will be the best thing for the both of us.

Yea, she'll realize it. Maybe not tomorrow, but she'll forget about me.

She'll be ok.

She'll be ok.

I'll be ok.

I'll be ok.

I'll keep telling myself that because I have to. I'll pound it into my head until I've brainwashed myself into thinking it for both of us.

Love is truth, truth is love.

CHAPTER 19

Cruz & Harlow

Harlow~

4 Months Later...

It's not like I want to come back here, ever, but I know my friends will keep him away from me if I see him. If he sees me.

I'm doing ok. I'm only down to three sessions a week with Dr. Goldberg, and I'm only on the anti-depressant now. No more anxiety pills. Yoga helps. Therapy helps. Teaching helps, and knowing that to me, he no longer exists in my life, helps too. I've worked on it... Well, on myself.

So what has happened in the last four months of my life? Not a suicide attempt, that I'll tell you. Locking myself in my condo for a week, wallowing in self-pity and calling out sick with the flu, yes, that happened. Craw, Willow and Thea bringing me food that I didn't eat, yes, that happened too.

The girls helping me bathe my disgusting body, yes, that happened as well. Then it came to me. My self worth. I don't need anyone to love me. I have to love myself first and take it from there.

Doing that doesn't mend everything, obviously, that's why I see Dr. Goldberg three days a week.

Teaching helps. My mind is consumed with those kids and their bright minds. It's amazing what I can see from my point of view when I'm teaching them. It opens my mind up to the infinite possibilities that there's more to life than depending on one person to make you happy. You have to be happy with yourself first and foremost.

A few weeks after we broke up, I started to keep a journal. I write down every single thought I have in my head. Dr. Goldberg said it's a good outlet. I have to agree. I don't hate him for what he's done. I have come to forgive him. He was right. I couldn't change him from what he was like before. A leopard doesn't change his spots. When I heard that person in his room, I knew that we were done. Up until that point, I think I would have fought harder, but cheating and saying the things he said in the process… Well, it doesn't fly with me. I put up with it from Chad for years. Sneaking around behind my back, smelling like a different girl all the time. I won't allow myself to be made a fool of again. I'm stronger than that now. Why should I always fight to be someones first choice? I should automatically be theirs.

Willow forced me to come just for the weekend. It is Memorial Day. The start of the summer. I'm only staying for the night. That's all I can handle right now.

Porter kicked Cruz out of his house as soon as we came back that day. Drove down himself, but Cruz was already gone. Odd, but I'm guessing he already knew that Willow would rat him out, and I'm like another cousin to Porter, so he wouldn't put up with me being hurt. He hasn't talked to him since. Max told him he's living in Sandy Cove somewhere, but didn't say where exactly. Craw is the one I was worried about. He went down to Sandy Cove looking for him. I tried to stop him, but he didn't find him anyway. He wasn't even on duty.

So here we are at The Boat Stop. The place that opened last summer. I wanted to come here instead of Jax. I didn't want to go there. Too many memories. I'd probably take up ten pages in my journal from one night at Jax.

I casually sip on a beer and sit at a table with the girls and Porter.

"Max coming down?" Willow asks.

"He's around here somewhere I think. Why do you want to know?"

"No reason." And she goes back to drinking her beer and avoiding any kind of eye contact with us.

"Son of a bitch. Here comes Chad." Willow growls and is ready to pounce. I hold her arm down as she attempts to stand up to probably knock him out.

"Wills, it's ok. We've run into each other a few times around home and we have spoken, briefly, but we have." She gives me an ominous look which I can't avoid.

"It's just talking. Believe me, once with him was enough." I see Chad approach cautiously, and I muster up the confidence to give him a friendly grin.

"Hey, Harlow."

"Hey, Chad. How are you?"

"Good, good. You look great. Can I… Um… Buy you a drink?"

I raise my almost full beer to him.

"No, I'm good." He leans in slightly to me, trying not to

allow anyone to hear him.

The anyone means Willow.

"Har, do you think we can talk? Please. There's some stuff I need to say."

Now do I stay, or do I go? The old me says to go to him, the new me says to stay away, but since we've talked back home, I'm not afraid. It's not like I'm going to fall for his charms again. Be the prey of the hunter. I'm fine on my own. Don't get me wrong, he is the devil, but maybe he wants to apologize for all he's done to me. I have learned to be a forgiving person. I can't forget. What happened with us, it changed my life, but I can forgive.

"Sure." I tell him.

"Harlow. Are you crazy?" Willow yells above the crowd.

"It's fine. My God. What do you think is going to happen? He's not going to kidnap me." I push back my chair and follow Chad outside to the makeshift beach area off the side of the restaurant part of the place.

We stand here. He's far from me which is good. So I'll wait to hear what he has to say.

Cruz

"She's in there. I know she is, Cruz. Go in there and get her back."

Max paces in front of my patrol car in his Chucks, and he's going to wear them out if he keeps it up.

"I'm not going in there, man. Plus I'm on duty. I can't do it. She hates my fucking guts."

Max jumped in front of my patrol car at the station as I was pulling out to go on duty. He told me Porter had called him to tell him that Harlow, Willow and Thea were here and for him to meet them at The Boat Stop. Two reasons why I'm not going in.

Number one, obviously Harlow, and two, Porter. He will kick my ass. He hates me for what I did, and we haven't spoken since he kicked me out of the house. Just another thing I lost in the process of breaking the girl's heart. I lost one of my best friends. I tell myself it was all worth it. I know she's ok. She's better off without me. Max gets updates from Porter, and Max tells me, not that I want to hear because it kills me. It fucking kills me to even hear the sound of her name. From what I hear, our breakup put her back in therapy a few more days a week, and they were all pretty worried about her once she got back that day after I ended it. I threw up when I heard that. I knew what she went through before and how she wound up in therapy because of Chad. It crushes me to think about how this time I was the cause of her going through another breakdown.

If I thought I turned into a pussy when I was with her, ha, ha, you should see me now. Watching those old black and white movies she loves so much, just so I can feel like I'm still a part of her. She'd turn one on when we were snuggling on the sofa and the look in her eyes when the movies started, damn you'd think they just announced she won the lottery or something. That look in her eyes made me love her even more. Seeing someone you love so much adore something so much makes all the problems you have seem to melt away. Temporarily.

I go to the beach sometimes and just dip my toes in the water and imagine how it felt for her to be so scared of it.

When I'm on duty, and I have to drive by a school at dismissal time, I think of her, and I look at my watch, thinking that this is the time she'd be done with her day, saying goodbye to her students. I imagine her with her black rimmed glasses on, her hair frazzled by the end of the day, but once she's home, her heels come off. The fuzzy slipper socks go on, and a cold beer is on her mind then in her hand. I think about her mostly the nights when I'm not on duty. The nights where I lie awake and wish things were different. Hell, who am I kidding. I think about her every second, of every day.

Her scent is gone from the pillow I stole. It just smells like... Well, nothing now. The strands of her hair have fallen off of it, and I'm left with one picture of us. The one we took in the car, the one she had in her place that was framed. The one she put in a frame for me and gave to me on New Years Eve. The others, I burned them on the dock, our dock. I mean the dock, and let them fall into the water. I can't have that much to look at of her. The one picture I just couldn't do it. I couldn't destroy it, like I destroyed her.

Pictures are just pieces of paper. The memories I have of her, of us, play like a movie in my head. Constantly.

To answer all further questions, I have callouses on my hands. Yes, I said callouses. I haven't been with anyone that way, but my hand since I left her the day after New Years. I mean I haven't completed the job. I can't do it. I tried... But Morty, well, I guess he's mad at me. I kissed a few girls, but all I see is her face, smell her scent. The bodies don't feel the same. The softness of her hair, her skin, her breasts. Her taste, no other could ever compare to her. I am always talking myself out of her memory. I've even murmured her name a few times while making out with someone. Got a kick to Morty and a few slaps to the face for those. But I deserve it. A few more months and she'll be out of my head.

"You're a dumb mother fucker, you know that? I've had

to deal with your miserable ass for months now, and you know what conclusion I've come to?"

I roll my eyes at him. "What's that, Max?"

"You're a fucking pussy bitch. You're not the tough guy, the man-whore. You're nothing that you want everyone to think you are. You're nothing but a selfish, fucking prick."

Little bastard. Whose he think he's talking to?

He steps closer to me, and I give him a warning look.

"You had something you wanted your whole life in your hands, right there." His hands are cupped out in front of me, palms up.

"Fucking love. You let it go because you think you're not good enough. Did you ever stop and think that maybe you are and you never even gave Harlow the chance to base her own decision on the facts? You never even gave her a chance to hate you, not that I ever thought she would. I always thought she'd understand about your family and your fucked up life. And fuck what Granny does and says. She may be powerful in Princeton, but who's to say she has it anywhere else."

Jesus, what if he's right.

Oh, God. What the hell have I done?

I get my bearings and start to pace like Max, and he can see the trepidation in my movements. He stops and looks at me.

"You're going to go get her aren't you?"

I take off my cap and pull at my hair.

"She'll hate me, Max. I fucking destroyed her. I did. What I said to her, I can't make her see that it was to protect her."

"Try, Cruz. Just try."

I spin around 'cause I hear her name. I hear someone call her fucking name, and I follow the voices that I hear speaking. Max is close behind. I look around the other side of the building.

She's here. My Turnip is here.

With Knox.

Harlow~

"What was it you wanted to say, Chad? I really don't have a lot of time."

Here we stand practically face to face. He looks uncomfortable and edgy.

"I just wanted to say the thing I've wanted to say for a long time, and it's sorry."

I smirk. "Took you long enough, Chad. It's all fine though. I've learned to forgive you and myself. We just need to move on." He steps closer to me, and I don't want him to so I step back.

He calls out my name, "Harlow, please."

"Turnip." I turn around, startled by the name I just heard and from the voice it came from.

He steps towards me, my heart races. My mouth goes dry, and I look at him, and my heart weeps. It weeps and melts because I love him so much still. I know it as soon as I see his beautiful face.

However, he dismantled me and I struggle with it everyday, no matter how busy I keep myself. So now I'm stuck. Do I run to him and tell him I still love him, or do I turn the other way and not look back?

Be the bigger person here, Harlow.

"What the hell are you doing here?"

"I heard you were going to be here tonight and I need to talk to you." I turn back in the direction of Chad.

"I don't want to hear anything you have to say."

Chad grabs my hand. "Come on, Har. Let's go talk some more. I'm not finished saying what I have to say and I need you to listen to me, please." He tugs me, and I step into pace with him.

"Daddy's boat is here. We can talk privately there." We go towards the dock where the boat is.

"Harlow, wait. I have some things to say too. Just don't go with him." His voice pleads with me. "Please, just stop, stop and listen to me."

Cruz

She stops, but doesn't turn around. Her head is bent down, then I see her slowly raise it.

"Harlow!" I demand.

She turns sharply in my direction.

"What? What do you want, Cruz? What could you possibly want with me? Can't go back and change stuff, remember? One pussy is not good enough for you, your words, not mine."

"No you don't understand…" She stops me from speaking.

"No you don't understand. You told me I'm too messed up in here." She points to her head, and I feel sick.

"You told me I was a convenience. Like a friend with benefits. Well, I'm no one's second choice. I won't be, not ever again. I told you that the day you wrecked me. I was your experiment, wasn't I? Your test of the sloppy seconds endurance. Well, you succeeded in your quest for the truth."

Asshole Knox grabs her hand again.

"Come on, baby, we need to talk."

I step closer to him.

"Fuck you, asshole. I need to talk to her."

He smirks at me and laughs.

"You had your chance with her before you screwed it all up. Don't think I don't know what happened. Princeton's not such a big town."

I charge at him with all the adrenaline I have in my body. Knox lunges for me as well, but Harlow steps between us and Max hold my arms back.

"Both of you, stop it now. Chad, go to the boat, I'll be there in a minute. I need to deal with this."

Harlow puts up her hand and points to the boat.

"Go!" He doesn't move. Harlow squeezes her eyes shut tightly and yells, "I said now, Chad!" He walks away backwards, not looking away from my eyes.

He yells to me, "We're not done here, Officer. She knows what she wants, and that's not you."

"Fuck you," I yell back to him.

I try and move a little closer to her, but she takes a step back when I do.

That's fine. I'll tell her all the things I have to say to her from a short distance.

"Harlow... Turnip."

She looks away from me. "Don't call me that."

"Harlow, it was a mistake. I made a mistake and I need to tell you everything. I need to tell you all of it. Beginning to end. Will you listen?"

She shakes her head from side to side, folding her arms across her chest. I'm so afraid she's going to say no.

"Want to know what your only mistake was? Better yet what mine was? Looking at you from across the bar that night we first met. Just the little eye contact we shared was the first in a long line of mistakes I've made along the way with you. So when you say it was a mistake, yea, Cruz it was. From that first night till now. All of it was a mistake."

I grab her arm, gently as she begins to walk away. She whips her body around, her hair spinning like a windmill, and I look at it knowing how much I've missed touching the silky strands, and all I want to do at this moment is wrap my hands up in it, but I can't. I need to slow this, slow myself. I'm in love with her, and I have to tell her... Now.

A voice comes over my radio that's attached to my shoulder.

"Officer Cruz. We have a domestic disturbance at 321 Anchor Lane, and we need back up, do you read me?"

Fuck!

I hold up my finger to her.

"Officer Cruz here. I'll be there."

I have to leave. I don't want to walk away. I'm afraid if I do, she'll go to Chad. He's put her under some trance. He'll tell her all kinds of bullshit and my chance will be gone, but I have to.

"I have to go, but please, I really need to talk to you. Meet me later around midnight. Please, Harlow?"

Her eyes are so distant, but with mine, I plead to her. I need her to listen to me and understand why I did what I did.

"I... I can't, Cruz. It's taken me four months to forget what you said to me, and no matter what you say now, it doesn't change the fact that you said them. You can say sorry all you want, it doesn't change things."

The voice comes over the CB again, but I don't care.

"What if... What if I told you I loved you? That I didn't mean a word of anything I said to you that day."

She laughs, an uncontrolled vibrating laugh, that goes

through me and hurts because I know she doesn't believe me.

"Oh, please. You're incapable of it. You don't know the meaning of it. I told you I loved you and you treated it as though it was just another word in the English language. But it isn't, at least to me. You didn't love me, Cruz. I was the game. The game you lost, or won, however you want to look at it. When you love someone you feel it everywhere, you live it, you breathe it. It's not something to toy with or take advantage of. But to someone like you... You wouldn't understand that concept or even try to."

I'm losing her. I can feel it. She steps away with her head held high, looking directly at me. She doesn't see it. She doesn't see how much I love her.

"I gave my whole heart to you, you threw it back. What am I supposed to do with that knowledge now?" I reach for her, but she retreats.

"I have to go. Leave me alone."

She runs away towards the boat where Knox is.

Mother fucker.

I'm not giving up. Not by a long shot. I'm not letting her go without a fight.

CHAPTER 20

I Should Have Given In

Cruz

We need all available officers in the area to report to The Sandy Cove Marina immediately. We have a hospital case boating accident with multiple injuries, possible fatalities and coast guard rescue is en route. Do you copy?

"Copy."

Great. My night will be full of activity so I don't have to sit here and think about how I lost the only thing that matters, or mattered in my life.

Damn it, I should have done so many things differently.

I turn on my sirens and race over to the marina. There's already a slew of police vehicles and several ambulances. I'm hoping there aren't any fatalities. Not sure I can handle that tonight. When I step out of the car I can hear screams, as I get closer I can see a girl on the ground rocking back and forth and someone behind her rubbing her shoulders.

Willow!

I run full speed and crash to the ground in front of her. Porter is behind her consoling her.

"Willow? Porter? You guys ok? What the hell happened?"

She's crying so hard, she can't speak.

"Thea, sit here with her." Porter releases Willow's shoulders and takes my arm to pull me to the side. They all seem to be ok, no injuries, so why's everyone so fucking upset?

"What the hell is wrong with Willow? She know anyone in that accident?"

He braces my shoulders, crying as he does so.

"Cruz, there's... Oh, God, there's been an accident."

"Yea, I got the call, that's why I'm here. Why are you all so upset? Is it someone we know?"

"Cruz, look at me. Look. At. Me. It's Harlow. She was on Chad Knox's boat, he was driving and they hit another boat. She was knocked unconscious and she was in the water for a long time. She's wasn't breathing when they pulled her out."

"What do you mean she's not breathing?"

I think what he just said is a dream. I'm so confused. That can't be the truth. He's lying. He's fucking lying. I just saw her... It's not her.

"She can't swim." My voice is small when I say the words, because she can't, and I'm scared. I tried so many times to teach her, even going as far as getting her those damn swim lessons.

"I know, buddy that's why..." He stops talking to me and looks over my shoulder.

"There's Knox."

I'll fucking kill that bastard. I run over to him. He's

sitting on a curb wrapped in a blanket. Police surround him, and an EMT is listening to his heart. I rush over to Knox, pushing everyone out of my way. I grab his shirt and tug him upwards. I shake him not bothering to see if he's hurt. I don't fucking care.

"What did you do, you fucking prick? What did you do to her? I'll kill you, Knox. If she doesn't survive you will wish you were dead. Do you hear me, damn you?"

I can feel hands on me trying to get me to let go of him. I want to hit him so bad. Pulverize him. He just stands there, speechless. The bastard looks fine. Why the hell were they even out on the water anyway? She hates the water, she's terrified of it. How could she agree to it?

All I hear him say is, "I'm sorry. I'm so sorry."

If I had my way, they would be the last words Chad Knox would ever speak.

Out of the corner of my eye, I see the EMT's pull Harlow onto a gurney, and I fly over to where they are. I run through the mass of people surrounding the marina and all I know is I have to get to her. I have to see if she's ok.

"Harlow, Harlow!" I'm screaming her name, but I don't hear myself. "Harlow, baby!"

She's blue, and there's a deep laceration to her head.

I hear someone tell me to get back, but I pay no attention.

"That's my girlfriend, damn it! What happened? Why... why isn't she breathing?" No one is answering me.

"Harlow, baby, can you hear me? Please wake up, baby and look at me. I'm here. You're going to be ok." I touch her hand, but that's all they will let me touch before they try and pull me away again.

"Sir, we have to get her to the trauma unit. She was in the water for a while before the coast guard got to her. We need to help her now, please step aside and let us do our jobs." I look to the EMT, and if he thinks I'm leaving her side, he's nuts. Swiping at my face, the tears flow faster than I can wipe them away. I grab her hand again and tell them I'm going with them. I see Porter stand by holding Willow and Thea. I yell out to him that I'm going in the ambulance.

"We'll be right behind you." I think I hear him say.

They put Harlow in the back and I follow.

On the drive I hear words that scare me.

Coding.

Unresponsive.

Intubate.

They put some electrical thing on her chest and her body jumps, and I cry harder. I haven't cried since I was... I can't even remember. This is the love of my life here, and I'm so afraid of losing her... Again. There's no color to her face, they stick a tube down her throat, her beautiful hair, now blood-soaked. All I can do is sit here and watch them try to bring her back to life. They stick her with needles, lift the lids of her eyes and shine lights in them. They poke and prod and speak a language I don't understand. We're moving so fast it's like we are in some kind of high powered death trap. Every bump, every pothole we hit on the road, I feel. My body bouncing upwards in my seat. They won't let me hold her hand. They won't let me near her. I can't help her. For once, I can't help her.

EPILOGUE

Week Four

Cruz

I have my routine down pat. I sleep in this chair next to her bed. Bella and Tony bring me new clothes every few days. I shower at ten a.m. when the Physical Therapist comes in to do exercises with her. I finish and step outside for a brief few minutes just so I can get fresh air. I don't stay away too long. What if she wakes up and I'm not there.

At noon, the nurses bring me lunch, but I never eat it. Max and Porter will bring me in a sandwich from my favorite deli when they come to visit. At one, the nurses come in and bathe her. After they are done they leave the hair brushing to me.

That's my job.

I usually spend upwards to a half hour doing it. It relaxes me. The feeling of her hair in my hands.

I usually doze off from two to two forty-five.

The residents usually come in to assess her, and I wake up and it's my cue to go into the hall.

Around four, I log on to my online class and do a bit of homework. I lost my job on the force because I refuse to leave here, but it's ok. I have plenty in savings and they told me I'll always have a rent-a-cop job here when I'm ready. I gave up my apartment. My stuff is at Bella and Tony's for now.

The words visiting hours don't exist in my world. This is my home until she goes home.

Harlow's mom sleeps at the house she and her dad rented in Sandy Cove since the accident. Other than that, she's here sitting with me, beside Harlow from sun up to sun down. Her dad is here almost as much. Craw is here everyday. He decided to take a leave of absence from his final semester and temporarily moved down here. He started talking to me again once I told him everything. The information I gave him was after he threw a couple of punches at me, and I let him. I let him curse me out, spew hateful words to me, which I deserved. Her parents never questioned why I did what I did. They understood. They were there once. I'll tell you one thing though, I'd hate to be Evelyn Hannum because after Joe and Annabeth confronted her about what she did and said to me, she is no longer in their lives. That's including Greta's too. Speaking of Greta, she's almost six months pregnant and isn't having a great pregnancy, so she and her husband will only take the drive once a week to see her. What's to see though...

She began breathing on her own after about a week and that awful tube was ejected from her throat. Now there's a thin, white tube that goes into her nose and down her throat. That gives her the nourishment she needs. All those tubes she was attached to looked like something out of a

Sci-Fi movie. You could hardly see her beautiful face. The bandage has come off her head, and the stitches have been removed. The wound is healing nicely, or at least that's what they tell me. She shows all signs of brain activity, which is miraculous. Her legs… That's a different story. They were a bit mangled. We won't know anymore until she wakes up, but to their knowledge there is no spinal cord injury.

I'm not a praying man. I've never had a lot to pray for in my life, but with Harlow, praying and hoping is all I have.

At six, I try to eat a little something, but again, I never do. Food is the last thing on my mind. My stomach is in a constant state of churning. My mind, it's in a constant state of denial.

Denial that this has all happened. Sometimes when I fall asleep in the chair next to her bed, I dream about her laughing, dancing, being carefree. In my dreams, her strawberry-colored hair twirls around her as she spins at the water's edge. She calls my name and holds out her hand for me to join her. She wraps her arms around my neck and whispers to me how happy she is and how her love for me has changed her, how my love for her has changed her.

Then I'm awakened to the nightmare.

At night before her mom, her dad and Craw leave, her mom always gently kisses my head and tells me she knows she's in good hands if I'm here. That brings no comfort to me even though I know she means well. I let her go that night. This is all because of me. She's lying here because I didn't give in. I didn't give in to the love even though I felt it within my soul. With every nerve, every ounce of blood pumping through my veins, with my whole heart, I loved her… I love her. I was just too damn afraid to admit it to her.

I squeeze her hand, I gently stroke her fingers. They're

still cold, bruised and a yellowish color has developed on the surface from the I.V.'s going in and out of her. Her skin so very delicate, like her. I just want her to wake up and look at me. I want her to smile at me with those freckles reaching across her face when she does so. I know the nurses tell me to talk to her, that she can hear me, but it just doesn't seem possible. When I sleep and dream I'm in another world. Maybe that's what it's like for Harlow.

I swallow hard, lean my head on her hand that's resting on her bed, and I speak. Feeling out of sorts when I do, but I do.

"Turnip, remember when you tried to explain to me what love is like, what being loved is like? I get it now." I smile as a single tear rolls down my face.

"Love is the only thing I think you can't fake, no matter what. It's when you look into the eyes of the person meant for you, and you can see into their soul. I'm pretty sure you can't lie when you truly look into the depths of them. There's a resemblance there, a home, somewhere you can put your trust into, someone you can tell your deepest, darkest fears to, and no matter their opinion of them, it really has no bearing. They will be beside you. They will watch you succeed, and they will watch you fail, but the love is so strong, they will see past it. See past all the bad and take the good... A good hard look at the good."

I just want her to give me a sign she hears me, that she understands what I'm trying to say.

I love her.

I love her.

I love her.

She didn't believe me though. Not that I gave her any reasons to believe me.

Oh, God, why does this have to hurt so damn bad? I've

never been one to feel anything, but she made me feel, and I'm not scared of feeling anymore. I'm not afraid to love for fear of not having it in return because she loved me, and I believed it because I felt it.

I raise my head off of her bed and realization steps in. Just when I thought I had all the answers and I questioned myself over and over again, now I know.

Love is real. Harlow's love is real.

I take her hand and bring it to my face, stroking it along my rough skin, her softness against it. I feel her, kissing each finger, each knuckle, as my salty tears coat her hand.

I stand up and lay in the bed next to her. It's against all the rules, but rules don't apply to me. I don't move her body, but somehow my large frame fits beside her, without disruption. I stroke her hair, and lean into her ear and whisper, "Loving someone is when you make the other person a better one. You did that, my Turnip. You made me a man. You changed me from that silly person who thought he was a man. I'm whole when I'm with you, I'm better Har, I'm better. Please believe me, hear me… Just hear me. Listen to my words. Oh, God, Turnip, I hope you can hear me. I can't help but to cry. I think there's about twenty four years of pent up tears. I'm so afraid everyday that once I start, I won't be able to stop.

My tears dampen her hair as I nuzzle my face in it, and I need her to know everything. So I whisper in her ear.

"Turnip, I'm not leaving you. I'm not going anywhere until you open your eyes and I see their color. I want to see the blue that sparkles when you smile at me. I will never leave you again. You're mine, Harlow Hannum, you are mine and when you wake up I'll spend the rest of my life proving to you how much I do love you. We are meant to be and I'll give you the world if I have it to give. I need you to believe me, trust in my love, it's all I have. Your love is all I have. Wake up, baby, so we can start our life together, so I can explain to you why I did what I did." I wipe my face with the back of my hand.

"Just open your eyes love of my life."

I rest my chin between her shoulder blade and the crook of her neck, and I listen to her breathe. I listen to the sound of life as she exhales. I listen to the slow, rhythmic sounds of the monitors, the faint sounds of the nurses talking out in the halls. I don't really want to hear any of it. I just want to hear her voice. The voice of the one I love. She's all that will ever matter.

Harlow gave me the courage to accept love in my heart, and she didn't even know it. I won't rest until she knows it, until she knows that I finally gave in.

To Be Continued...

www.goodreads.com/author/show/6936575.M_R_Joseph

facebook.com/reunionbookseries

www.amazon.com/M.R.-Joseph/e/B00E7TME2C/ref=ntt_athr_dp_pel_1

11809651R00176

Made in the USA
San Bernardino, CA
30 May 2014